EASY LOVE

BOOK ONE IN THE BOUDREAUX SERIES

KRISTEN PROBY

This book is dedicated to K.P. Simmon. Because you're not just the best publicist in the history of publicists, you're also my best friend. You have my back, and I have yours.

Also, Eli loves you, too.

OTHER BOOKS BY KRISTEN PROBY

PROLOGUE
Eli

"You work too hard." The voice comes from behind me. I'm standing behind my desk, gazing out over the French Quarter and the Mississippi River from my fifty-fourth floor office windows in New Orleans. The sun is blazing already. It's only eight in the morning, but it's a stifling eighty-six humid-filled degrees out there, much hotter than the cool comfort of my office.

It seems all I do is watch the world from this office window.

And where the fuck did that thought come from?

"Earth to Eli," Savannah says dryly from behind me.

"I heard you." I shove my hands in my pockets, fingering the silver half-dollar that my father gave me when I took this position, and turn to find my sister standing before my desk in her usual crisp suit, blue today, her thick dark hair pinned up and worry in her hazel gaze. "And, hello, pot, I'm kettle."

"You're tired."

"I'm fine." She narrows her eyes at me and takes a deep breath, making my lips twitch into a half smile. I love getting her riled up.

It's ridiculously easy.

"Did you even go home last night?"

"I don't have time for this, Van." I lower into my chair and motion for her to do the same, which she does after shoving a banana under my nose.

"But you have time to stare out the window?"

"Are you trying to pick a fight today? Because I'll oblige you, but first tell me what the fuck we're fighting about." I peel the banana and take a bite, realizing that I'm starving.

Savannah blows out a deep breath and shakes her head, while mumbling something about pigheaded men.

I smile brightly now.

"Lance giving you problems?" My hands flex in and out of fists at the idea of finally laying that fucker flat. Savannah's husband is not one of my favorite people.

"No." Her cheeks redden, but she won't look me in the eye. "Van."

"Oh, good, you're both here," Beau says, as he marches into my office, shuts the door behind him, takes the seat next to Savannah, steals my half-eaten banana out of my hand, and proceeds to eat the rest of it in two bites.

"That was mine." My stomach gives a low growl, not satisfied in the least, and I give a brief thought to asking my assistant to run out for beignets.

"God, you're a baby," Beau replies, and tosses the peel in the garbage. My older brother is taller than my six-foot-four by one inch and as lean as he was in high school. But I can still take him.

"Why the fuck are you two in my office?" I sit back and run my hand over my mouth. "I'm quite sure you both have plenty to do."

"Maybe we missed you," Savannah says with a fake grin and bats her eyelashes at me.

"You're a smart ass."

She just nods knowingly, but then she and Beau exchange a look that has the hairs on the back of my neck standing up.

"What's going on?"

"Someone is stealing from us." Beau tosses a file full of spreadsheets in my direction. His jaw ticks as I open it and see columns of numbers.

"Where?"

"That's what we don't know," Savannah adds quietly, but her voice is full of steel. "Whoever's doing it is hiding it well."

"How did you find it?"

"By accident, actually," she replies crisply, all business now. "We know it has to be happening in accounting, but it's buried so deep that the who and how is a mystery."

"Fire the whole department and start over." I shut the file and lean back, just as Beau laughs.

"We can't fire more than forty people, most of whom are innocent, Eli. It doesn't work like that."

"There has to be a paper trail," I begin, but Savannah cuts me off with a shake of her head.

"We're paperless, remember?"

"Oh, yeah, saving the fucking trees. Are you telling me that no one knows what the fuck is going on?"

"It's not a huge amount of money, but it's big enough to piss me off," Beau says quietly.

"How much?"

"Just over one hundred G's. That we've found so far."

"Yeah, that's enough to piss me off too. They're not just stealing post-its out of the supply closet."

"And it's not predictable. If it was a regular amount, on a routine, we could find it no problem. But I don't want to cause mass hysteria in the company. I don't want everyone to think that we're looking over all of their shoulders every damn minute."

"Someone is stealing, and you're worried about the employees' feelings?" I ask with a raised brow. "Who the fuck are you?"

"He's right," Savannah adds. "Having the co-CEOs of the company on everyone's asses isn't good for morale."

"What about having the CFO do it?" I ask, referring to Savannah, who shakes her head and laughs.

"No, I don't think so."

"So, we just sit back and let whoever the fucker is use us as his own private ATM?"

"Nope." Savannah smiles brightly, her pretty face lighting up. "I want to bring Kate O'Shaughnessy in."

"Your college friend?" I glance at Beau, who has no expression on his face whatsoever. Typical.

"This is what she does for a living."

"She looks over people's shoulders for a living? She must be everyone's favorite person."

"You're on a roll today," Beau says quietly.

"Kate works with companies who are dealing with embezzlement. She comes in as a regular employee and blends in, investigating on the down-low."

"Can she actually do the job? It won't work if she doesn't know what she's doing."

"She has an MBA, Eli. But I want to put her in as an administrative assistant. They see and know everything, and they talk to each other. She's likable."

"Okay, works for me." I glance at Beau. "You?"

"I think it's the way to go," he agrees. "None of us have time to do it ourselves, and I don't trust handing this off to anyone else. Like Van said, people talk. I'd like to keep this quiet. Kate will sign all the necessary non-disclosure agreements, and from what I've heard, she's excellent at her job."

"One thing," Van says, and leans forward to stare at me, the way she does when I'm about to be in deep trouble. "You're not allowed to mess around with her."

"I'm not an asshole, Van…"

"No, you're not allowed to get your man-whore hands on her."

"Hey! I am not—"

"Yeah, you are," Beau says with a grin.

I sigh and roll my shoulders. "Not having the same date twice doesn't make me a whore."

Van simply raises a brow. "Leave her be."

"I'm a professional, Van. I don't sleep with the employees."

"Is that what you said to that assistant that sued us a few years back?"

"Anymore."

"God." Van shakes her head as Beau laughs. "She's a nice woman, Eli."

Instead of replying, I simply narrow my eyes at my sister and swivel in my chair. Kate's a grown woman; one I'm most likely not attracted to anyway.

It's been a few years since much of anything has held my interest for long. That would require feeling something.

"Call her."

CHAPTER ONE
KATE

"Hello?" I ask breathlessly, as the cab I'm in whizzes down the interstate, heading directly for the heart of New Orleans.

"Where are you?" Savannah asks with a smile in her voice.

"In the cab on the way from the airport. Are you sure I shouldn't check into a hotel room?"

"No way, Bayou Industries owns a beautiful loft that we'll pretend you're renting while you're here. Come directly to the office. I have a meeting, so I won't be able to greet you, I'm sorry."

"It's okay," I reply and bite my lip as the cabbie cuts off another motorist and my stomach rolls. "I'm hoping to make it alive. I might not survive the cab ride."

Savannah chuckles in my ear, and then I hear her murmuring to someone else in her office. "I have to go. Eli will meet you."

"Eli? I thought I'd meet with Beau—"

"Eli's not as scary as we've all led you to believe. I promise." And then she's gone. The cab swerves again, and I send up a prayer of thanks that I didn't eat breakfast this morning as I use my hand to fan my face.

It's darn hot in the Big Easy.

During all the years I went to college with Savannah and her twin brother, Declan, I never did make it down here to visit them, and I can't wait to explore the French Quarter, eat beignets, have my tarot cards read, and soak it all in.

Of course, I'd rather soak it all in while not wearing so many clothes. Who knew it would be so hot in May? I shimmy out of my suit jacket, fold the sleeves over so they don't wrinkle, and watch as above ground cemeteries, old buildings, and lots of people zoom by.

Eli is the one Boudreaux sibling I've never met. I've seen photos of the handsome brother, and heard many stories about his stoic, tough, playboy ways. Van says the stories are exaggerated. I guess I'll find out for myself.

Well, not the playboy part. That's just none of my business.

Finally, we come to an abrupt stop. There's a red cable-car on one side and mountains of concrete on the other. I stumble out into the hot Monday afternoon, and sweat immediately beads on my forehead.

It's not just hot. It's sticky.

But I smile despite the discomfort, tip the reckless cabbie, and roll my suitcase behind me into the blessedly cool building, where a woman sits behind a long, ornate desk, typing furiously on a computer while speaking on the phone.

"Mr. Boudreaux is unavailable at this time, but I'll put you through to his assistant, one moment." She quickly pushes a series of keys, then smiles up at me.

She's very smiley.

"I'm Kate O'Shaughnessy."

"Welcome, Ms. O'Shaughnessy," she says, holding that smile in place. "Mr. Boudreaux is expecting you." She types furiously and begins speaking into her phone again. "Hello, Miss Carter, Ms. O'Shaughnessy is here for Mr. Boudreaux. Yes, ma'am." She clicks off efficiently. "Please have a seat. Can I get you some water?"

"No, thank you."

Miss Efficient simply nods and returns to her ringing phones. Before I have a chance to sit, a tall woman in black slacks and a red sleeveless blouse walks out of the elevator and straight to me.

"Ms. O'Shaughnessy?"

"Kate, please."

"Hello, Kate. Mr. Boudreaux is in his office. Follow me." She smiles and offers to take my suitcase, but I shake my head and follow her into the elevator. She doesn't ask me any questions, and I'm thankful. I've learned to lie well in this business, but I don't know what she's already been told. I'm led past an office area and into the largest office I've ever seen. The massive black desk sits before a wall of floor-to-ceiling windows. The furniture is big and expensive. Comfortable. There are two doors, each on opposite sides of the room, and I can't help but wonder what they lead to.

"Ms. O'Shaughnessy is here, sir."

"Kate," I add without thinking, and then any hope of being able to think at all is tossed right out of those spectacular windows, when the tall man standing before them turns to look at me. The photos didn't do him justice.

Yum.

The door closes behind me and I take a deep breath and walk toward him, hiding the fact that my knees have officially turned to mush.

"Kate," I repeat, and hold my hand out to shake his over his desk. His lips twitch as he watches me, his whiskey-colored eyes sharp and assessing as they take a slow stroll down my body, then back up to my face. Jeez, he's taller than I expected. And broader. And he wears a suit like he was born to it.

Which, I suppose he was. Bayou Enterprises has been around for five generations, and Eli Boudreaux is the sharpest CEO it's seen in years.

He moves around his desk and takes my hand in his, but rather than shake it, he raises it to his lips and places a soft kiss on my knuckles.

"Pleasure," he says in a slow New Orleans drawl. Dear God, I might explode right here. "I'm Eli."

"I know." He raises a brow in question. "I've seen photos over the years."

He nods once, but doesn't let go. His thumb is circling softly over the back of my hand, sending my body into a tailspin. My nipples have tightened, pressing against my white blouse, and now I wish with all my might that I hadn't taken off my jacket.

"Please, have a seat," he says, and motions to the black chair behind me. Rather than sit behind his desk, he sits in the chair next to mine and watches me with those amazing eyes of his.

A lock of dark hair has fallen over his forehead and my fingers itch to brush it back for him.

Calm the eff down, Mary Katherine. You'd think I'd never seen a hot man before.

Because I have.

Declan, the youngest of the Boudreaux brothers, is no slouch in the looks department, and he's one of my best friends. But being near him never made my knees weak or made me yearn for a tall glass of ice water. Or a bed. Or to rip his clothes off his body.

Whoa.

"Did Savannah fill you in on what's happening?" Eli asks calmly, his face revealing nothing. He crosses an ankle over the opposite knee and steeples his fingers, watching me.

"Yes, she and I have talked extensively, and she's emailed me all of the new-hire paperwork, as well as the NDA's, which I've printed and signed." I pull the papers out of my briefcase and pass them to Eli. Our fingers brush, making my thighs clench, but he seems unaffected.

Typical. I don't usually inspire hot lust from the opposite sex. Especially not men who look like Eli. Which is fine, because he's my boss and my best friends' brother and I'm here to work.

I clear my throat and push my auburn hair behind my ear. With all of this humidity, it's going to be a curly mess in no time.

"That's a beautiful ring," he says unexpectedly, nodding toward my right hand, still raised near my ear.

"Thank you."

"Gift?"

He's a man of few words.

"Yes, from my grandmother," I reply, and tuck my hands in my lap. He simply nods once and glances down at the papers in his hand. He frowns and glances up at me, but before he can say anything, his office door swings open and Declan walks in with a wide smile on his handsome face.

"There's my superstar." I squeal and leap up and into his arms, and Dec squeezes me tight and turns a circle in the middle of the wide office. He finally sets me on my feet, cups my face in his hands, and kisses me square on the mouth, then hugs me again, more gently this time. "You okay?" he whispers in my ear.

"I'm great." I gaze up into Dec's sweet face and years of memories and emotion fall around me. Laughter and tears, love, sadness, affection. "It's so good to see you."

"Have you done anything fun since you got to town?"

"I almost lost my life in a cab," I reply with a laugh. "I came straight here."

"I'll take you out tonight. Show you the French Quarter. I know this great restaurant—"

"That won't be necessary," Eli interrupts. His voice is calm. He's standing now, his hands shoved in his pockets, his wide shoulders making the large office feel small. "You have a gig tonight," he reminds Declan.

"I can take you out before."

"Don't worry about Kate this evening," Eli replies, still perfectly calm, but his jaw ticks.

I feel like I'm watching a tennis match as my head swivels back and forth, watching them both with curiosity.

"You know what Savannah told you," Declan says softly to Eli.

No response.

Declan glances back down to me. "I really don't mind calling the gig off tonight and settling you in."

"I'll be fine, Dec." I grin and pat his chest. "Where will you be playing?"

"The Voodoo Lounge."

"I might just show up." I push up onto my tiptoes and kiss his cheek.

"I don't want you wandering around the French Quarter after dark."

"I'll take her," Eli offers, earning a speculative look from Declan, who then gazes down at me and kisses my forehead softly.

"I'll save a seat for both of you then," he replies with a happy smile. "Have a good afternoon. Don't let the boss man run you ragged." He winks at me and grins at Eli, then slips back out the door.

"You and Declan are close," Eli says when I turn back around. His hands are still in his pockets as he rocks back on his heels.

"Yes. He, Savannah, and I were sort of the three amigos in college."

"Are you planning on fucking him?"

"Excuse me?" I feel my jaw drop as I stare at the formidable man before me. I prop my hands on my hips and glare at him. "That's none of your darn business."

He purses his lips as though he's trying not to laugh. "It's none of my *darn* business?"

"That's what I said."

He tilts his head and looks like he's about to say more, but then he saunters to my suitcase and pulls it behind him, as he gestures for me to follow him.

He's kicking me out?

"Miss Carter, I'll be out the rest of the day. Reschedule my appointments."

His assistant gapes at him and then sputters, "But, Mr. Freemont has been waiting…"

"I don't care. Reschedule. I'll see you tomorrow." Eli calls the elevator, his eyes never leaving me as we wait for the car to arrive. "Do you have a change of casual clothes in here?"

"Yes. The rest of my things are being shipped down and should arrive tomorrow afternoon."

He nods and motions for me to lead him into the elevator. "Eli?"

The air literally crackles around us as he glances down at me and raises a brow. He's barely touched me and my body is on high alert and my mind is empty.

"Where are we going?"

"To your place."

"You know where my place is?"

"I own it, *cher*." He sighs and finally reaches over and tucks my hair behind my ear, making me shiver. "Are you cold?"

"No." I clear my throat and step away from him. "If you'll just give me the address, I'll take a cab to my place."

"I wouldn't dream of endangering your life again," he replies with a half-smile, and every hair on my body stands on end. Good Lord, what this man can do with a smile.

I need to get my hormones under control. It's simply been too long since I got laid, that's all. And I'm not going to scratch this particular itch with this particular man. He's my boss. My best friends' brother.

No way, nohow.

"You coming?" he asks.

Yes, please.

I realize the elevator has opened and he's standing next to me, waiting for me to go first.

"Of course."

"Of course," he chuckles. "We can walk it…it's not far, but it's hot out, so we'll drive."

I nod and follow him to his sleek, black Mercedes, which he expertly drives down the narrow streets of the French Quarter. I can't help but practically press my face to the window, trying to take in everything I see at once.

"It's so beautiful," I murmur.

"Have you been here before?"

"No. I can't wait to walk around and soak it all in."

He parks less than three minutes after we set off, and kills the engine. "We're here."

"Already?"

"I told you, it's not far."

"I could have walked that, even with the heat."

"It's not necessary to make you uncomfortable," he replies simply and climbs out of the car, gathers my bag, and with his hand on the small of my back, leads me up to a loft that sits above an herb shop called Bayou Botanicals. I can smell sage and lavender as Eli unlocks the front door and ushers me inside, where I stop on a dime and take in the beautiful.

The outside of the building is well kept and beautiful with worn red bricks and green iron railings, but the inside is brand new and simply opulent.

"I'm staying *here*?"

"That you are," he confirms, his accent sliding along my skin like honey. "You'll consider this your home while you're with us. Here are your keys." He passes the keys to me, then turns his back and leads me to the kitchen, which boasts brand new appliances, dark oak cabinets, and matching granite countertops. "The bedroom is through there," he continues, and leads me into a beautiful room with a four-poster bed. "The linens are clean and fresh. The bathroom is there." He points to the left, but my eyes are stuck on the doors that lead out to the balcony, which offers a beautiful view of the street below and Jackson Square just a block away.

"There are times that it gets noisy with music and people, but there's never a dull moment in the French Quarter."

I nod and turn back to him. "Thank you. Shall we go back to the office?"

"It's mid-afternoon, Kate. Take the rest of the day to settle in."

"Oh, but, I'm here to work. Surely, I could—"

"It would look odd to bring on a new hire in the middle of the day, don't you think?"

Of course it would.

I smile sheepishly and nod. "You're right. I'll work from here." I toss my jacket onto the bed, pull my laptop out of my briefcase, and walk briskly into the kitchen. "It's going to be a process."

"Kate, I don't want—"

"I'm not going to be able to just dig in and start investigating. Van's right to give me an assistant position, but that's going to be even tougher." I tie my hair back off my face and lower into a kitchen chair as I talk briskly. If I talk about work, I won't be ogling him, and thus losing more brain cells.

"Kate."

"I'm going to have to play by the rules for a while, a couple weeks at least. I need people to trust me, so they'll open up to me."

"Kate."

"I—"

"Enough," he says sharply.

CHAPTER TWO

My head whips up to stare at Eli. He shoves his hands in his pockets and swears under his breath as he hangs his head then glances back up at me, looking at me like he doesn't really want to be here, and he's not quite sure if he likes me.

"You don't have to stay," I inform him stiffly.

"I don't expect you to work today at all, from here or the office."

"Why ever not?" I lean back in the chair and frown up at him. "You're paying me to work."

"You've travelled all morning, Kate. Settle in. Eat something. In fact, let me take you out to eat something."

"I don't think that's necessary."

"I do." He removes his suit jacket after taking his sunglasses out of the inside pocket and drapes it over the back of the sofa. He rolls the sleeves of the white shirt that molds over his muscled torso all the way up to his elbows, unbuttons the top two buttons, and removes his soft blue tie. "That's better. Go change into something more comfortable, and I'll feed you the best jambalaya you've ever had."

"I've never had jambalaya before," I reply with a raspy voice. I can't tear my eyes off his broad shoulders.

"This will ruin you for all other jambalaya; I promise you."

I frown and meet his gaze, trying to figure him out. "Are you sure?"

He nods and waits expectantly. I have a feeling not many people say no to Eli Boudreaux.

"I'm not going to sleep with you." The words are out of my mouth before I can reel them back in. I feel my face flame, but I tilt my chin up and square my shoulders firmly.

"I didn't invite you to," he replies calmly, but his eyes are full of humor.

I nod and walk back to the bedroom to change into a light summer dress, slather on sunblock with SPF 4000 to protect my white, freckled skin, and then rejoin Eli, who is now looking out my windows.

"You're always looking out windows," I remark with a smile. He turns to me and his eyes heat as he looks me up and down, and I suddenly feel very exposed.

"You'll burn, *cher*."

"I'm wearing sunblock."

"Do you always argue?" he asks.

"I don't argue."

He holds my gaze for a moment and then tosses his head back and laughs, shakes his head, and leads me out into the hot afternoon.

"Let's go this way first." He turns to the left and rests his hand on the small of my back again, ever the gentleman, walking me down Royal Street. If you'd asked me yesterday if I thought I'd be walking in the French Quarter with the sexiest man I'd ever seen by my side, I would have told you to consult a doctor.

And Eli Boudreaux *is* sexy. But he's not mine, and he never will be. He's my boss, and he's being kind.

I take a deep breath, determined to pull my head out of the gutter and enjoy New Orleans, when Eli pulls me into a trendy shoe and accessory shop called *Head Over Heels*.

"Shoes!" I exclaim, already salivating. Okay, so the man is showing me shoes. I might sleep with him after all.

"Hats," he corrects me.

"Holy crap, what are you doing here?" A woman with short, dark hair and full lips smiles from behind the counter.

"Kate needs a hat," Eli replies and grins as his sister launches herself into his arms and holds on tight.

"Been a minute," she whispers in his ear in the same New Orleans drawl. Eli grins.

"You saw me at Mama's last Sunday."

"Been a minute," she replies and steps back, smiling at me. "Hi, Kate. It's good to see you again."

"You too, Charly." I'm pulled into another hug—the Boudreaux family is an affectionate bunch, and the middle sister, Charlotte, is no different from the rest.

"What can I do for you two?"

"Kate needs a hat," Eli repeats.

"I do?"

"Oh, yes, sugar, you do," Charly replies with a nod. "We need to keep the sun off your face and shoulders. Let's see…" She leads us to the back of the shop and pulls three hats off the wall, all wide-brimmed and pretty. "I think green is your color, with that beautiful auburn hair and your pretty green eyes."

"Thank you, but this hair is about to be a curly tangled mess with all this humidity."

"I know the feeling. I'll make a list of hair products to use while you try these on." She jogs back to her counter as I plop the first hat on my head. It's pink, not quite as widely brimmed as the green, and makes me look like a mushroom.

"Try the green one," Eli suggests, but instead I pull on one with a rainbow of colors. It looks like a box of Crayolas exploded all over it. Eli just watches me in the mirror with humor-filled eyes and crosses his arms over his impressive chest. "You do have beautiful hair."

"Thank you." His jaw ticks. If he doesn't like giving out compliments, why does he say anything at all?

"Oh no, dawlin', the green one," Charly says as she rejoins us. I smirk as I put the green hat on and sigh as I realize that she and Eli were right.

"Looks like this is the winner," I say with a grin. "I'll take it." I pull my wallet out of my handbag, but Eli lays his hand over mine and shakes his head.

"Bill me," he tells Charly, who smiles and nods happily, while handing me a list of hair products to try, waving at us as Eli leads me back out into the heat. "Feel better?"

"Hmm," I murmur, but, oh, God, yes, it feels so much better. "Thanks for the hat."

"You are welcome," he replies, his accent making me squirm again. I met this man just a few hours ago, and so far, everything he does makes me squirm.

Not good. Not good at all.

"Tell me about yourself," I say, surprising myself. All I know is, I need to get my brain on something other than the mass of testosterone walking next to me. We cross the street, me on the outside, and Eli immediately trades places with me, tucking me next to him away from the street. "Chivalry isn't dead," I whisper.

"No, dawlin', it's not." He flashes me a quick smile before leading me to a café with beautiful courtyard seating.

"It's surprisingly cool in here," I murmur after we're seated.

"The trees keep it cool," the waitress says with a smile. "Need a minute with the menu?"

"Do you eat seafood?" Eli asks me.

"Yes," I reply.

"Good. We'll both have the seafood jambalaya, please."

The waitress nods and walks away, leaving us alone.

"Now, tell me more about your plans to catch the person stealing from my company."

"You didn't answer my question first," I reply, and butter a piece of the bread the waitress just set down for us.

"What question?"

"Tell me about you."

"I don't matter." His voice is calm, but sure. Final. He leans back, folds his arms, and shutters immediately close over his eyes.

Interesting.

"It's your company, so yes, I do believe you matter."

"All you need to know about me is that I'm your boss, you'll be paid timely, and I expect nothing but your best on this job."

I set my bread on a small white plate and lean back, mirroring his pose with my arms crossed. "Actually, I believe it was Savannah who hired me, and I don't ever give less than my best. Ever."

He raises a brow and cocks his head to the side. "Beau, Savannah, and I hold equal shares and equal interest in the company. All three of us are your bosses, Kate."

"Understood." He watches me for several minutes. I can't figure him out. He has moments of being so kind, *nice*, and I think he may be attracted to me, and then the walls come slamming down and he's distant, impersonal, and borderline rude.

Which is it?

Not that it really matters, because starting tomorrow I'll answer to Savannah, and I'll hardly ever see the mysterious and sexy Eli.

I hope.

I tilt my head back, close my eyes, and take a deep breath of the thick New Orleans air. There's a light breeze now, cooling my heated skin. The trees above are green and lush, and I can see sprinkles of sunshine as it fights its way through the leaves.

Our meal is served and I stare down at the bowl of rice, shrimp, mussels and a bunch of stuff I can't make out dubiously, then glance up to Eli, who has already dug into his bowl heartily.

"You won't regret it," he says simply, and shovels another spoonful into his mouth. I watch his square jaw as he chews, and then glance back down at my own bowl.

Why not? I take a bite and my gaze finds his in surprise. "It's good."

"I wouldn't feed you something bad, Kate." He chuckles and reaches for the bread. The jambalaya is delicious, and I'm hungrier than I thought, devouring the bowl in just a few minutes. Finally, I sit back and pat my flat belly.

"That was great."

When the bill is paid and we're back on the sidewalk, walking back toward my loft, Eli glances down at me, and then sighs and pushes his hand through his hair.

"How did you get into your profession?" he asks softly.

"Oh, we're talking about ourselves now?" I raise a brow. "Look, you don't have to be nice to me. It's okay if you don't like me. I'll do my job, very well I might add, and be out of New Orleans in four to six weeks."

"Four to six weeks?" he asks incredulously.

"Yes. I told you earlier, it takes time to settle in, gain my coworkers' trust and confidence. I can't just sit down at a desk and start pilfering through files. I'm supposed to be a new hire, on the down low, remember?"

He shakes his head thoughtfully. "I didn't think it would be that involved."

"It's harder than it looks; otherwise, you wouldn't need me."

"Who said I don't like you?" he asks abruptly.

"What?"

"You just said 'it's okay if you don't like me.' What makes you think I don't like you?"

I stop on the sidewalk, stare up at him for a long minute, and then chuckle at the bewildered expression on his wickedly handsome face. "It doesn't matter, Eli."

I begin to walk again, and he hangs back, walking just a few paces behind me. I can hear the wheels turning in his head from here.

Finally, we reach my door. I glance back at him as he catches up to me. "Thanks for the hat, and for the meal."

"You're welcome."

I turn to let myself inside and move to shut the door, but Eli nudges his way inside and pushes the door shut behind him.

"Um, come on in?"

"I do like you."

I roll my eyes and toss my handbag on the couch, my hat on top of it, and see his jacket and his tie where he left them earlier.

"Oh, you almost forgot—"

Eli's very firm chest presses to my back as he reaches around me and takes the coat out of my hands and sets it aside, then swivels me around to face him.

"I do like you," he repeats. When I would look down, he catches my chin with his finger and tilts my head up. "But this is a bad idea."

"What is?" I whisper, hating the shakiness in my voice.

"This." He lowers his face to mine and sweeps his nose across my own, gently. His lips haven't touched mine yet, but they're tingling, already yearning for him. His hands glide up my bare arms to my neck, his thumbs gently draw circles along my jawline as he places a light, barely-there kiss on the corner of my lips. I hear a soft moan, and would be mortified to know that it came from me, if I could find my brain cells.

This man is dangerous. Everything about him screams *RUN!* but instead, I grip onto his lean hips and tug him closer. He needs no further invitation. He slips those amazing lips of his over mine, licks my bottom lip, and when I gasp at the fission of pure lust that moves through me, he moves in for the kill.

His tastes like the after-meal peppermint we both ate, and the light one or two day scruff on his chin rasps against my skin in the most tantalizing way. I can't help but wonder how it would feel on other parts of my body…behind my knees, between my breasts, between my legs.

Holy shit, I bet he would feel amazing between my legs.

I grip onto his biceps and realize that the one arm he's slung around the small of my back is the only thing keeping me upright. My knees no longer exist. We're both breathing hard as he drags his fingers down my cheek and pulls back, nibbling the edge of my lips once more, and then he's gone, staring down at me with shining whiskey eyes.

"That. That's a bad idea."

CHAPTER THREE
ELI

"So how was your date?" Beau asks, just before he attacks me from behind, his arm wrapped around my neck. I slip out of his grip, flip him onto his back, and glare down at him, sweaty and panting.

"What date?"

"Heard you left out of here for the day with Van's friend Kate," Ben Preston, a life-long friend of ours, and the Krav Maga expert that comes to train us four times a week, says with a smug grin. He's already shirtless and sweaty, but barely panting. Ben's not as tall as Beau and me, but he's much stronger, and he's fucking badass. "After Van told you to keep your hands off. She's pissed, by the way."

"It wasn't a fucking date," I mutter, and wipe the sweat off my forehead with a towel before switching my attention to Ben and throwing a punch, which he deflects, and we spar for a few long, hard minutes before I can continue. "Beau and Van were in a meeting. Someone had to meet her and show her the loft."

"And buy her a hat and take her lunch?" Beau asks with a wide grin. "Van's gonna cut your balls off."

"What are you, a bunch of gossiping women?" I whip my soaking wet T-shirt over my head, then prop my hands on my hips.

"Charly called me after you left her shop. She said you looked love sick."

"Fuck that," I mutter with disgust. "I don't do love sick, and you know it. So, Charly called you, and you used the family phone tree to spread the news that I was being nice to Kate?"

Beau and Ben both laugh, then Ben catches me off guard and takes me down to the mat. Motherfucker. "So, you're not taking her to Dec's gig tonight?"

"Do you want Mama's recipe for her pecan pie too?" I snarl.

"Wow, you're very defensive for someone who's not interested in the pretty Kate."

"She's not pretty," I mutter. *She's fucking beautiful.*

"Yeah, I'm not really into redheads with freckles myself. But the last time I saw her, she had a sexy little body," Beau continues, speaking to Ben, who nods thoughtfully.

I'm going to kill them both.

With my bare hands.

"When did you see her?"

"During one of my trips to visit Dec and Van at college." Beau strips out of his own shirt and tosses it away. "That was a while ago, though. Maybe she got fat."

"She's not fat," I reply, walking right into his trap. "Look, I'm just being nice to her."

"Right," Ben nods, just before he takes Beau down to the mat, but Beau pulls out, rolls Ben beneath him, and pulls up to throw a punch, which Ben rolls out of, and for the next few minutes they try to best each other.

I am *not* lovesick over Kate. Sure, she's sexy with her thick auburn hair and big green eyes, and the freckles on her face and shoulders simply beg to be kissed and traced, but for the love of fuck, she's an employee. It's just been longer than I care to admit since I last got laid.

That's a detail easily taken care of.

But the thought of any of the usual women I call to scratch that particular itch holds no interest.

Fuck.

"Not paying attention gets your ass kicked, man," Beau warns, just before he pulls my torso down and knees me in the stomach, then throws an elbow up, but I throw him off balance and he misses. Barely.

"Stop daydreaming about hot redheads and pay attention," Ben snarls.

"I'm done," I mutter, and suck down a bottle of water.

"We have ten minutes left," Beau says.

"You go ahead."

"Dude." Beau, panting and sweaty himself, props his hands on his hips and levels me with a somber look. "Be careful."

"I haven't done a fucking thing," I reply, but the memory of that hot kiss in her loft is right there, front and center. Her sweet body pressed to mine, her hair tangled in my fingers, and those bright green eyes, full of lust and mistrust, pinned to mine as I backed away and ran like a bat out of hell.

"Okay." Beau shrugs and shakes his head. "But if you decide to do the fucking thing, be honest with her."

"What the hell is that supposed to mean?"

"You have a habit of making women fall for you, and then you squish them like bugs," Ben adds.

"I do not."

"Yeah, you do. Dad never meant for you to—"

"This isn't therapy," I interrupt, and turn my back on both of them, headed to the shower. "I'm fine. Kate's safe from me. I'll make sure she gets to Dec's gig safely, and then I'll probably rarely see her after that."

"Eli."

I turn at Ben's voice.

"I do want that recipe. Your mom's pecan pie is the best."

I smirk, shake my head, and leave to the loud grunts of Beau getting his ass kicked.

***

Kate answers her door and I just about swallow my tongue at the sight of her. Her hair has been swept up onto her head, with soft wavy strands hanging around her face. She's in a silk black tank top that flows from the tops of her breasts to her waist, and white Capri pants.

And the sexiest strappy black heels I've ever fucking seen.

She's safe from me. No messing with her.

"Eli."

"Right the first time," I reply, and offer her a smile. I seem to smile at this woman a lot.

"What are you doing here?"

"I told you I'd take you to Declan's gig tonight." I raise a brow as she bites her lip and winces. "Problem?"

"I kind of figured that offer was off the table. Especially after—"

"After what?" She glances down at my chest and her eyes dilate. Oh, she's interested, all right. The chemistry is off the charts.

"After you kissed me." Her eyes return to mine, and she tilts her chin up defiantly. She's not going to back down and get shy, or play coy.

Good girl.

"I don't play games, *cher.*" She frowns slightly at the nickname.

"What does that mean?"

"It means that I won't kiss you and then ignore you."

"No, *cher.* What does it mean?"

I grin and skim the tip of my finger down her nose. I can't seem to keep my hands off this woman. So much for not playing games.

Jesus, get it together, Boudreaux.

"It's a Creole term that means dear or darling. Are we going to stand in your doorway all night?"

She shakes her head and steps back, allowing me to pass. The place already smells like her, like honey.

"You really don't have to take me. Declan texted me with the address. According to my Google Maps app, it's not far."

"You shouldn't be walking around the Quarter after dark by yourself. You don't know your way around, and anything could happen. Besides, his club is on Bourbon. You're not walking down Bourbon looking like that."

"Looking like what?" she demands, and props her hands on her hips, making her shirt lift just an inch, giving me a glimpse of creamy white skin.

"Like a walking wet dream," I mutter and shove my hand through my hair.

"I live here. How can I never walk around after dark?" She raises a brow and is doing her best to look unaffected by me, but her cheeks have reddened and she keeps licking those plump lips of hers in agitation.

Those lips that taste like heaven and move effortlessly beneath my own.

I narrow my eyes and watch as she tosses her phone, cash, and other mysterious things that women carry with them into a small handbag and turns back to me.

"I'd feel better if I walked you."

"Suit yourself." She shrugs and glances around, as if she thinks she might be forgetting something. "How far is the walk?"

"About ten minutes."

I almost tell her that those heels are going to be a pain in the ass on the cobblestones and uneven sidewalks, but then decide against it. If the thought of keeping her held against me to make sure she's safe makes me an asshole, so be it.

I *am* an asshole.

Kate follows me down her stairs to the sidewalk below, and we set off toward Bourbon Street and Declan's gig.

"Are you sure you're up for this? You've had a long day." I catch her elbow as she cautiously makes her way around a wide hole in the sidewalk, then settle my hand on the small of her back. It just seems to fit there.

"I haven't heard Dec play in years," she replies with a smile. "I miss it. He's so talented. He could be doing so much more with his music than he is."

"New Orleans is his home," I reply softly, but with complete agreement. "He was in Memphis last month working on an album."

"I know. I was in town on a job, so we met for dinner, but I didn't get to hear him play."

"So, how close are you really?" I do my best to ignore the stab of fucking jealously that spears my gut.

"Very close." She nods and reaches for my arm as we cross a cobblestoned street, when she almost loses her balance on those sexy shoes. "He and Savannah and I were roommates. Declan is one of my dearest friends."

Naked friends?

I want to ask, but hold my tongue. She was right this afternoon; it's none of my fucking business if she and Declan have a physical relationship.

Ah, fuck it.

"Have you two ever—"

"I believe we already had this conversation," she says with a laugh.

"I don't think it's funny."

"The thought of me having sex with Declan is hilarious," she replies and smiles up at me, her gorgeous green eyes glowing under the streetlights. "He's like a brother to me, Eli."

I nod and lead her to the left, down Bourbon Street, the hubbub of the French Quarter. At night, at least.

"Holy moly," she breathes, and takes in all the lights, the loud music, and the people leaning on the railings above the street. "It's like Vegas on steroids."

I laugh and tuck her hand in mine, linking our fingers. "That it is. It's still early, so this is pretty tame."

The streets have been blocked off for foot traffic only.

"There are a lot of sex shops on this street." Her frank observation startles a laugh from me, and I glance down to find her smiling up at me.

"It's Bourbon," I reply with a shrug. "The club that Declan is playing at is actually pretty classy. I think you'll like it."

"I think I like it all," she replies softly. "It's hard to believe this is the same city from one block over."

I nod and lead her through an iron gate into a wide courtyard with lights twinkling in the trees overhead. I introduce myself to the hostess, and she immediately guides us to the front of the crowd to two seats right in front of the stage, where Declan is playing a jazz song on the piano.

Dec's voice is deep and croony, reminiscent of Dean Martin and Frank Sinatra. He has a decent voice, but it's what he can do with a musical instrument—any instrument—that makes him stand out.

He's a freaking genius.

"Did it bother you that he chose music over the family company?" Kate asks from beside me, swaying back and forth to the song.

"No. That would be stupid. Listen to him."

She nods and then smiles up at me, a full-on smile that lights up her face, and I find that I have to swallow hard and fist my hands to keep from reaching out and cupping that amazing face in the palm of my hand and leaning in for a kiss.

No more kissing.

I make myself look back up at Dec, who's watching us. He shakes his head and finishes his song to delighted applause.

"Ah, that's awfully kind of you," he drawls, and winks at a woman in the front row who winks back. And they call me the man-whore. "I have some special guests here tonight, ladies and gentlemen."

He stands from the piano and reaches for a guitar, then pulls two chairs to the edge of the stage and grabs an extra mic as well.

Kate is already shaking her head no.

Interesting.

"My brother, Eli, is here tonight." He smiles down at me, and I just grin and raise a brow. "And a very old friend from college is here too. In fact, Kate and I used to sing together all the time, and I'm going to talk her into coming up here and joining me right now."

The room erupts into applause, but Kate is vehemently shaking her head and saying "No. Heck no."

Heck no.

Her aversion to cursing turns me on. I wonder what it would take to get her to talk dirty.

I'm going to hell.

"Come on, Kate. New Orleans wants to hear you sing."

I nudge her with my elbow and grin at the look of terror on her face. Finally, she swallows hard and stands, climbs the steps to the stage, sits next to Declan, and raises the mic to her mouth.

"Was this necessary?"

"Well, it's not as fun if you sing from down there," Declan replies and kisses her cheek. "Isn't she pretty?"

Why does everyone call her *pretty*? Can't they see that she's unbelievable?

I applaud with the rest of the crowd, and then Declan begins to strum the guitar. "Remember this one?" he asks her.

"I remember belting this one out after having a few too many drinks in Memphis at that dive bar you played in during college."

"That's the one," he confirms with a grin. And suddenly, Kate begins to sing *Crazy* by Patsy Cline, as if she was made to. It's effortless for her. Declan joins her on the chorus, adding harmony, and when the song is over, they're given a standing ovation. Kate stands and bows, kisses Declan's cheek, and returns to her seat at my side.

"Wow." It's all I can manage.

"He'll pay for that later." She takes a deep breath and clenches her shaking hands together.

"You have a beautiful voice."

She jerks one shoulder in a shrug and then settles back to listen to the rest of Declan's set. She gradually relaxes, moving in her seat, singing along with the songs she knows. And when it's all over, she stands and whoops and hollers, making Declan laugh from the stage.

"Thanks for coming, superstar," Declan says, as he pulls Kate in for a hug. "And you too," he says to me. "It's been a minute since you came to a show."

"Too long. I enjoyed it."

This seems to surprise him, and I feel like an ass. It has been too long.

"I'd walk you home, but—" Declan looks over at the girl in the front row he winked at earlier and shoots her a smile.

"I see things haven't changed," Kate mutters and shakes her head. "I'm fine. Eli walked me over."

"Do you mind walking her home?"

"If it's out of your way—" Kate begins, but I shake my head.

"Of course. Have a good night."

"He's so formal," Declan says with a grin.

"Not always," Kate replies, and then kisses Declan's cheek again, and before he can ask what she means by that, she says, "call me soon. We'll have lunch or something."

And with that, we leave, winding our way through the crowd.

"Would you like a drink for the walk home? There's no open container law here."

"Sure. I'd love some white wine, please."

I order two glasses, and we set off toward home, walking slower so she can absorb everything happening around us.

"We can walk up a block and get out of the crazy."

"No, I don't mind." Her eyes are pinned on a couple practically having sex against the wall of a building as we pass.

I take her hand in mine and keep her close, glowering at the drunker than fuck men that leer at her as we pass.

I'd rather not have her in the middle of this, and steer her down a block to walk up Royal, which is much more tame.

"I really didn't mind," she insists and sips her wine.

"I did." I glance down at her and lead her around the gaping hole in the sidewalk. "Promise me you won't go back there alone."

"Oh, I'm fine."

"Promise me, Kate."

"It's no big deal."

I sigh and stop us, right there on the sidewalk, steps from her front door, and turn her to face me. "Please, as a favor to me, don't go back to Bourbon Street at night alone. People get shot, raped, beat up down there all the time, *cher*. If you want to go, take someone with you."

Her eyes are wide as she watches me, her hand flat on my chest. I pulled her against me without even realizing it, and now the zing of awareness is a pulsing need. I can feel her, from knee to chest, and it immediately makes my dick stand up and beg.

This woman is going to be the death of me.

And she's off-limits.

"Kate."

"I won't," she whispers, and watches my lips as she licks her own. An involuntary growl slips from my throat as I tip my head down and lean my forehead against hers, breathing her in. "This is a bad idea," she whispers.

"Very bad," I agree, and reluctantly pull away and walk her down the block to her loft.

"This house is pretty," she says, gesturing to the four-story single family home right next to the building that holds her loft.

"Thank you," I reply.

"You own that one too?"

"I do. That's my house."

"You live there?"

I nod and watch her carefully.

"So, we're neighbors."

"We are."

"Well, thanks for taking me," she says, and doesn't meet my eyes as she climbs the stairs. "You don't have to walk me to the door."

"It's not a problem," I reply, but she stops me with a hand to my chest.

"I don't want you to walk me to the door, Eli. Have a good night."

And with that, she climbs the last of the stairs and lets herself inside without a backwards glance.

I stand on the sidewalk and watch her turn the lights on in her loft, then walk to my place and pour myself another glass of wine before I change into basketball shorts. It's hot enough outside to forgo a shirt. I sit on the balcony, listening to the music coming from Jackson Square, and settle in for a long sleepless night.

An hour later, Kate's lights go out, putting an end to a very long day. I picture her with her hair loose, climbing into bed, slipping between the sheets wearing nothing at all, and swear under my breath as I walk inside and close the doors.

Tomorrow will be business as usual. Forget her. I have no room in my life for a woman, least of all a woman who has forever and white picket fences written all over her.

I gave all of that up long ago.

CHAPTER FOUR
KATE

"Good mornin'," Savannah says with a smile and hugs me after leading me into her office. "Thanks for coming in so early."

"I figured we could go over the details before I head down to HR and meet my new boss." I set my purse on the floor next to the chair and take in Van's office. "Nice place you have here."

"Thanks." Van grins. "Quite a step up from that apartment we all shared at college."

"It wasn't so bad," I reply. "But, yes, this is great. I'm proud of you."

"Okay, so tell me what happens now."

"Well, not much for the next few weeks. I need my coworkers to believe that I'm just another assistant. Then, as things settle and I'm not being watched as much, I'll start investigating. You know I'm good with the computer, I can hack and sneak around and no one will ever know I've been there."

"Do we lie and say we don't know each other?" Van asks with a frown.

"No." I shake my head and smile ruefully. "This is new for me, in that I've never worked in a place where I know the owners, but I think that if anyone asks, I'll just say that I went to college with you. Leave it at that."

"Why do I think we won't be having lunches together?"

"Because we won't. I need people to feel comfortable talking to me, and they won't if they think that I'm best friends with the boss."

"You are best friends with the boss."

I shrug. "They don't have to know that."

"This whole thing pisses me off," Van says with a sigh. "I love having you here, but I hate that someone is stealing from us."

"We'll find them. It's just going to take a little time." I reach across the desk and grip Van's arm reassuringly. "I promise."

She nods and then frowns. "Okay, change of subject. I'm sorry I wasn't available to meet you yesterday."

I sit back in my seat and school my features. "I told you, it was fine."

"Was Eli okay?"

"What do you mean?" I ask with a raised brow.

"I'm sure he was perfectly nice, but was he...*too nice*?"

"What are you asking me, Van?"

"Look, I told him to leave you alone, and then I practically dumped you at his feet yesterday."

"Wait." I hold my hand up and glare at my friend. "You told him to *leave me alone*?"

"Of course I did."

I blink at her and then stand and pace across the room. So, was he just hanging out with me, kissing me, yesterday as a rebellious act against his bossy sister?

"Why?" I turn and face her, hands propped on my hips. She looks down at her desk, suddenly looking flummoxed.

"Well, because, you know Eli—"

"Actually, I don't." I cross my arms. "I'd never met him before yesterday. But I'll tell you this," I lean on her desk, towering over her, suddenly so angry on both my and Eli's behalf that I'd be baffled if I stopped and gave it too much thought. "Eli was nothing but polite yesterday. He escorted me to my loft and to Declan's show last night."

"Look, Kate, I didn't mean—"

"I don't know why you think you had to warn your brother off me. I'm a grown woman, a professional woman, who certainly doesn't flop down on her back for any man who smiles at her and crooks his finger, which your brother *did not*. So, I think you've misjudged both of us."

"Wow, you're pissed."

"I am *so* bloody mad at you right now."

"When you get mad, your Irish shows through." Her lips twitch, but I'm not done being mad at her yet.

"I'm here to do a job, not start an affair. I won't be here that long."

"You like him," Van murmurs with narrowed eyes.

"I don't *know* him!" I repeat in exasperation. *Yes, I like him! He kisses like a dream, and I want to climb his hot body and have my wicked way with him!*

Not that I'm going to tell her that.

"I just didn't want him to set his sights on you and have you eventually hurt. I know you're still—"

"I'm fine." I shake my head, not wanting to go down this road with Van, not today. I have a long day ahead of a new job, and bringing my own baggage into it won't be productive. "I promise, I'm fine. Now, I need to get down to HR. I don't want to be late on my first day."

"I'll walk you down." She stands, but I shake my head.

"No thanks. No favoritism, remember?" I shoot her a grin and walk toward her door.

"Kate, if you want to talk about—"

"Do you want to talk about Lance?" I ask without turning around, and the room is suddenly filled with a heavy silence as I shake my head and open her door. "I didn't think so. Love you."

"Love you, too."

***

"This is Hilary," Linda Beals, the head of HR informs me as she leads me to my new office. "She's been promoted to another position here in the company, but is going to stay with you today to show you the ropes."

Hilary, a woman who looks to be a few years older than me smiles and stands, offering her hand to shake. "Pleasure," she says.

"Hello," I reply and smile at Linda, as she assures me that I'm in good hands, and leaves me with Hilary.

"So, you're taking over as Mr. Rudolph's assistant," Hilary says, stating the obvious.

"It seems so," I reply and sit in the desk chair next to hers behind my new desk. "How long have you been with him?"

"Oh, gosh, about twelve years now, I guess." Hilary leans in as if she's about to tell me a big secret. "He's really very easy to work with, as long as you make his coffee just so."

"You make his coffee?" I ask with a raised brow. "That's a little old school."

She shrugs and starts pulling files out of her drawer. "I don't mind. Now, let's get started. You only have me for today, but I'll just be one floor up, so if you ever have questions, don't hesitate to call me."

"Thanks."

"Did Linda show you around?"

"No, she just brought me down here after she went over my paperwork." I glance around my small, simple office, and see exactly why Van put me here. It's a corner space, and I'm able to see down two corridors of offices, and into the windows of said offices.

"Sounds about right," Hilary replies with a roll of the eyes. "After we go over these things, we'll take a break, and I'll give you a grand tour."

"Sounds good."

"Are you new to town?"

"Yes, very new."

"Well, I think you and I will be good friends." She smiles and then stands when a man walks in, looking harried and busy. "Mr. Rudolph, this is your new assistant, Kate."

"Hello," he says with a distracted smile and shakes my hand, his grip firm. He's probably in his early forties, with thinning hair over a handsome face, with a nose just a couple sizes too big, and he wears thick-rimmed glasses on his face. He's not terribly tall, but he's wiry thin. "Hilary will show you the ropes, but let me know if you have any questions." And with that, he disappears into his office just off of mine and shuts the door firmly behind him.

"He's a man of few words," I remark with a smile.

"Yeah, he's not terribly chatty," Hilary confirms.

"Miss O'Shaughnessy?" A man asks as he walks into my office, carrying a large bouquet of happy sunflowers.

"Yes," I reply with surprise.

"These are for you."

I gape in surprise as he sets the flowers on my desk, waits for my signature, and then leaves.

"Wow, sugar, those are impressive."

I nod and pull the small envelope out of the plastic holder in the center of the bouquet and open it, facing away from Hilary, so she can't read over my shoulder.

Kate-
Welcome. Have a good first day.
Best Wishes,
Eli

"Who are they from?" Hilary asks.

The sexiest man I've ever seen in my life, but I have no idea why he sent them because nothing good can come of it.

"My parents," I lie easily, and shove the card in my pocket. Eli said he doesn't play games, yet he kisses me like he'd like to devour me, says it's a bad idea, and then sends me flowers?

"Oh, how lovely." Hilary begins to chat about her own family while she sets me up with new passwords on the several software programs we use and shows me her routine, and all the while my mind wanders exactly where it shouldn't: to Eli.

Does he think he can sweet talk me with a few pretty blooms?

Okay, maybe the flowers are sweet, but I don't get it. I was up long after I turned off the lights and climbed into bed last night. I could still feel him against me, hear his low, rumbly voice. My body was on fire, and the man had really barely touched me. Sure, that kiss was combustible, and just the casual way he laid his hand on my back, or linked our fingers, sent my body into a tailspin unlike any I've ever felt.

Even with my ex-husband, and I don't know for sure what that says about me.

By lunch time, I've been shown Hilary's complete routine from start to finish, I've been given a tour of the building and introduced to everyone in the department, and Hilary was kind enough to show me exactly how Mr. Rudolph likes to have his coffee made.

Oh, and it must be on his desk by 8:05 every morning. Sharp.

Because, apparently, this is 1956, and it's important to bring the boss man his coffee.

Hilary and two other assistants from our department, Suzanne and Taylor, invite me to join them for lunch, and I eagerly accept, hoping against hope that one of them lets something slip and I can wrap this case up early.

Of course, I'm not that lucky.

"So, where are you from, Kate?" Taylor asks, as she munches on her sandwich, careful not to get her perfectly manicured hands dirty. She's short and lusciously curvy with dark hair that is styled in a short bob and has big brown eyes.

"Yes, tell us about you," Suzanne, Taylor's exact opposite with blonde hair, tall, statuesque figure, and bright blue eyes agrees, while Hilary nods expectantly and pops a chip in her mouth.

"Well, I grew up in the Denver area," I reply, easily keeping the details vague. "Are you all from here?"

"Hilary and I are," Suzanne replies, "but Taylor just moved here from Florida last year."

"What part of Florida?" I ask.

"Orlando," she replies with a wrinkle of the nose. "I left one hot, humid city for another."

"What were you thinkin'?" Suzanne asks with a laugh. "I think we're going to try to take the kids to Disney World next year."

And just like that, the subject is redirected from me, and I sit in silence and listen while I nibble my sandwich and chips and sip my diet soda.

**

My phone is vibrating in my handbag as I push my way into my loft after a long day in the office. I drop my keys and briefcase on the kitchen table and dig out the phone, grinning when I see Van's name on the caller ID.

"Hey, boss lady."

"How was your first day, dear?" I can hear the smile in her voice.

"Pretty much the usual. Choose forty-five different passwords, each with a different number, symbol, and the blood of a virgin, then gossip about the boss, not *my* boss, mind you, and the two assistants having an affair three offices over, learn how to make the boss his coffee, and walk home in the sweltering heat in a suit jacket."

"So, it wasn't boring then," she replies dryly, as I eye the boxes that were delivered this afternoon and are now stacked in my living room.

"Nope, not boring." *Tedious, long, and I wanted to poke my own eye out with something hot and sharp, but not boring.* "I just got home."

"Do you like the loft?" I can hear Lance's voice in the background, asking Van something about where his golf glove is, to which she says no.

"It's really beautiful. I love the balcony off the bedroom. I think I'll have some wine out there before bed tonight. My stuff arrived today."

"Good. Settle in and make yourself at home. Do you want to have breakfast in my office in the morning? You could come the same time as today and I'll have everything ready."

"Sneaky breakfast, I like it." I grin and sigh happily. I missed her. "You don't mind going in that early?"

"Pshaw, no. I usually show up that early every day. This will be a much better start to my day."

I bite my lip to keep from asking her why she shows up to work before seven in the morning every day, because I already know.

Lance.

I wish she'd talk about it, but I know she won't. Maybe one night I'll ply her with a bottle of wine and get her to unload on me.

"Okay, I'll see you tomorrow morning then."

"It's a date. 'Night."

"'Night," I reply and end the call, then order in pizza and put the bottle of wine I bought on my way home from work into the fridge on my way to the bathroom for a long, cool shower.

It's bloody hot outside.

I need to start dressing in layers for work, with something light under my jackets, so I'm not so damn hot by the time I get home.

The shower is cool and rejuvenates me. Just when I'm pulling on my shorts and a tank top, the doorbell rings.

Thank God, I'm starving.

I carry the pizza to the kitchen, grabbing my iPad on the way, pour myself a glass of wine, then decide screw it and tuck the whole bottle under my arm and walk through my bedroom to the balcony. There is a small wrought iron table with two comfortable, plush chairs out here, and I settle in to watch the sun set and the people wander through the Quarter on their way home from work or walking their dogs, tourists wandering.

It's like a moving painting, never the same, but familiar. The person who owns the herb shop below me must have got some fresh lavender in today, because the smell is brighter and lovelier than yesterday.

I prop my feet up on the unused chair and nibble on a slice of pizza and sip my wine, perfectly content to stay right here until bedtime.

"Did you get my flowers?"

I turn my head to the left, and there is my neighbor, Eli, sitting in a similar chair, only about ten feet away. And, instantly, I'm pulled toward him in the most elemental way possible.

Which is ridiculous. He's only a man.

"I didn't hear you come outside," I reply.

"You were too busy munching on that pizza and looked about a million miles away." He props his feet up, laces his fingers behind his head, and flashes me a smile that I feel all the way to my core.

Does he have to be this handsome? Seriously?

I take a sip of my wine, finishing the glass, and refill it.

"Have you had dinner?" I ask.

"No, ma'am."

"Here." I pass the pizza box over the ornate railing that separates our balconies. "I have lots of food." Then I fill my glass and pass him the bottle of wine as well. "But only one glass."

He stands and disappears into his house, then quickly returns with his own glass and flashes me that heart-stopping smile as he reclaims his seat and takes a big bite of pizza.

"This is good."

"Hilary said they were the best in the neighborhood," I inform him.

"Who's Hilary?" He frowns in confusion, making me grin.

"The woman whose position I took. She trained me today."

"So, it went well then?" His gaze is sober, and if I'm not mistaken, concerned, making me soften toward him even more.

"It did. No problems."

"Good." He chews on his crust and tilts his head at me. "Did you get my flowers?"

I nod slowly. "Why did you send them?"

He opens his mouth to answer, and then chuckles and shakes his head. "I'm not sure. It just felt like the right thing to do."

"Because you kissed me?"

His smile fades as he watches me over the railing, and I know that the replay of yesterday is running through his head just like it is mine. "No."

"Did you kiss me because Van told you not to?"

He narrows his eyes in temper, his jaw ticking, and then simply says, "No."

"Why?"

"The kiss or the flowers?"

"The flowers." I can figure out the kiss on my own. It's called chemistry, and we've got it in spades.

He frowns and looks into his wine glass. "I don't know."

"That's…not helpful." I chuckle and offer him another slice of pizza, which he declines with a shake of the head.

"Honestly?"

"Well, I don't want you to lie to me."

"I've been asking myself why all day. And the only thing I can come up with is, I like you, and I wanted you to have a good day."

I sit and stare at him and realize that he's telling me the honest truth, and that he might be as confused by it as I am.

Huh.

"Well, they're beautiful. Thank you."

"You're welcome." He grins, as if he's thinking of an inside joke, and I can't help but smile back.

"What are you thinking?"

"The sunflowers reminded me of you."

"Big and yellow?"

"Happy. You have a great smile."

I exhale loudly and watch him carefully. "You confuse me."

"We're on the same page there."

"You said this is a bad idea, and you're right. Bad idea is tattooed all over it with huge neon letters."

He nods. "I know. So, for tonight, I'm going to stay over here and you're going to stay over there, and we're just going to enjoy the evening and this wine."

I watch as he raises a brow and waits for my response.

"When was the last time you sat out on the balcony to watch the sunset?" I ask.

"I haven't been home before the sunset in years," he replies honestly.

"Why tonight?"

He shakes his head again and watches a man jog by with a huge black lab on a leash. "I couldn't say."

I want to ask him if he *can't* or *won't*, but instead, I just nod and leave it be for tonight. "It's a good evening for sitting outside," I say instead.

"That it is."

CHAPTER FIVE

It's been a hell of a week.

By Friday night, I'm exhausted. Administrative assistants work their asses off. Not that I didn't already know this; I've just never personally worked as one, regardless of what my resume on file in Linda's office says. I'm ready to take a cool shower and curl up with a good book and a glass of wine.

I make it through the shower and change into sweat shorts and a tank, just as my doorbell rings.

I frown, tempted to ignore it, but when the bell rings for the third time, and then a fist pounds on the wood with a loud, "We know you're in there!" I walk over and swing open the door.

"Did I forget that we were having dinner?" I ask and watch with a wry grin as Savannah and Declan both push their way inside, stopping to kiss my cheek as they pass, their hands and arms loaded down with bags of food.

"We decided to surprise you." Declan sets down his bags and pulls me in for a big hug. "We're gonna sit around and eat fattening food and drink wine. Well, I have to leave after dinner for tonight's gig, but I'm still having a little wine."

"Just like the old days," Savannah adds with a grin. My cheek is pressed to Dec's chest, listening to his heartbeat, as he rubs his hands up and down my back. I didn't realize how badly I needed a hug until this very minute.

"You okay?" he asks and plants his lips on my head.

"Yeah." I don't pull away, and instead watch Savannah as she pulls white Styrofoam containers out of plastic bags, laying the food out buffet style on my table. She has dark circles under her tired hazel eyes, and she looks way too thin in her jeans and plain black T-shirt.

"You survived your first week," Van says, as she opens a bottle of wine and pours it into three glasses.

"Did you think I wouldn't?" I ask with a laugh, as I pull away from Dec and accept a glass.

"No, I just figured we'd use that as an excuse to celebrate," she replies with a wink. "I brought your favorite: Italian. With fattening Alfredo sauce and lots of extra bread."

"You do love me." I offer Van a wide smile and snatch the bread first. "God, I love carbs. Why do I love carbs so much?"

"Because they're bad for you," Van replies. "They're every woman's kryptonite."

"I thought that was shoes," Declan says, as he piles his own plate high with pasta, sauce, and bread.

"No, shoes are a necessity," I inform him soberly. "Like water."

"Women are weird," Dec says with a laugh, and makes himself at home on the floor, his back leaning against my sofa. His long, lean body is relaxed as he eats his dinner, and he reminds me of his older brother. Dec's just as tall and broad in the shoulders as Eli.

The Boudreaux men are prime examples of the male species.

"I don't think we're supposed to fully understand each other," I reply, and lick sauce off my finger.

"How are you?" Van asks, as she nibbles on a piece of bread. She barely took any food. I eye her plate and then stare her in the eye, but she shakes her head and narrows her eyes at me.

"I'm fine," I reply.

"No, really," Dec says, his usually smiling face sober now.

"No, really," I insist. "I'm fine."

"When was the divorce final?" Van asks.

"Sixty-four days ago," I reply before I can catch myself, then wince when they both turn surprised gazes on me, and share a glance with each other.

"You're counting the days and you're *fine*?" Dec asks.

"Heck, yes, I'm counting the days. That divorce was hard won." I stuff more chicken and pasta in my mouth and point at both of them with my fork. "You know that."

"You should have let me deck him," Declan insists. He lowers his fork to his plate, his eyes hot with temper as he glances at me. "Only a lowlife son of a bitch does what he did to you."

"It might have been satisfying to watch you hit him." I lick my fork clean as I think of my strong friend kicking my ex-husband's ass. "Do you still do that Krave Magnus stuff?"

"Krav Maga," he corrects me with a laugh. "And you should do it too. It's great self defense."

"I'll just add that to my list of things to do." I tilt my head as I watch Van push her pasta around her plate, lost in thought. "I'm thinking about becoming a lesbian and joining a nudist colony."

"Now, that, I'd like to see," Declan declares with a roguish grin, but then follows my gaze and swears under his breath. "She's not listening."

"Not even a little bit," I agree. "Earth to Van."

"Huh?" She jerks her gaze up and takes another long sip of her wine, then refills her glass.

"Now it's your turn to talk."

"We haven't finished with you," she says, but I just grin at her.

"Yes, we have. Dec and I just discussed me turning lesbo and joining a nudist colony."

"I'm all for it," Declan agrees, earning a glare from his twin sister.

"How bad are things, Van? And don't deny it. You look like poop, and you deflect when asked. I'm the master of those tactics."

She glances nervously at her brother and then back at me. "You don't need to worry—"

"Spill it, Van." Dec's voice is calm, his posture relaxed, but every muscle in his body is on high alert.

He's ready to kick butt.

And so am I, for that matter.

"Things just aren't going very well," Savannah murmurs softly.

"Is he hurting you?" Declan asks.

"He's…ignoring me." She sets her plate aside and pulls her knees up into her chest, hugging her legs tight. "Unless he can't find something, he just pretty much does his own thing."

"Who else is he doing?" I ask, and set my own finished dinner aside, then just raise a brow when Van stares at me and chews her bottom lip.

"I don't know."

"I'm going to grab Eli and Beau, and we're going to—"

"Nothing," Van insists, laying her hand on Dec's shoulder. "You're going to do *nothing*."

"Fuck that, Vanny," he says and stares at her as if she's lost her mind. "He's fucking around on you and you want us to ignore it?"

"I don't have proof." She shrugs and smiles sadly. "It's just a hunch."

"Promise me," Dec says and pulls her close to hug her, "that you'll call me, day or night, if you need me."

"I will."

"If you find proof—" I begin.

"I'll kick his ass myself," she finishes. She pulls out of Declan's embrace and begins cleaning up.

"See, this is exactly why I'm not ever getting married," Dec says. "I'd kill myself before I'd hurt a woman, and that seems to be all marriage is good for. Pain."

"Mom and Dad were married for more than thirty-five years," Van reminds him.

"Mine have been married for thirty-five," I add. "They're not all bad."

"Still, I'll stick to the way things have always been."

"Why are all my brothers man-whores?" Van asks me, as if Dec's not sitting right next to her.

"Because they're all hot and sexy and have women falling at their feet?"

"You think I'm hot and sexy?" Dec asks with a charming smile. "Aww, dawlin'. That's the sweetest thing you've ever said."

"Are you falling at Eli's feet?" Van asks, surprising me. Declan sobers and they both stare at me with matching hazel eyes.

"Heck no," I insist. "I don't fall at any man's feet."

"Atta girl." Van salutes me with her wine and drains the glass.

"Oh, by the way, Mama has given us instructions to bring you to dinner on Sunday." Declan grins. "I'll pick you up on my way over."

"I don't want to intrude on your family dinner."

"She might kill us if we don't bring you," Van assures me.

"Or not feed us, which would be worse," Declan adds. "You're coming."

"Thank you," I reply and grin at my friends. "It's good to see you guys."

"It's you we're happy to see, dawlin'," Declan replies with a wink. "Did you bring dessert, Vanny?"

"Of course."

"Stop holdin' out on me."

***

I sleep late the next morning. My biggest vice is sleeping late on the weekends. I despise the alarm clock. I open my eyes slowly and stretch in the soft king sized bed, then lie on my back and stare out the French doors at the bright blue sky.

As I begin to ponder what might be on today's agenda, my doorbell rings.

I glance at the clock and scowl. It's nine in the freaking morning on a Saturday. Who in the world could be ringing my bell?

I climb out of bed and don't even bother to throw a robe over my tank and pink frilly panties. Whoever is stupid enough to show up at my place at this hour is just going to have to take me the way they get me.

It's most likely Savannah anyway. She always was a morning person.

I hate that.

I yank the door open and scrub my free hand over my face. "Seriously, Van, you just left here like six hours ago. Did you forget something?"

"Savannah was here until three this morning?"

I drop my hand and stare up in shock at a grinning Eli. His whiskey eyes are shining as he takes in my sleepy appearance, from the top of my ratted head, down my braless front, making my nipples pucker, thank you very much, to my pink tipped toes. On his way back up, his jaw drops when he sees my panties.

"Yes," I squeak and cross my arms over my chest. "She and Declan came over for dinner and ended up staying. We always could talk for hours."

"Did I wake you?" he asks, his voice low and intimate as he steps toward me. I move back, letting him inside, and close the door.

"No, I was just waking up." I bite my lip. "Um, what are you doing here?"

"I need a favor."

I feel my eyebrows climb into my hairline as I watch his eyes smile, but he purses his lips to keep the smile at bay. It's... endearing.

"A favor?"

"Yes, dawlin', a very important one."

I tilt my head and feel my lips quirk into a half smile. "I'm listening."

"I need an escort around the Quarter this mornin'."

I prop my hands on my hips, and Eli's eyes slowly sober, heat, and move from my eyes to my mouth and down to my breasts. He swears under his breath as I remember that I'm showing him way more than I should and recross my arms.

"You need an escort?"

He nods and catches my gaze in his again. "Yes, please."

"I don't know my way around," I reply softly.

"I do."

"So, why—"

"I'd like to show you around our neighborhood, *cher*," he says softly. "What do you say?"

I chew my lip for a few seconds, and finally smile gratefully. I've been dying to walk around and explore the famous French Quarter. "I'd be happy to escort you."

"You might want to choose a different outfit," he says, as he gestures to my clothes. "I would hate to have to beat every man we walk past into the sidewalk for looking at you."

I wave him off and turn to walk into my bedroom, but hear him mutter, "Although, you look amazing in anything you wear."

This is not helping my nipples calm down. I close the door to the bedroom, lean back on it, and take a deep breath. This man is pure walking temptation. But he didn't touch me. He smiled and invited me on a tour of the neighborhood. Sure, he checked out my chest, but I am braless, and my damn body reacts to him on a purely visceral level.

I can control myself for the day. No problem.

I nod and mentally pat myself on the back, then quickly tame my hair, brush my teeth, and pull on some denim capris and a blue sleeveless blouse. On my way out of the bedroom, I grab the green hat Eli bought me the other day, and slip my feet into a comfortable pair of Toms.

"Okay, I'm ready."

Eli is standing at my window, his hands in the front pockets of jeans that mold to his bottom and thighs just perfectly. His black T-shirt is stretched over his broad shoulders, and his dark hair is still wet around the collar from his shower.

He turns and smiles when he sees me holding the hat.

"Good plan. It's going to get hot today."

"It's hot every day," I reply with a wry grin. He hands me my handbag and escorts me down to the sidewalk.

"This way." He leads me to the right, his hand in its spot on the small of my back, and within two blocks, we're at Jackson Square, in front of the St. Louis Cathedral where jazz musicians play enthusiastically on a variety of instruments, palm readers are just setting up their tables, and artists have set up their canvases on the iron fence surrounding the beautiful park that holds the large statue of President Jackson on his horse, giving the square it's name.

"It's beautiful down here," I murmur, and smile at a man as he plays his saxophone.

"That it is," Eli agrees, and leads me around the park toward a green building with a green and white awning and dozens of round tables with chairs under it. "We'll start with breakfast."

"There's a long line," I reply, and eye the line of people waiting patiently for a table.

"It moves fast," he assures me, and leads me to the end of the line. "And it's worth it."

"Okay, tell me about Café du Monde," I request, reading the sign on the awning.

"Best beignets in New Orleans," he assures me. "This place has been here forever and hasn't changed much."

Before I know it, we move up the line and find a table near the sidewalk.

"The menu is on the napkin dispenser," Eli informs me, and tilts it toward me. "But do you mind if I order for you?"

"I don't mind." I sit back and listen as Eli informs our server that we'll each have an order of beignets and a frozen café au lait. I watch in fascination as horse-drawn carriages glide down the street before us, the drivers giving their passengers all kinds of information about Jackson Square, which is directly across the street from us. "Thank you for bringing me out today."

Eli quirks a brow. "It's *you* escorting *me*, remember?"

I grin and nod. "Right. Except you're showing me around."

"You're new to town." He shrugs as if it's no big thing, but somehow I think it is a big deal. "And I haven't wandered around in a long while."

"Does it change much?"

"Not much," he says with a smile, as the beignets and coffees are delivered. "My father used to bring all six of us here every Saturday morning for as long as I can remember. We came until he passed away."

He stops talking and frowns, his eyes trained with determination on his beignets.

"I'm sorry for your loss," I say softly. I know his dad passed away two years ago, and I remember the heartbreak of the entire family with the loss of the larger than life patriarch of the family. "Oh, my gosh," I whisper, eyeing the square doughnuts covered in a heaping pile of powdered sugar. "This is just…"

"The best," Eli finishes on a groan and eats one of the treats in two bites. He licks his lips, and my ninety-dollar black lace panties are soaking wet.

This man should come with a warning label.

"Are you going to eat them or continue to stare at me?" he asks with a laugh.

I shake my head, pulling myself out of the trance of watching Eli, and take a bite. "Oh, wow."

"Right?"

"I need these every day."

"I can arrange that." His eyes are perfectly sober as he watches me.

"I'm kidding. I'd weigh four hundred pounds within a month."

"No, you wouldn't, and I'm not kidding. Say the word, and I'll get them for you."

I sit back in my seat and watch him as I chew the doughy goodness. What can I say to that? Instead of responding, I finish my beignets, then drink the delicious frozen coffee and wipe my mouth and brush the fallen powdered sugar off my shirt and pants.

"Ready for what comes next?" he asks and stands, holding his hand out for mine.

"Sure." He leads me to the sidewalk, settles my hat on my head, and leads me up and down the streets, wandering through gift shops and antique stores, jewelry stores, and even novelty voodoo shops. I soak it all in, looking in every nook and cranny of every store, and Eli patiently waits for me, not saying much, letting me lead him where I want to go.

He's protective while we're walking from store to store, sure to keep his hand on the small of my back, but when I'm poking around, he gives me space to explore.

In an antique jewelry store, I find a silver and ivory cameo locket that I must have for my mother for Mother's Day. When I pull my wallet out to pay, Eli beats me to it, handing the clerk his card.

"Eli, I'm buying this for my mom."

"She'll love it."

"Yes, but *you* just bought it."

He raises a brow and watches me with an amused tilt to his lips, as the clerk bags it up and hands it to me. "You're not paying for anything when you're with me, *cher*."

Before I can respond, he turns and leads me out of the store, and we're back to the palm readers and musicians before Jackson Square. A woman with deep mocha skin and a bight white smile waves at me, and I immediately sit at her table and pay her before Eli can blink, making him glare at me.

I stick my tongue out at him.

"Well, hello there, I'm Madame Sophia." She grins and begins to rub hand sanitizer on her hands.

At least she's a clean palm reader.

"Will I be reading both of your palms, then?"

"No," Eli replies and shoves both his hands in his pockets. He always does that when he's uncomfortable.

It's kind of adorable.

"Scared?" I ask with a grin.

"Skeptical," he replies, matching my grin and sending me off my axis.

"That's okay, baby girl, he can just listen. Please give me the hand you're most comfortable writing with." I lay my right hand in hers, palm up, and settle in to be entertained.

"Ah," she whispers and traces her finger around the outside of my palm. "You're an emotional one, aren't you, baby girl? You wear your heart on your sleeve."

I bite my lip and glance up at Eli, who rolls his eyes. I know what he's thinking: half the population does that.

"A smart one, you are. Oh, look at that! You're a good liar." She glances up at me, narrows her eyes, and then looks back down.

I lie for a living.

"Oh, baby girl." She's not looking at my palm anymore. Now she's looking me in the eye, her chocolate brown eyes full of sympathy. "He didn't deserve you, and you're better off without him."

I frown and glance at Eli, then back at Sophia. "I don't think—"

"But you gonna be just fine," she continues without a beat. "Sometimes, love be right under your nose, y'know?"

"I don't think I really need love advice," I reply nervously. She winks at me, and then returns to my palm.

"Ah, you're stubborn, but that's good. You don't let people take advantage, but you are a sucker for the puppy dog eyes." She chuckles when I simply blink at her. "Your parents miss you, way over there in Ireland."

I gasp and move to pull my hand away. "How did you know—?"

"It's just here," she replies. "You'll get a call soon that will change things for you."

"Change them how?"

"That's enough," Eli says, and lays his hand on my shoulder, sending electricity down my chest, making my nipples pucker and Sophia's eyes widen as she looks between the two of us, her hand still hanging on to mine.

"This is a powerful connection."

"I said that's enough. Thank you for your time," he says and helps me to my feet.

"I don't think she was done," I say with a frown, and glance back to see Madam Sophia watching us walk away with a thoughtful frown on her worn face.

"She was done."

His jaw is clenched and his eyes are narrowed as he leads me down the cobblestone street.

"Eli."

He doesn't stop, so I dig in my heels and pull him to a stop next to me.

"I'm fine."

He tucks my hair behind my ear. "You should be wearing your hat."

I settle it on my head, tipped a bit too far forward, so he has to bend at the knees to see my face. Finally, he smiles and tips the brim back.

"Why did that freak you out?"

He shrugs. "She was upsetting you."

She was freaking me out.

"I'm fine," I repeat stubbornly. He simply smirks and kisses my forehead.

"Are you ready for lunch?"

"More food?"

"You're in New Orleans, dawlin'. There's always more food."

***

"I'm exhausted," I sigh, as Eli walks me up to my door several hours, many shops, and two meals later.

"In a good way, I hope."

"Definitely a good way. I had so much fun today."

He smiles softly and takes my hat off my head, then tucks my hair behind my ear and drags his fingertip down my jawline. "I had fun too."

"I'm glad you rang my bell at the crack of dawn."

"I believe it was nine, not the crack of dawn."

I shrug. "Same difference."

He chuckles as I fish my keys out of my handbag and unlock my door.

"Do you want to come in?" I ask.

"I have a bit of work to do this evening," he replies. His eyes look almost…determined.

"Okay, well thanks again."

He nods as I close the door and toss my hat on the sofa. Holy crap, today was fun. The chemistry is still off the charts, but he was a perfect gentleman the whole day. He barely touched me, but we laughed a lot and he was…*friendly.*

Huh. Eli Boudreaux and I are friends.

I grin as I walk through my loft, and my iPhone lights up with a FaceTime call from my cousin Rhys. I grin as I press accept and sit out on my balcony to take the call.

"Well, hello, gorgeous. You are a sight for sore eyes."

"Hey, handsome. Back at you."

CHAPTER SIX
ELI

"Do you want to come in?" she asks, her green eyes smiling up at me.

Fuck, yes, I want to come in. Which means, I'd better not go in there because I've kept my hands off of her all day and my resistance is dying a slow, painful death.

"I have a bit of work to do this evening," I lie easily. She immediately looks down, disappointment shadowing her eyes, and I feel like the first-class asshole I'm known to be. But I'd be an even bigger asshole if I followed her in and seduced those expensive panties off her.

"Okay, well thanks again." She offers me another of her sweet smiles, then closes the door behind her and flips the deadbolt lock with a loud click.

I lean my forehead on her door and quietly take a long, deep breath.

I can still smell her.

I walk down her stairs and stroll to my own empty house, thoughts of Kate still running through my head. I don't remember the last time I took a whole day away from the office, and I certainly don't remember the last time I enjoyed myself so much.

Kate's enthusiasm for everything new is contagious. Her love of the music, the food, hell…even that crazy palm reader.

She jumps in with both feet and relishes the experience, making being in her company simply effortless.

And maybe that's what has me scared shitless.

I've taken my home for granted my whole life. My father always pointed out to us that we live in a special place, but until I spent the past week sharing it with Kate, it never occurred to me to truly appreciate it.

Her delight in red beans and rice and a shrimp po' boy this afternoon brings a smile to my lips. The woman can eat unlike anyone else I've ever been with. Most women pick at lettuce and turn their nose up at walking *anywhere*, not to mention walking for blocks and blocks, wandering through shops full of overpriced gaudy knick-knacks.

Not that I typically pay attention to those sorts of things, as long as they're fun in bed and don't get too attached.

But Kate's different. Yes, I want to tumble her into bed and mess her up more than I want my next breath, but I enjoy her company just as much. Making her smile makes my stomach clench. Listening to her laugh makes my chest ache.

And when she slid her hand in mine and linked our fingers when we crossed the street, it was the easiest touch I've ever had.

I walk up the stairs to the master bedroom, toe off my shoes, and stare at my balcony, wondering if she'll go out to enjoy the rest of her evening.

And if so, would she mind if I join her?

God, I've become a pussy.

I just saw her five minutes ago, and I'm already craving her company. And that's exactly what it is: I crave her. Her body, her thoughts, her smile.

All of her.

She's made parts of me come alive that have been long dead, and I'm not sure if I can trust this yearning in my gut, yet I can't stop it.

I cross to the doors and open them, but before I can step out onto the balcony, I can hear her voice. And a man's.

I shove my hands in my pockets and finger the half-dollar in my right hand.

"Well, hello, gorgeous. You're a sight for sore eyes."

"Hey, handsome. Back at you."

"How are you down there in the Big Easy?"

I inch outside and see that her back is to me, and she's talking via FaceTime on her iPhone.

"Things are great down here. How are you? Are you taking care of yourself? I know you work so hard, and I worry, you know."

"Stop worrying about me, love. I'm strong as an ox." I raise a brow at the term of endearment, and feel my breath catch in my throat.

"Stubborn as one, too," she replies. I can hear the smile in her voice.

"You miss me and you know it."

"I do," she replies with a sigh. "I miss you very much. When do I get to see you?"

I turn and quietly let myself back into my house, gently closing the doors behind me. So, she does have someone. I shake my head and laugh ruefully. I'm such a fucking fool. Sharing beignets and palm readings means nothing.

She means nothing.

I can hear her laugh trickle in from my door, and every hair stands up on the back of my neck.

She's not nothing. She's the least nothing I've ever met in my life. And I can't have her.

***

"Uncle Eli, I want to go outside and play catch." My youngest sister's son, Sam, is staring at me with hopeful hazel eyes, his Chicago Cubs hat planted firmly on his head, baseball mitt and ball in his grubby little boy hands.

"I know you don't have a hat on in my kitchen," Mom gives Sam a stern look, and he takes the hat off and lowers his chin to his chest.

"No, ma'am."

"After dinner," I inform him, and pull him in for a hug and to ruffle his shaggy dark hair. "You can take both me and Beau on."

"I throw better than both of you," Sam says, and grins at Beau, who is chopping vegetables for Mom on the other side of the counter, across from where Sam, Gabby, and I are sitting.

"You don't throw better than me," Beau insists with a frown.

"Do too," Sam says, and eyes the pecan pie sitting on the counter cooling. "Nannan, can I have some pie?"

"Don't even think about touching that pie until after dinner." Mom shakes her spatula at Sam, making him grin. "You're just like your uncles. Always diving into dessert first."

"I'm a growing boy. Right, Mama?"

Gabby smiles down at her son and kisses his head before he can pull away with a cringe. "You are a growing boy. Growing on my nerves."

Sam smiles and walks toward the back door. "I'm gonna go toss the ball in the air until dinner."

"Good plan. Stay close!" Gabby calls, as the screen door slams.

"He's adorable," Charly, at the stove next to Mom, says with a grin. "And knows it."

"He's seven going on thirty-five," Beau says with a laugh. "He tried to talk me out of twenty bucks the other day when he dragged the garbage cans down to the road."

"He what?" Gabby asks with a gasp. "I'll kill him."

"Oh, please," Mom says with a scoff. "Y'all tried to pull off more 'n that with your daddy 'n me when you were young."

"Never got away with it, either," Charly says happily, and tosses some corn on the cob into a boiling pot. We've been wealthy for generations, but we've never hired household staff. Mama and Dad always said that there was no reason to live in a house too big for the eight of us to take care of. Mama loves to cook, loved raising us kids, and we had our own share of chores growing up. "Where are Savannah and Dec?"

"Here we are," Van answers, as she comes into the kitchen, passing hugs and kisses out to everyone.

"You did not!"

I freeze at the sound of her voice, then feel my hands clench into fists and my eyes narrow when Kate and Declan walk into the kitchen, his arm around her shoulders and hers around his waist, leaning into each other and laughing their fucking asses off. It's the leaning that pisses me off the most. They're way too cozy for my comfort level.

What is she doing here?

"Kate!" Mama exclaims, and hurries around the kitchen counter to pull Kate in for a hug. "Ah, dawlin', it's been too long since I laid eyes on you."

"You look wonderful, as always," Kate returns and hugs my mom tightly. "Thank you for inviting me."

"You're family, babe. You don't need an invitation. You'll come for Sunday dinner while you're still in town."

I take a deep breath, but feel my blood boil. She was invited, but she didn't call me to give her a ride? Instead, she chose to ride with Declan?

What the fuck?

Suddenly, Sam comes running in from outside, letting the screen slam loudly behind him. "Mama! I threw the ball way up high and it hit the oak tree and bounced off the trunk and hit the roof!" He comes to an abrupt stop when he sees Kate, pulls his hat off his head, and shuffles the toe of his worn sneaker on the hardwood floor. "Ma'am."

"Sam, this is Kate," Declan says, smiling at our nephew. "She's a very good friend of the family."

"It's a pleasure, ma'am." He holds out his hand to shake Kate's, making us all grin. Gabby's raising Sam very well.

"The pleasure is all mine, Sam. It's nice to meet you."

"Yes, ma'am."

"What were you saying about your baseball?"

Sam smiles widely, the excitement filling his dark brown eyes again. "It hit the roof and then rolled off and I caught it!"

"Good job," Kate says with a smile. God, her smile kills me every time, even when it's aimed at someone else.

"Don't you hit any of my windows, now," Mom warns and kisses Sam's head as she passes back into the kitchen.

"No, Nannan," Sam agrees. "I'm still working off the last window." He cringes and glances at his mom.

"He broke another window?" Charly asks with a laugh.

"Hey, don't laugh, that's the third one in six months," Gabby replies, but can't help the smile that forms on her pretty, young face.

"I do chores to pay for them," Sam informs us all. "When can we have pie?"

"Come on, shorty." Declan snags Sam's ball from his mitt. "Let's go out and toss some."

"You don't have a mitt!"

"I'll make do." Dec winks at Kate, setting my teeth on edge, and follows Sam outside.

"Lance isn't coming?" Beau asks Van. She just shakes her head no, and Beau's gaze meets mine.

Yeah, he and I are going to have to have a conversation with Lance soon. Something's going on there, and it isn't good. Seeing Van hurting is killing all of us.

"I got some new shoes in, ladies," Charly says with a sly smile. "Some really gorgeous, knock you on your behind, beautiful shoes."

"I'll be there tomorrow," Van says and links her arm through Kate's. "I'll bring Kate too. We'll clean you out."

"Not fair," Gabby says with a scowl. "This is what sucks about living so far out of town. I don't get to just walk down the street and shop."

"I brought you some in your size," Charly replies and winks at our baby sister. "I can't have you living in the Bayou with ugly shoes."

"You're my favorite sibling. You know that, right?"

"Hey!" Beau scowls at Gabby and wags his sharp knife at her. "I'm the one that lives out there with you, so you're not alone, and commute in to work every day."

"I've been telling you for months to move into town," Gabby replies and leans her elbows on the counter.

"I don't want you out there by yourself either," I reply. "You and Sam alone in the Bayou makes us all nervous."

"I'm not alone. I run a very successful bed and breakfast, thank you very much. There are always people around."

"People we don't know," Charly replies, and Mama nods in agreement.

"We love you, babe," Mama adds and cups Gabby's face in her hand. "Beau's keeping you safe."

"Beau needs to get himself a woman and leave me alone," Gabby replies, glaring at Beau, who just shakes his head and laughs.

"Tell me about the bed and breakfast," Kate says and fishes a carrot out of the salad bowl. God, I love her appetite. She looks amazing today in a soft, flowy black skirt and a green button-down top with a black belt cinched around her slim waist. She left her hair down and applied minimal makeup, leaving her gorgeous freckles uncovered, and has clear gloss on her lips.

Fuck, I want to kiss those lips.

"I turned the family plantation house into an inn," Gabby replies proudly. We're all fucking proud of her. Inn Boudreaux is thriving and booked solid for months.

"Oh, that's awesome," Kate says. "I bet it's amazing. Is it right on the river?"

"Yes. You can't see the river because of the levy, but yes. Guests love the old oak trees, and we've restored some of the slave quarters and stuff so they can also wander around and learn about the plantation."

"I'd love to see it," Kate says, and I immediately decide to take her out there next weekend. She'll love it. "Maybe I can get my parents to come visit and stay out there. It would be right up their alley."

"Are they still in Ireland?" Savannah asks.

"Yes, and they love it there. But I miss them."

"What about Rhys?" Charly asks, as Gabby and I set the table and Mama sets bowls and platters full of way too much food on the table as well. I still at Charly's question and watch Kate.

"He's great. Busy. I haven't seen him in a couple months."

"He's adorable," Charly says with a grin. "In a sexy, delicious kind of way. Is he available?"

"This is Rhys we're talking about," Kate says with a laugh. "Who knows? But I was able to FaceTime with him last night, and he looks as great as ever, and still stubborn as heck."

So, she was FaceTiming with this Rhys guy.

None of my business.

"Boys!" Mama calls out the back door. "Dinner's ready! Come eat these groceries!"

Kate sits next to me at the table and smiles up at me sweetly, and I find myself returning it, despite this perpetual frustration I can't shake.

"You okay?" she asks softly.

"Why wouldn't I be?"

"You haven't said two words to me since I got here."

"Hello, Kate." She narrows her eyes and tilts her head, but before she can ask any further questions, Sam and Declan join us and we all dig in. I glance up to find Charly watching Kate and me with a raised brow, but I shake my head, giving her the silent message to leave it be, and eat silently.

Kate laughs, asking more questions about Gabby's inn, Charly's shop, and how Sam likes the second grade, charming my whole family. How has she been friends with Dec and Van for so long and I'd never met her before?

Because you've been too busy keeping the business the way Dad wanted you to.

"Eli, you're more quiet than normal," Mama says softly, watching me with shrewd eyes. "What's going on with you?"

I shake my head and wipe my mouth with a napkin. "Just the same old thing, Mama."

"Hmph," she replies and glances around the table. "Why do I feel like I'm out of the loop here?"

"You're not," I reply with a smile. "Work as usual."

"You work too much."

"Not you too," I reply, and rub my forehead with the tips of my fingers. "I get this lecture from Savannah at least once a week."

"Well, you'll be gettin' it from me too. You're *my* baby boy."

Oh, God.

Kate smirks next to me and hides her smile behind a tall glass of lemonade.

"I'm fine, I promise."

"He even took the day off yesterday," Kate adds nonchalantly. Mama's eyes widen as she looks between Kate and me.

"He did?"

"Yes, ma'am."

"How do you know?"

Don't say it. I lay my hand on Kate's thigh, but she ignores me and says it anyway.

"Because he was with me. He showed me around the French Quarter all day. It's his fault that I'm now addicted to beignets from Café du Monde."

The table is silent for a few beats, then Mama clears her throat.

"You went to Café du Monde on Saturday mornin'?"

I meet her bright eyes with my own and nod. "Yes, ma'am."

"I've always wanted to see the French Quarter. It was amazing," Kate continues, oblivious to the tension between us siblings. They're all staring at me like I've grown a second head.

Finally, in the innocent way that only a seven-year-old can, Sam speaks up.

"Pawpaw used to take us there on Saturdays," he says, and takes a bite of the corn on the cob, missing some pieces, thanks to the gap in his front teeth. "It was fun."

"That's right," Gabby says and runs her hand over her son's hair.

Suddenly, Kate lays *her* hand on *my* thigh and I glance down into understanding eyes, and it's all I can take.

"I'm sorry, Mama, but I just remembered that I have some work to catch up on." I stand quickly and take care of my own dishes, then kiss her cheek. "Thank you for dinner. I'll call you tomorrow."

"Eli—"

But I don't stop to hear what she has to say. I walk quickly to my car and peel out of the driveway. My heart is beating quickly, and for the first time in more than two years, I'm consumed with *emotion*.

What in the hell is wrong with me?

And who the fuck is Rhys?

This is all Kate's fault. Before she showed up with her gorgeous green eyes and touchable red hair, I was fine, consumed by work. I had a routine that worked well for me, with no interruptions.

Certainly no Saturdays spent in the Quarter and evenings listening to Dec's gigs.

I just need to get laid. That's all there is to it. It's been more than a minute since I last enjoyed the company of a warm, willing woman.

Yes, that's it.

Before long, I'm back at my house, pacing through the silent, empty rooms, my phone in my hand, paging through my contacts list. I'm going to scratch this itch and get over it. Erase Kate from my mind completely.

I pour myself three fingers of brandy, sit behind my desk, and thumb through my electronic black book.

Ah, yes, I could call Amanda. She's always fun. Tall, leggy. But she has strawberry blonde hair, and that'll just remind me too much of Kate.

I skip to the next name.

Collette! I met Collette three years ago at a charity function. She's smart as a whip and likes to be blindfolded. I grin, but then I remember that Collette has freckles on her shoulders, and that won't do.

Fuck.

Fredericka. I haven't seen her in a while. She's curvy in all the right places with the best tits I've ever seen.

Scratch that. Kate has the best tits I've ever seen.

And I've never actually *seen* them.

I sigh loudly and swallow the rest of the brandy, then smile when I see Stephanie's name.

Steph and I have had a mutually satisfying arrangement for the better part of five years. She's long and lean with a runner's body and an enthusiasm in bed that can't be matched. She has jet-black hair and chocolate brown eyes with the whitest, smoothest skin I've ever seen. She's not afraid to make noise, and she can suck a cock like no one else.

Yes, I do believe I'll call Steph.

My thumb hovers over her name, but suddenly I see laughing green eyes smiling up at me as she gets her palm read, her face set in rapture when she first tasted the beignets. God, my dick throbs at the thought of what those eyes will look like when I'm buried so deep inside her I can't tell where she ends and I begin.

Motherfucker.

I throw my phone across the room, aiming for the couch, so it doesn't break, then pick up my glass and consider throwing that too, needing to hear the shatter of glass, when Charly's voice comes from the doorway.

"Sam would be impressed with that arm."

I whirl and glare at my sister. "What the fuck are you doing here?"

"Well, I'm not here for your sparkling personality," she replies, and plants her hands on her hips.

"Look, I'm not really fit for company tonight, Char."

"Clearly." She smiles, her hazel eyes softening, and I feel my chest loosen too. "You're handsome when you're pissed."

"Don't try to charm me."

She tosses her head back and laughs, then plops down on my couch and rescues my phone from the cushions. "What did your phone do to you?"

"Nothing."

"Wanna talk about Kate?"

"Fuck no."

"Wanna talk about anything?"

I glare at her and cross my arms over my chest.

"That may work in the boardroom, but it doesn't work with me."

"You're a pain in my ass." I sigh and stare at Charly. She's the second to the youngest, and I've been wrapped around her little finger since the day Mama and Dad brought her home from the hospital.

"You love me."

I simply grunt and then cave under her hard stare and scrub my hands over my face.

"You took her for beignets."

"Shut up, Char."

"I'm just saying, you haven't had beignets since Daddy—"

"I've had beignets since Dad died."

"Yeah, the ones you make your assistant go get for you. But you never go there."

I raise a brow and smirk at her. "I'm a bit too busy to just run out for beignets when the mood strikes."

"You know, I may not be the genius of the family, leading the family business into the new millennium, but I'm not slow, Eli."

"I'm sorry." I close my eyes and pinch the bridge of my nose. "I don't know what you want me to say."

"Say that you like Kate."

"It's not a matter of liking her."

"Well, why are you here, alone, while she's right next door, also alone? That's ridiculous."

"Because she's an employee, a friend of the family, and it sounds like she already has someone in her life."

"Yeah, an asshole of an ex-husband."

My jaw drops as I stare at Charly. "Rhys?"

"What?" She frowns and shakes her head. "No, Rhys is her cousin. Her very hot, baseball star cousin. Daniel is her asshole of an ex."

I stand, circle my desk, lean my hips against it, and push my hands into my pockets. "What did he do to her?"

"Oh, no, that's her story to tell." Charly shakes her head as she stands and crosses to me, wraps her arms around my waist, and hugs me tight. "Daddy wouldn't want you to live like this, Eli."

I cringe, but don't reply. No one was in that room with Dad and me right before he died. No one else knows what he said.

What, exactly, he expected of me after his death.

"I'm fine, *bebe*," I reply, and smile reassuringly as she pulls away.

"But you want me to leave now."

"No, you know you can stay here for as long as you want." There are four women in my life that I'd do anything in the world for. My three sisters and my mother.

Scratch that. Five. It seems Kate has wormed her way onto the short list.

"I love you, big brother."

"I love you too, brat." I grin as she laughs and walks back out of the room.

"Get some sleep! You look like shit!"

"Thank you!" I call just before the front door closes. She really is a pain in my ass. I pour three more fingers and let myself out onto the balcony, my eyes immediately turning to the left, and sure enough, Kate is sitting out with a glass of wine in her small, perfect hand.

She turns her head, leveling me with a cool glare.

"Problem?" I ask and sink into my chair. She's sitting only a few feet away, with a simple wrought iron railing separating us. I could reach out and touch her.

But I don't.

"Yeah, I think there is a problem," she replies, as calmly as if we're talking about the weather.

"Would you care to share it?"

She's quiet for a moment, then sets her wine on the table beside her and turns to face me, and her green eyes, full of anger and frustration, take my breath away.

"I promised myself that I would never again let a man determine the way I feel about myself. I wouldn't play games. I'm worth more than that."

I raise a brow. "Agreed."

She laughs humorlessly and stands to pace around her small balcony.

"You confuse the heck out of me! You were so fun and easy to be with yesterday. I actually thought we were...*friends.*"

Friends. That particular word leaves a bad taste in my mouth.

"And then I see you today and you barely speak to me, then run out on your own family dinner!"

I stand and lean my hands on the railing, looking her in the eye. "I'm trying to keep my hands off of you, Kate."

"Oh, please." She rolls her eyes and crosses her arms over her chest. "I'm not irresistible, Eli. Trust me, I know."

"You're wrong. You're practically family—"

"I'm *not* part of your family."

"And I didn't know if you were already taken."

"I wouldn't have spent all day with you yesterday, not to mention let you *kiss me* the way you do, if I were taken."

"Is your divorce final?"

This makes her pause. "Of course it is."

"And Rhys is your cousin?"

She scowls. "Are you kidding me right now? You can't be jealous of my *cousin*."

"Oh, dawlin', it seems I'm jealous of my own fucking brother when it comes to you. I wanted to rip Dec's arm off his body when y'all came in Mama's kitchen today."

"Declan and I are *friends!*" She stomps away again, really worked up now, and I have to work to keep the smile off my face.

My God, she's magnificent.

"*Friends* the way you and I are friends, Kate? Does he kiss you like I do?"

"It's none of your bloody business!" She points her finger at me and keeps railing. "You don't want me anyway! I'm bloody divorced, and I have bloody male friends, and I'm not going to apologize about any of that to you!"

"Come here," I reply softly. She stops in her tracks and stares at me, chest heaving with temper.

"No."

"I won't tell you again, *cher*."

She narrows her eyes and steps closer. "You don't get to talk to me like—"

Before she can finish, I cup her face in my hand and brush my thumb across her soft cheek. Her skin is smooth and simply irresistible. I lean across the railing and stop my lips from covering hers by just a breath.

"Say *fuck*, Kate, it's okay."

"I don't swear," she whispers. "I have enough Catholic guilt as it is."

"Just this once. I won't tell." My lips are tickling hers as I talk, and I feel the shiver run through her. She licks her lips and swallows thickly, and I've never been so hard in my damn life. "Say it."

"Fuck," she whispers, and I crush my mouth to hers, kissing her with all the pent up frustration and need that I have inside me. I push both hands to the nape of her neck, holding her still as my tongue tangles with hers, then lick to the corner of her mouth to tease.

She moans, gripping onto my forearms, but not pushing me away. I want to be in her arms. I want to wrap my arms around her and pull her into me and lose myself in her.

I want to strip her bare and feast on her.

But I pull away, gently caressing her face, tucking her auburn hair behind her ears, keeping her gaze caught in my own.

"Say goodnight, Kate."

"Bad idea," she whispers, still gripping my arms with all she's worth.

"Maybe not such a bad idea," I reply hoarsely. *But not tonight.*

"Eli—"

"Say goodnight, Kate," I repeat and back away when I'm sure she has her feet under her.

"Goodnight, Kate." She presses her fingertips to her mouth and watches me with wide green eyes for a long moment, then turns and walks into her loft, locking the door behind her.

Chapter Seven
Kate

It's too hot in here. I jerk my right leg out from under the covers and roll to my left side, staring into the darkness. I swear I can still taste Eli, but it's been hours since that crazy kiss on the balcony.

He confuses me unlike anyone I've ever met, including Daniel. It's clear that he's attracted to me, and let's face it, it's reciprocated. But he's fighting it as if he's almost *afraid* of it.

How could he possibly be afraid of me?

And, honestly, it's probably for the best that he fight it, and I should be fighting it too. I'm only here for six weeks, tops. I love his siblings as if they were my own, and sleeping with Eli could make things awkward.

Although, things seem to be awkward already, so that's probably not a great argument.

Now I'm too bloody cold.

I pull the covers back over me and roll onto my back, staring at the ceiling. A car drives by outside, sending light and shadows over the walls, and then my phone pings next to me.

I frown and reach for it. Who the heck is texting me in the middle of the night?

I'm thinking of you.

Eli.

I bite my lip and reply. *Why are you awake?*

A moment later, he responds with: *Because I'm thinking of you.*

And now I'm too hot. I whip my covers off me, but before I can reply to him, he sends another message. *Did I wake you?*

No.

Why are you awake?

I shrug, even though he can't see me.

Dunno.

His next message makes me smile. *Do you need anything?*

I shake my head and answer. *No.*

Are you only going to give one word answers?

I laugh. *I have lots of words for you, but for now? Yes.*

It takes a minute for his response. Long enough for me to get too cold and then too hot and too cold again.

Okay, then just listen. I enjoy making you smile. Your smile slays me. You taste sweeter than any beignet, and I want to spend more time with you tomorrow after work.

I sigh, suddenly way too warm, and it has nothing to do with the temperature in the room, and everything to do with this confusing man.

Are you trying to charm me?

I bite my lip as I wait for his response.

Maybe.

I giggle and turn on my side. Now he's giving me the one-word answers.

It might be working. What do you have in mind for after work?

I grin and bite my lip as I wait for his answer. *I have many things in mind.*

Oh, flirty Eli is so fun!

I look forward to hearing about those things.

Meet me on the balcony?

I want to say yes, jump up, and run out there to see him, just for a few minutes, but instead, I take a deep breath and reply with: *No, thank you. Say goodnight, Eli.*

My eyes are getting heavy as I wait for his response. Finally, long minutes later, he replies.

Goodnight, Eli.

***

When I woke up this morning, there were no more text messages from Eli. I almost thought I'd dreamed them, but when I looked, there they were.

He likes making me smile.

And now that I stop to think about it, he does make me smile. Quite often, actually. He has the best smile, and when he laughs, his whole face lights up, showing off a small dimple in his right cheek. His whiskey eyes are intoxicating, and when he pins me in his sexy I-want-you stare, well, he makes my panties melt right off me.

Yeah, I enjoy making him smile too.

"Earth to Kate." I blink rapidly and glance up to find Hilary laughing at me.

"I'm sorry."

"Hon, you were a million miles away."

I cringe and glance at my computer, which has been idle so long it went to sleep.

"Yeah, daydreaming. Sorry." I smile and gesture for her to sit in the chair across from me. "What can I do for you?"

"Oh, nothing. I decided to take my lunch break a few minutes early and come see how you're gettin' on here."

"Is it lunch time already?" I check my watch, and sure enough, the day is half gone. "Wow, time flies. I'm doing well. How are you?"

"Oh, I'm just fine." Hilary pats her pretty blonde hair and grins. "I had a date on Friday."

"Really? How did that go?"

"Well, it ended on Sunday afternoon, so I'd say it went well."

We both giggle, and suddenly there's a delivery boy at my doorway. "Miss O'Shaughnessy?"

"Yes."

"I have your lunch order here."

I frown, but quickly recover, playing along. I don't want Hilary to suspect anything.

"How much do I owe you?"

"Nothin', ma'am. Have a nice day."

There's a note stapled to the plain brown paper bag.

Kate,

This should hold you over until tonight.

E.

I tuck the note in my pocket, my heart suddenly beating fast and doing the happy dance in my head, as Hilary watches with blatant curiosity. I open the bag and practically groan.

"Shrimp po' boy and red beans and rice," I announce. "I can't eat all of this. Please, tell me you'll stay and help me."

"I've never passed up a po' boy," Hilary says with a grin, as I split everything in half and we settle in to eat at my desk.

"So, tell me more about this two-day date." I take a bite of my sandwich and sigh with happiness. The man does feed me the best food.

"Well, his name is Louis, which made me think that he'd be a bit of a geek at first. I mean, his name is *Louis*."

I nod as I chew, and chuckle as Hilary gets the dopey I-got-laid look on her face.

"Where did you meet him?"

"Online." She blushes and then shrugs. "Once you reach a certain age, it's hard to meet people."

"You can't be more than thirty," I reply, and take a heaping bite of the red beans and rice.

"I'm thirty-two. No, not old, but I work all the time, and it's not like I go to school or meet new people all the time. So, I'm doing the online thing. So far, it doesn't suck."

"What does Louis do?"

"Well, he does this thing with his tongue—"

"Ew! No, what does he do for a living?" I laugh and throw a plastic-wrapped spork at her, making her giggle.

"I don't know. I think he said he works at a Starbucks."

I raise an eyebrow. "Not that I'm judging, but *you think*?"

"Honey, once he took his shirt off, and I got a look at his chest and abs, he could have told me he hunts whales for a living, and I still would have gotten naked for him."

I smirk, but I know exactly what she means. I wonder what Eli looks like under all of his perfectly tailored suits, worn blue jeans and hot T-shirts. He's muscular, I know that much just based on the little I've touched him. I wonder if he has tattoos?

"Also, Louis has these tattoos," she continues, as though she can read my mind, "all down his left arm. I spent a good few hours tracing them with my tongue."

"*Hours?*" I ask with a snort.

"Trust me; it was totally worth it," she replies with a wink. "He used his tongue in other ways that made me a very happy woman."

"Oh, my gosh, stop it with the tongue talk!" I cover my ears with my hands and shake my head. "I beg you!"

"He was begging all right."

I dissolve in a fit of giggles. "I like you."

"I like you too." She sighs and sips half my Coke. "So, who put that look I saw on your face when I walked in here?"

I shake my head adamantly. "No one."

"Bullshit."

"Seriously. I'm not currently having sex."

"No, you're currently having lunch with me. But you were thinking about having sex. I know that look." Hilary narrows her eyes. "Spill it."

"Honestly, I'm not seeing anyone, naked or clothed. I am, however, going to go buy some new shoes after work."

"New shoes are almost as good as really good sex," she concedes, and I silently blow out a long breath. "Not quite, but almost."

"New shoes are great, but I'm even more addicted to handbags."

"Me too!" she exclaims and shimmies in her seat. "Have you seen what's coming this fall from MK?"

"No, is it delicious?" I ask, and suck Coke through my straw.

"To die for," she confirms with a nod. "And I just picked up a cute little number at the Coach outlet last week."

"The outlets are my weakness." I grin at Hilary. I really do like her. She's someone I could be friends with. I'm glad she's decided to befriend me here at work.

"Now, tell me you like to read, and we'll be soulmates."

"My iPad is full of trashy romance novels."

A slow smile spreads across her pretty face. "I'm keeping you."

***

"You keep feeding me," I say to Eli as he escorts me, hand in hand, down Royal Street to the pretty little restaurant that he's taking me to for dinner.

"You like to eat. I like that in a woman." I laugh up at him, and then sigh as he leads me across the street, protectively laying his hand on the small of my back.

"How was your day?" He links his fingers with mine again as we stroll down the street.

"Long. I found out that I have to leave tomorrow morning for a business trip to New York. I also kept thinking about getting you alone. Do you know what a pain in the ass it is having you in the same building as me all day long and not being able to walk into your office and kiss you whenever I want to?"

"No, why don't you tell me."

His lips quirk as he glances down at me. "You're sassy. One of these days I'll just have my assistant send down for you and you can come to my office."

"Just so you can kiss me?"

"We can start with that, yes." His voice is suddenly rough, and my knees turn to jelly at the thought of being in Eli's office with him, and all the things we could do in that office.

"I don't think that's a good idea. People will talk, and we can't have that."

"So professional," he murmurs, then stops us on the sidewalk and leans in to whisper in my ear. "I can't wait to see you all flummoxed and writhing and *unprofessional* beneath me, *cher.* Trust me, we're about to get as unprofessional as possible."

My breath catches in my throat as he leans back and pins me in his hot stare. He drags his fingertip over the pulse in my throat. "I see that thought turns you on."

Heck yes that turns me on! I can only swallow hard and watch as he pulls away and leads me to the restaurant.

"Café Amelie," I read aloud. "That's a pretty name."

"And good food." He turns to the hostess. "Reservation for Boudreaux."

"Of course." She grins and grabs two menus. "Would you prefer courtyard seating?"

Eli raises an eyebrow at me. It's cooler this evening, and the courtyard is pretty with lights in the trees above. "The courtyard is beautiful."

"The lady wishes to sit in the courtyard," Eli replies with a soft smile, his eyes never leaving mine.

This man is potent.

We're seated in the corner of the courtyard, giving the table an intimate atmosphere. Soon, a very tall, handsome waiter arrives to take our drink order and to tell us about the specials.

"I'd enjoy a lemon drop martini, please." I smile at Eli as he orders his own drink and tells Joe the waiter that we need a few minutes with the menu.

"You're not ordering for me?" I ask when Joe leaves.

"Do you want me to?" Eli asks. "I certainly can."

I shrug a shoulder. "It's not necessary. You just usually enjoy ordering for me."

Joe delivers our drinks and takes our order. Eli orders an appetizer of Brussels sprouts sautéed in butter and bacon with dates, and assures me they are to die for.

"They're Brussels sprouts."

"You'll like them," he insists, and takes my hand in his as I drink my lemon drop.

"This is delicious." I take another sip. "So, you're leaving tomorrow?" I try to keep my voice nonchalant, but my stomach is suddenly tight. I don't want him to leave.

"Just until Friday afternoon." He kisses my palm. "I'll miss you."

"You'll be too busy to miss me."

"I'll miss you," he insists. "How was *your* day?" he asks and leans in, giving me all of his attention.

"It was good, despite not getting a lot of sleep last night. A handsome man sent me lunch."

"He did," he replies with a satisfied grin. "Did you enjoy it?"

"Yes, I loved it. I also shared it with a co-worker, because it was way too much food for just me."

"And this handsome man? Do you like him?"

"Well, he can be frustrating, but he's also fun and charming. Yes, I like him."

His eyes heat as he watches me talk. His thumb is tracing circles over the back of my hand.

"Another lemon drop, miss?" Joe asks as he walks by.

"Yes, please." Joe nods and leaves. "Thank you for lunch."

"You're welcome. I would have delivered it myself, but—"

"But people will talk." I chuckle and shake my head. "It's okay. It was a nice surprise."

"I have to tell you, I'm a bit confused as to why I didn't know you were recently divorced." His face sobers with the change of conversation, and I cringe, the subject of my ex being the very last thing I want to talk about.

"It really isn't a secret." He raises a brow. "It's been several months since the divorce was final, but I haven't lived with him in more than two years, Eli. It's not something I talk about freely, certainly not with someone I don't know well."

"Why did the divorce take so long?" he asks and leans back, but doesn't let go of my hand. I eagerly sip the fresh drink that Joe just set at my elbow.

"Because Daniel is a selfish, proud, arrogant man who didn't like having the word *divorcee* after his name. Well, until he was ready to marry again, anyway."

"He's remarried already?"

"One week after the divorce was final, yes." I sigh and then just shrug. "Honestly, I didn't care. I wasn't in a position emotionally to be dating anyone, and the important thing was to simply not be living with him anymore. The rest was just gravy."

"Did he hurt you?"

"Oh, he hurt me more than any one person should be allowed to hurt another," I reply easily, but sip my drink to hide my face behind the glass for just a moment to gather my wits around me.

"Look at me."

I raise my gaze to find Eli's eyes hot with anger and his jaw ticking, but the hand holding mine is still amazingly tender. This man has amazing control.

"Did he hit you?"

"Yes."

"*Fuck*," he whispers.

"But that wasn't the worst part."

He cocks his head and raises a brow when I don't want to answer. My lips are starting to feel numb.

"These drinks are strong. They make my lips talk."

His sexy lips quirk up in a smile. "They make your lips talk?"

"Yep."

"Okay, so keep talking. What was the worst part?"

I shake my head and finish the second drink, then signal to Joe for another. I can't tell him the very worst part. Not yet. "He would yell at me. He was a bully. Sometimes it's better if they just hit you once and then get on with their day."

"Bullshit," he says calmly. "I could teach you some self-defense, you know."

"Oh, I took self defense classes." I wave him off and drink the new lemon drop. "He used to call me a whore." I giggle, barely noticing that Eli has pulled his hand away and curled it into a fist. "Which is actually pretty funny."

"Why in the fucking hell is that funny?"

"Because, counting him, I've only been with…" I count in my fuzzy head. "Two and a half men. Hey, isn't that a TV show?"

"How is it possible that you were with half of a man?" he asks with a surprised laugh.

"Because he never got it in. It didn't count." I slap my hand over my mouth and giggle. "These drinks are really delicious. You should have one."

"That's okay, one of us will have to get you up to your front door."

"I can walk." I compose my face and sit up straight. "See? I'm perfectly sober."

"Right. So, back to what you were talking about. Why couldn't he get it in?"

"Who couldn't get what in?" I ask with a frown, and then prop my chin in my hand as I watch Eli smile across from me. "Gosh, you're pretty."

"Excuse me?" He laughs and tucks my hair behind my ear. His fingers feel good on my skin.

"I bet they'd feel good everywhere."

"I think I just missed half of that conversation," he replies. "You're hilarious when you've had too much to drink. I think you've had enough." He takes my drink away, earning a scowl from me.

"I have not."

"What would feel good everywhere?" he asks, distracting me.

"Your fingers."

This makes him pause. He blinks rapidly, and if I'm not mistaken, all three of him blush.

"You're blushing after what you said to me on the sidewalk?"

"I'm certainly not blushing," he replies. "And, yes, I do believe my fingers would feel good everywhere."

"I have no doubt," I reply, and reach up to push his dark hair off his forehead. "You are pretty."

"You already said that."

"It's true."

"I think our sprouts are here," he replies and kisses my hand before leaning away.

"Well, hello, Joe." I smile up at the sexy waiter as he sets my food before me.

"Hello there," he replies with a grin.

"You're handsome," I inform him. "May I please have another lemon drop?"

"You're flirting with the waiter?" Eli asks with a laugh.

"He brings me delicious drinks," I reply seriously and turn to Joe. "I would flirt with my date, but he took my drink away. That means no flirts for him."

"I would be happy to bring you a water," Joe replies and sets his hand on my shoulder. "And then another lemon drop after you get some food in you."

"You have strong hands, Joe." Eli growls next to me, but I ignore him. "Are you sure I can't have just one little teeny tiny drink now?"

I bat my eyelashes, but Joe just laughs. *Laughs!* Maybe my flirter is broken.

"I'll be right back with that water."

"My flirter is broken."

"No, it's doing just fine," Eli replies and holds a Brussels sprout up on the end of his fork for me to eat. "Try this."

"It's a bloody Brussels sprout."

His eyes flare at the word *bloody*, and suddenly I'm thinking about his lips against mine telling me to say fuck.

"Fuck," I whisper, watching his lips. He swears under his breath, then leans in to whisper in my ear.

"Eat, Kate. Please. You're killing me here."

"I am?" I smile widely, ridiculously proud of myself.

"Yes." He takes my hand in his and guides it under the table to his lap. "See?"

"Wow," I whisper, letting my hand roam over the bulge in his pants. "This is impressive."

"Thank you." He laughs and takes a drink of water, and when I squeeze my hand, just a little, he chokes on it. "Kate."

"I mean, you won't have any problem getting this in."

"Stop." He tugs my hand away, kisses my palm, and lays my hand back on the table. "The bartender gave you some strong drinks."

He offers me the Brussels sprout again, and I open my mouth, obliging him.

"It's good," I say, surprised.

"Told you."

"You're good at food."

"I'm glad you think so."

I eat two more of the delicious vegetables. "I do."

"Here's your water, miss." Joe smiles down at me with those super blue eyes, and I sigh, just a little.

"It's too bad you didn't give in to my flirting, Joe. You're almost as delicious as these Brussels sprouts."

"Kate." I glance at Eli, who is pinching the bridge of his nose with his thumb and forefinger.

"What?"

"So, liquor makes you come on to men, then? Is it true that tequila makes your clothes fall off?"

"No, tequila makes me throw up. Vodka makes my clothes fall off." I grin and sip my water. "You might want to take notes."

"No need. I don't think I'll ever forget anything about you."

"Oh." I sigh and lick my lips. "You say really great things."

"Only the truth."

I want to say more, but I clench my lips together, determined to not give too much away in my drunken stupor. Thankfully, Joe returns with our entrees, and Eli and I both dig in, enjoying the sounds of the diners around us, the night birds, and crickets. My cheeks feel warm from the alcohol, but the fuzzy haze is clearing from my head a bit with the food. Eli finally places the rest of the lemon drop he confiscated in front of me to finish with a grin.

"I've learned something about you tonight, *cher*."

"Yeah? What's that?"

"You have a three drink limit," he replies with a laugh. "And, from now on, I'm asking for the oldest, ugliest waiter on staff."

"I probably wouldn't have dumped you for Joe," I inform him with a grin. "Although, the man is pretty hot. And has strong hands. And brings me drinks."

"Are those your requirements?" Eli asks.

"Some of them."

"What are the rest?"

"What are your requirements?" I ask, rather than answer him.

"As of about a week ago, I only have one requirement. That she be *you*."

I blink at him, unsure that those words actually came out of his mouth.

"You're charming."

He shrugs one shoulder, watching me closely. "Call it what you want."

Eli settles the check and then holds his hand out for mine, pulling me to my feet. He leans in and kisses the corner of my mouth sweetly, then whispers in my ear, "You're all I want, Kate."

My nipples tighten, and the expensive lacy panties I'm wearing under my black maxi skirt are soaked as he leads me back to the sidewalk and toward our homes. I slip my hand in his and link our fingers, loving the way his big hand feels in mine. I lean back just a bit and take a quick look at his tight butt in his khaki slacks. He's wearing a white button-down with the sleeves rolls up on his forearms, showing off the sinewy muscles that flex and move under his skin.

"You okay?"

"Yep, I was just checking out your butt."

He shakes his head and laughs. "And?"

"It's there."

"Is that all?"

"And it's impressive."

He moves my hand to his other hand and cups my ass in the palm of his hand, gives it a pat, then takes my hand back in his. "Likewise, dawlin'."

"My loft feels really far away right now."

"It's right there," he says, and points to the building just a half of a block away.

"Really far."

But, before I know it, we're climbing the stairs to my door, and when we reach the top, Eli spins me, pins me to the door, and kisses me like a man starving. I grip his hair in my hands, loving the way the soft strands feel between my fingers, and press my belly against his pelvis. He's hard and thick, and I need to get him naked.

He pushes his hand under the hem of my top and glides his magical hand up to cup my breast over the lace of my bra.

"God, I fucking love your lingerie choices," he mutters, and drags his lips down my jawline to my neck, nibbling as he goes, sending shivers all over my body.

"I have a thing for pretty underwear."

"Thank Christ." His other hand cups my ass and he boosts me up high on his thigh. I shamelessly rub myself on his thigh, needing to get closer. God, he's just hard, *everywhere.*

"Come inside," I murmur and kiss his cheek when he rests his temple on my forehead, then turns his face and kisses me lightly on the lips. His thumb brushes my nipple again, making me gasp and press harder on his thigh, but he pulls away, breathing hard, and swallows thickly.

"I can't."

"What?" My eyes snap up to his. He's panting, and just as turned on as I am.

"Kate—"

"No, it's okay." I look down, disappointment singing through my veins, but he tilts my head up and kisses me sweetly.

"I'm not turning you down, and trust me when I say, I'm going to have you in every way there is to have you, but you've had too much to drink, and I'm not convinced that you trust me all the way yet. We're getting there, *cher*."

"I trust you. I trust you to give me a few of the best orgasms of my life."

"Killing me," he whispers, before planting his lips on my forehead and taking a deep breath.

"It's this door." I pull the hem of my shirt down and try to gain my balance. "I think you have an aversion to this door. Should I buy a new one? Is it the color you don't like?"

He laughs and cages me between his hands. "I don't want to fuck this up before we really get started, Kate."

"And then you say things like that that make me swoon and my panties all wet."

"Are your panties wet, Kate?"

"My panties have been wet for a week, Eli."

"Good." He kisses me softly, ending it on a growl. "Please tell me you can get yourself to bed."

"I can't get myself to bed." I grin and bat my eyelashes. "You might have to help me."

"Why do I think you're not as impaired as I originally thought?"

"I'm fine." I clear my throat and rest my hand on his rock-hard chest. "I'll get myself to bed."

He nods and steps away. "I'll see you Friday."

"Friday."

CHAPTER EIGHT

It's early and I'm dragging, getting ready for work, when there's a loud knock on my door. I check the clock and frown, wondering who in the world would be here at six in the morning.

Did Eli come home early?

My heart starts to beat frantically as I dash to the door.

"Oh, Declan."

He flashes a smile, and then laughs. "Gee, don't look so excited to see me, superstar."

"Of course I'm happy to see you." I step back and invite him in. "But *why* am I seeing you at this time of day? You're typically going to bed right about now."

"Yeah, well, I haven't been to bed yet." He smiles again, making me roll my eyes.

"You're a man-whore."

"The ladies like a man who knows his way around a musical instrument." He shrugs as though it's no big deal and yawns widely. "I've come to take you to breakfast."

"I have to be at work in two hours," I remind him.

"Plenty of time for breakfast," he insists.

"Let me finish my hair." I wave for him to follow me to the bathroom, where he leans his broad shoulder against the doorjamb and watches me with humor-filled hazel eyes.

Eyes just like his older brother's. I haven't heard one word from Eli in four days. No flirty texts or phone calls. I know he's away for work, and he's probably busy, but I can't help but be a little disappointed.

I miss the sexy charmer.

"Did you have a gig last night?" I ask and pull my flat iron through my hair.

"Yeah, at a new place. The owner is trying to get me to commit full time, but I like bouncing around."

"*Bouncing* being the operative word," I reply, and smile brightly at him in the mirror.

"There wasn't a lot of bouncing happening last night, actually."

"I don't want to know." I put the finishing touches on my hair, smooth gloss over my lips, and turn to Declan. "I'm ready."

"Good, I'm starving." He takes my hand in his and leads me out of the loft and down the street.

"So, who was the lucky lady this time?" I ask, as we stroll hand in hand into the heart of the Quarter.

"Clarice," he replies, and a slow grin spreads over his lips. "She's a dancer."

"Oh, God. Clarice? *Seriously?*" I giggle and lean my forehead on his strong bicep, then glance up into his handsome, frowning face. "Does she hear the lambs screaming?"

"Stop it right now. You know that movie scared the hell out of me."

I laugh loudly and shake my head. This is too good to pass up.

"Did you drink chianti?"

"Kate—"

"You're right. I'm sorry." I try to school my features, but it's no use. I dissolve into laughter again.

"I'm never going to be able to see her again after this," he complains. "Do you know how flexible dancers are?"

"Does she also have a moth collection?"

He glares at me as he holds the door to the restaurant open for me, making me laugh all the louder. We're seated quickly, not many people are out at this time of day, and I chuckle all the way to the table.

"Damn it. She was fun."

"Oh, come on. You had to know it was doomed from the beginning with a name like Clarice. You had nightmares about that movie for months. The only thing that would have made it worse is if you swung for the other team and went for someone named Hannibal."

"You got mean," he replies, glaring at me over his menu.

"You know I love you," I reply, and blow him a kiss. "I forgot how much fun it is to rile you up."

The waitress arrives and takes our order. When she leaves, I lean back in my chair and study my friend. "You look tired."

"I am tired."

"So, why are we out to breakfast?"

"Because I miss you."

I narrow my eyes and feel my heart catch. I love this man with my whole heart. He and Savannah are like siblings to me. But I can also tell when he's not telling me the whole truth.

"You just saw me on Tuesday when you and Van took me out for drinks after work."

He shrugs a shoulder and sips his coffee. "Eli's due home tomorrow."

Ah, there it is.

"Yes, that's what I heard." I sip my orange juice and study the little placard on the table, announcing the daily lunch specials.

"Okay, I'm not Van." He leans forward, getting right to the point, which is his usual M.O. "You're a grown woman, and my brother is a good man, so if y'all want to bounce on each other, who am I to say you shouldn't?"

I roll my eyes at the *bounce* word, but he keeps going.

"But I want you to be careful, and if he hurts you, I'll kill him. Brother or not."

"That's so sweet," I reply sarcastically, and fake a tear rolling down my cheek.

"I'm fucking serious, Kate."

"I love you, too," I reply, serious now. "Eli and me, well, it's been confusing and exhilarating at the same time. But I haven't even spoken to him since Sunday night."

I shrug, but I can't help the stab of pain in my chest. I miss his voice.

"He's working. He rarely calls home when he's working."

I nod and sip my juice, just as Dec's phone rings.

"Hello, Clarice," I whisper in a creepy voice. Dec flips me off as he answers his phone.

"Hello, big brother."

I still as my eyes whip up to find his. He simply nods.

It's Eli.

"Yes, I spoke with her. Beau is taking care of it today." He pauses. "I'm having breakfast right now with Kate."

I raise a brow and inwardly cringe as Eli's words from the other night fill my head. *It seems I'm jealous of my own fucking brother when it comes to you.*

"I'll tell her. Safe travels." He clicks off and sends me an apologetic smile. "He's heading into a meeting."

The waitress arrives with our food and I simply nod.

"If it helps, he didn't sound pleased that I'm here with you."

I laugh and wave him off. "I'm sure he doesn't care."

"Oh, I'm sure he does. He's been glaring at me since you came to town. I'm just too easygoing to call him out on it."

"I don't want to cause any issues in your family, Dec."

"Now, that's funny." He laughs and covers my hand with his. "Trust me, you haven't caused any issues. You're helping us fix some issues, and well, Eli just has *issues*. Mostly asshole issues." He smiles fondly, then looks at me and sobers. "I mean that in the best brotherly way possible. He's not really an asshole."

"I know." I chuckle and decide that we've talked about this long enough. "So, tell me more about the lovely and flexible *Clarice*."

"Damn it. I liked her."

***

I am sick of my own company. I check my phone for the hundredth time since I got home from work three hours ago and blow out a disgusted breath.

Nothing from Eli.

What in the world is wrong with me? I'm not this needy woman. So what if I haven't heard from him in three days? He gets home tomorrow.

It's not like we're sleeping together. We've only been out together a few times and shared some kisses.

Some amazing, mind-blowing, ruin me for all other kisses kisses, but just kisses all the same.

But I've missed seeing him on his balcony in the evenings.

Maybe he hasn't missed me.

I glare at my phone, then bring Eli's number up in my text box and send him a quick message: *How is your trip going?*

I bite my lip and hit send. It's a friendly message, but doesn't sound too needy.

Good Lord, I'm such a girl.

I flop onto the couch and turn the TV on, flipping through the channels and stopping on a show that I've heard good things about, but have never watched before, and try to get lost in the handsome actors and suspenseful story line.

Two hours later, after no response from Eli, and staring at the TV without following any of the shows that have played, I snap it off and scrub my hands over my face.

I want something sweet. That'll make me feel better. Now, ice cream or beignets? Café du Monde is open 24/7, thank goodness, because when I glance at the clock, I realize it's almost midnight.

Eli warned me not to wander around at night by myself, but the café is only a few blocks away. It'll take me less than five minutes each way to walk it. I can almost taste them now, and my mouth waters at the thought of the sugary goodness.

I'll stock my freezer with ice cream later for future emergencies such as this.

With a decisive nod, I slip my feet into my sneakers, grab my keys and some cash, and dash out the front door, walking briskly. There aren't many people out at this time of night. Some homeless people with their dogs curl up in doorways, sleeping. Someone is playing a saxophone on a balcony nearby, filling the night air with beautiful notes, making me think of Declan.

When I come upon Jackson Square, I decide to walk around the park rather than walk through it. That would just be asking for trouble.

Before long, I'm at the café and standing at the take out counter where I order a bag of the doughnuts and wait for just a few minutes while my order is filled. I glance around at the mostly empty café. There are a few people out, but it's mostly deserted, making me regret the walk out by myself.

I just have an uneasy feeling.

I check my phone, frowning when there still isn't a response from Eli. I understand that he's working, but he could have at least returned the message. Now, it's after one in the morning in New York, and he's most likely asleep.

Or with someone.

I shake my head in disgust, pay for my pastries, and set off back to my place. My stomach is in knots; this time, it's not because I miss Eli, but because it's actually kind of spooky in the Quarter at night.

"Really shouldn't have done this, Mary Katherine," I murmur to myself, as I clutch my warm bag of beignets to my chest and walk quickly, head up, constantly watching my surroundings. I pass Jackson Square and turn the corner near my loft when I see a taxi pass me and slow down, and then I'm suddenly jerked from behind.

"Scream and I'll kill you," a mean, hoarse voice snarls in my ear, as I feel something sharp pressed to my ribs. "Give me your money."

"I don't—" I begin, but lean forward, stomp on his foot, and smash the back of my head into the man's face, making him wail.

"Kate!"

I turn and jab my elbow into the man's stomach, but suddenly, I'm pulled away and Eli is there, landing a hard blow to the man's nose, knocking him cold.

"I almost had him," I say, panting and beginning to shiver as Eli dials 911 and reports the attempted mugging.

"What in the hell are you doing out here?" Eli spins, plants his hands on my shoulders and glares down at me.

CHAPTER NINE
ELI

"What were you doing?" I ask again when she only stares at me, her green eyes dilated in shock as she begins to shake. I pull her against me, wrap my arms around her shoulders and hold on tight, as sirens can be heard in the distance.

"Sir, the cab fare?" The cabbie approaches us, and I swear under my breath, wrap one arm around Kate and fish my wallet out of my pocket. I pay the cabbie and keep an eye on the man beginning to moan on the sidewalk.

"The luggage?"

"Leave it on the fucking sidewalk."

I want to fucking kill him.

"I'm sorry," Kate whispers in my arms. She's clinging to me now, her eyes pinned on the asshole waking up and dabbing at his nose.

"If you fucking move, I'll knock you back out."

"I just—"

"Shut the fuck up!" I reply, my voice hard and cold. Kate flinches, burying her face in my chest, then takes a deep breath and pulls away, meeting my eyes with hers.

"I'm okay."

"Kate—"

"I'm okay," she repeats stubbornly and glares at her mugger for roughly ten seconds until the police show up. For the next thirty minutes, Kate and I are questioned by the police, and the mugger is cuffed and taken away. We are finally given the okay to go home.

"I'm sorry about this," Kate says, as we reach my luggage on the sidewalk in front of my house. "Do you need help in with your bags?"

"No," I reply shortly. I'm so fucking pissed. Adrenaline is still coursing through me. I wanted to keep punching that fucker for just *thinking* of putting his hands on her.

"Well, I'll see you tomorrow."

"You're not going home," I reply, and take her hand in mine and lead her into my house.

"Eli, I'm fine."

"I'm not," I reply and unlock the front door, wait for her to walk in ahead of me, then leave my suitcase and briefcase just inside the door, lock it, and tug my tie off as I lead her up the stairs to the living area, shocked to discover that my own hands are shaking.

Kate stands in the middle of the room as I pour two glasses of brandy, pass her one, and take a long swallow, watching her as she also takes a drink and cringes as it burns on the way down.

"Why were you out there so late?"

"I wanted beignets," she whispers, her eyes trained on her drink.

"You wanted *beignets*?" I ask incredulously. "What the fuck, Kate?"

"Don't swear at me!" she shouts back, pointing her pink-tipped finger at me. "I was craving sugar, and it was either ice cream or beignets. The beignets were closer, darn it. I missed you, and you didn't answer my text, and I'm such a girl!"

She says this like I'm supposed to understand the logic, which I completely don't.

"What does your gender have to do with it?"

She glares at me like I'm being obstinate on purpose, then sets her glass on my desk and moves to walk out, but I catch her arm in my hand and pull her against me.

"You just scared ten years off my life, *cher*." I bury my face in her hair and take a deep breath. "I missed you too. I couldn't answer your text because I was on a flight home when it came in."

"Why are you home early?"

"Because I needed to see you." God, she smells amazing and feels incredible against me. "And then, when we drove past in the cab and I saw that fucker come up behind you, my heart stopped in my chest. God, Kate, he could have—"

"He didn't." I feel her smile against my chest. "I was kicking his ass."

"Yes, you were, tiger." I grin and plant my lips on her forehead. "You weren't lying when you said you took self defense classes."

"I'm no victim," she says fiercely, and another part of me softens.

"You're amazing," I reply and then sigh. "Scared me."

"Me too." She hugs me tightly before stepping away. "It's late, and I have to be at work in the morning."

"You're not going to work in the morning."

"Of course I am."

"No, you're not. I'm the boss, Kate. You were mugged tonight." Before she can shake her head and fight me further, I pick her up in my arms and carry her up another flight of stairs to my bedroom. "I want to spend tomorrow with you."

"Apparently, you're spending tonight with me too?" She pushes her fingers into my hair and smiles softly.

"I can't let you out of my sight tonight," I reply honestly, before sitting on the edge of the bed with her in my lap. "I need to keep you safe."

"Is that all?"

I bury my face in her neck, skim my nose up to her ear, and kiss her softly. She shivers, making me smile. "No, that's not all, *cher*."

"Have I mentioned that I'm glad you're home?" She cups my face in her hands and kisses my lips lightly.

"Are you?"

She nods, her fingers moving gently over my face. God, just having her against me has me hard, but her magical fingers, the way she's looking at me, has me tied in knots.

I need her.

And I don't need *anyone*.

"Kate, tell me now if you're not okay with me making love to you, because in about two point four seconds, I won't be able to control myself anymore."

Her lips curve in a purely feminine, seductive smile as she pulls herself out of my arms, stands, and in one fluid motion, whips her T-shirt over her head and tosses it on the floor by her feet. I'm struck dumb as she hooks her thumbs in the waist of her black leggings and works them down her legs, and suddenly she's standing before me in a matching lacy light pink bra and panty set.

Jesus Christ, she's breathtaking.

She moves to unhook her bra, but I shake my head and stand, just inches from her.

"You are stunning." My voice is nothing but a hoarse whisper as I take her in. She's slender, but has curves in all the right places. Her breasts...Fuck, I can't wait to get my hands on her breasts.

She lifts her hands and unbuttons my white shirt, then tosses it down with her things, and her intoxicating green eyes take a journey down my torso.

"Wow," she whispers, and traces the muscles of my chest and stomach with her fingertips, sending heat through me. "You're even better than I imagined."

Her hands land on the waist of my slacks and she pops the clasp open, and just as she slides her hands inside to nudge them down my hips, she leans in and plants her lips right over my heart.

Fuck me.

When my pants hit the floor, I lift Kate back into my arms and lay her in the center of the bed, then brace myself on my elbow next to her and run my fingers over the lace of her sexy as fuck underwear.

"I didn't hear from you this week," she murmurs, and watches my face as my hands roam over her body. "I thought maybe you'd changed your mind."

"Hell no," I reply and nudge her nose with mine. "I knew if I heard your voice I'd get on the next plane out and come straight here." My finger pushes under the cup of her bra and brushes over her nipple, making her gasp. "I've thought of nothing but you." I glide my finger to the other breast and repeat the movement, making her squirm next to me.

God, she's responsive.

Her hand cups my cock over my boxer-briefs, making my eyes cross. I take her hand, kiss her palm, then hold it over her head as I cover her body with mine and lay kisses on her lips, her neck, her collarbone, and begin working my way down her warm, writhing body.

"Oh, gosh," she breathes, shoving her hands in my hair.

"I want to learn every inch of you," I murmur, my lips against her belly. "I want to know what makes you gasp." I cup her sex in my hand and grin against her hip when she arches into my hand with a low groan. "God, you're soaked."

I glance up in time to see her bite her lip and her cheeks flush as I push one finger under the elastic of her panties and rub her wet pussy with just the fingertip, not sinking inside, just gliding over her lips and clit.

"Oh, that feels good," she whispers. I kiss my way across her lower belly to her other hip, then down to her thigh and hook my fingers into the material at her hips to pull them off, throw them over my shoulder, and spread her wide.

"Fucking hell, you're gorgeous, *cher*." And she is. God, her freckles are *everywhere*, sprinkled all over her body, even her pussy, which is waxed clean. I spread her wider and drag my fingertips up and down her thighs, making them quiver.

"Eli," she moans.

"Yes, babe, moan my name." And with that, I lean in and take one long swipe with my tongue from her wet opening, all the way up to her hard clit.

"Holy crap!" She jackknifes, but I press one splayed hand on her belly, holding her down, and nuzzle that hard nub with my nose as I pull her lips in my mouth and tug gently. "Eli, oh my."

I grin against her, still charmed that even in the throes of sex she refuses to swear.

I drag my fingertips down one thigh, around her ass to her crack and slide one finger over her anus and into her slick opening, making her moan all the more.

I love how fucking vocal she is.

I begin to slowly fuck her with my finger and kiss my way up her body. I tug on her nipples through the lace of her bra, kiss up her neck, and finally her lips. She wraps her arms tightly around my neck, holding me to her, still riding my hand and kissing me for all she's worth.

I'm going to fucking explode.

"Kate." Her feet are pushing my boxer briefs down my hips, just as anxious as I am for me to be inside her. "Kate."

"I'm sorry," she replies and arches against me. "Kate's not available right now."

I chuckle and bite her shoulder and her pussy clenches like a vise on my finger. "God, babe, you're so tight."

"Eli, I need you inside me."

Just the sound of her sweet voice against my neck while she's squeezing the fuck out of my finger makes me want to come. She's not going to get any more ready.

I reach into the bedside table and retrieve an unopened box of condoms to protect us both. I take myself in my hand and guide the tip through her slick folds, making us both moan.

"Are you trying to kill me?" she asks. Her eyes are bright green and wide as she pants and stares up at me in wonder and longing, matching every emotion running through me.

"No, *cher*, making sure you're ready."

"Never been more ready for anything in my life," she confirms and reaches between us, wraps her small hand around me and guides me to her opening. "Now."

I slide in, in one long, fluid motion and pause when I'm buried balls-deep. She's closed her eyes and is biting her lip, her fingernails digging into my shoulders.

"Open your eyes, dawlin'." She obliges and surprises me when she smiles up at me and circles her hips, inviting me to move. "You feel—" I shake my head, not having any words for the way it feels to be buried inside her.

And I know, in this moment, I'll never grow tired of her. I'll never want anyone else.

She rotates her hips again and I pull back, almost all the way, then push back and she closes her eyes.

"Keep them open," I instruct her. "I want you to see what you do to me."

Her eyes soften as she cups my face in her hands and kisses me deeply, and that's it. I can't stop my hips from setting a rhythm, moving in long strokes in and out of her, claiming her.

She's mine.

Her legs begin to shake and her whole body tenses. Her eyes widen in alarm.

"Oh, God."

"I'm right here," I whisper and nibble the corner of her lips. "It's okay."

I reach between us and press my thumb on her nub, and that's all it takes. She cries out, arching off the bed and coming spectacularly. I've never seen anything like it. Her pussy spasms around my cock, her arms tighten around my neck, and I have no choice but to follow her over into the most amazing orgasm of my life.

Our breathing is ragged and loud in the quiet room as I roll us and tuck her under my chin, cradling her on my chest. Her fingers are trailing up and down my ribs, in the same rhythm of my fingers on her back as we regain our senses.

"Eli?"

I plant my lips in her hair. "Yes."

"Kate's available now."

I chuckle and tilt her head back so I can look in her eyes, needing to see that she's okay. Her eyes are glassy with happiness, her cheeks flushed, and her hair a mess. She looks quite satisfied.

"She's about to be unavailable again."

"She might be tired."

I grin.

"I'll do all the work."

CHAPTER TEN
KATE

"Good morning, beautiful."

I feel my lips lift in a soft smile. Most of my face is buried in a pillow that smells of Eli, clean with a touch of his body wash. I'm lying on my stomach. We aren't touching, but I can feel the warmth from his body next to me.

He suddenly brushes a fingertip down my temple and hooks my hair behind my ear. I pry one eye open and gaze over at a rumpled, sleepy, deliciously sexy Eli.

"'Morning," I whisper. My arms are folded under the pillow, bracing my head. He drags his fingertips down my arm to my ribs, and traces the words tattooed from just under my armpit to just above my hip.

"*I am enough the way I am,*" he recites softly and smiles at me, his eyes bright with curiosity, but he doesn't ask why these words. He simply waits, that happy expression on his handsome face, and continues to lightly drag his fingertips over my skin, which is on hyper-alert after the night we just spent together.

I lost count how many times we made love, how many times he woke me up with his lips, his hands, his cock. My body is deliciously exhausted.

"You're not terribly chatty in the morning," he finally says quietly, and leans over to kiss the ball of my shoulder. I chuckle and bury my face in the pillow, then gaze over at him again.

"Good morning."

"There she is," he says. The house is quiet around us. It must be very early morning because of the gray light coming in through the windows. "How do you feel?"

"Hmm…" I take stock of my body and my heart, and smile. "I feel surprisingly limber and sated. You?"

"I don't think I've been better," he replies, and traces my tattoo again. "I was also surprised to find this during the night."

"Surprised good or bad?"

"It's sexy as hell, *cher*."

"Are you going to ask me about it?"

"No." He exhales deeply and finally pulls me into his arms, kisses my forehead, and tucks me against his chest. "You'll tell me about it when you're ready."

I grip onto his naked side and sigh in happiness. He's warm; his skin is smooth over toned muscles. He kisses my forehead, and his scruffy chin rasps against my skin.

It's sexy.

"We should be asleep," I murmur against his chest. "We couldn't have gotten more than a couple hours of rest."

"Go to sleep," he whispers against my hair. His hands are drawing patterns on my back, his lips are planted on my head, and with his heart beating in my ear, I could easily drift off and sleep happily for hours.

But it seems a shame to waste an opportunity to have Eli naked.

Again.

My hand drifts down beneath the sheet to cover his ass, which flexes under my touch. His body is just crazy. All of those hours I spent daydreaming about what he would look like beneath those suits of his were a waste of time, because the reality is just stellar.

"That's not going to sleep," he murmurs. I can feel him grin against my head as I turn my face and plant a kiss to his chest.

"Not particularly sleepy right now," I whisper, as I press my belly against his growing cock.

"No?"

"Nope."

He growls as I press him back onto the bed and pepper his torso with wet kisses, my hands roaming all over him in lazy caresses. His hands drift up my back to push my hair off of my face. When I glance up at him, he's grinning wickedly.

"You're so fucking beautiful, Kate."

I feel my face blush as I hide it against his hard abs. "Thank you."

Eli grips my shoulders and flips us, so I'm suddenly beneath him, his pelvis cradled between my legs, and his arms braced under my shoulders. He brushes my hair off my cheeks and stares down at me intently.

"You. Are. Beautiful," he repeats, kissing me deeply between each word, and my body flares to life beneath him, my nipples puckered against his chest and my hips circling against his hardness. "Jesus, just when I think I've had my fill, it's as though I've never touched you before."

"Love the way you touch me," I murmur against his lips. I freaking *love* the way he touches me.

"Do you like it when I do this?" He drags his nose down my jawline to my neck and lightly scrapes his teeth over my skin.

"Oh, gosh yes."

"Gosh yes," he repeats with a grin. "Oh, I think we can do better than that."

I whimper, knowing where this is going, but I have no energy to try to talk him out of it.

I'll say extra Hail Mary's the next time I go visit my parents.

"I want to hear that sweet mouth of yours get a little dirty, *cher*."

I bite my lip as he kisses down to my breasts and circles my nipple with his nose before taking it in his mouth and sucking firmly.

"We'll start with something easy. What's this?"

"My breast."

He tweaks my nipple, sending a zing up my spine. "Ow!"

"Dirty."

"Um, tit?"

"Very good." He laves the abused nub with his tongue, and then kisses his way down my stomach, nuzzles my navel and the piercing there, then scoots down the bed further and spreads my legs wide. "Look how wet you are."

I bury my hands in his hair and try to guide his mouth down to me, but he pulls away and grins. "Use your words."

"Eli…"

"Yes, that's a start. Keep going."

"Please, kiss me."

He presses his lips to the inside of my thigh and then grins up at me.

"Please kiss my…"

"Your what, Kate?"

"My." I swallow hard and clench my eyes closed. "Pussy."

He growls and licks me from my opening up to my clit, and then proceeds to drive me out of my ever loving mind with his lips and tongue, making my head thrash back and forth on the pillow.

"Do you want my fingers inside you?"

"Yes!"

"Ask me."

"Please put your fingers inside me."

"Inside your what?"

I lift my head and stare down at him in confusion. "My pussy."

"Say cunt, Kate."

I blink. *You're nothing but a fucking cunt. I can't stand the sight of you.*

"Never." I try to close my legs and move away from him, but he immediately covers me again with his body and holds me tenderly. Tears have sprung in my eyes, pissing me off. "I won't ever say that."

"Okay. I'm sorry."

"That word isn't okay. Ever."

He holds me to him, braced over me, and combs his fingers through my hair. "I'm sorry, *cher*. I didn't know that was a trigger for you."

"It's just that one word. I can't deal with it."

"Understood." He kisses my cheek and the corner of my mouth before pulling back and gazing down at me. His eyes look a bit angry, and I'm sure he has a million questions, but he simply offers me a soft smile and palms my breast once more. "No more c word. Any other words we should avoid?"

"I'm not particularly fond of being called a bitch either."

All humor leaves his face as his hand stills on my breast. His eyes narrow.

"Let's get something straight right now, *cher*. I would never call you that, or cunt, or any other despicable word that could hurt you. You are beautiful and sweet, and there will never come a day, regardless of what happens with us after today, that you or anyone else will ever deserve that. Are we clear?"

"Yes." I hate the relief in my voice, but my whole body relaxes beneath Eli as he watches me for another long moment, and then lays his lips over mine and kisses me sweetly. His hand resumes with its ministrations on my breast, making me tingle.

"I love your skin," he whispers against my neck. "You're so soft. And your freckles make me crazy."

"My freckles!" I giggle and slap his arm playfully. "They're out of control."

"They're amazing." He grins down at me. "You even have freckles on your pussy."

"I know." I wrinkle my nose, making him chuckle.

"Sexy."

"Silly."

He slowly shakes his head no and reaches over for a condom, slips it on, and settles between my legs.

"Are you sore?"

"In a good way."

"I'll do my best to take it easy."

I drag my fingertips down his cheek as he positions himself against my lips.

"What do you want, Kate?"

"You," I reply with a confused frown.

"What part of me?"

Ah, so we're back to the game.

"That large, impressive part of you."

He laughs and kisses my forehead. "Words, Kate."

"Eli."

He raises a brow.

"I'd very much enjoy feeling your *cock* inside me now, please."

His eyes darken as he slowly pushes inside me, all the way, and holds himself still.

"Say it again."

"Please."

His lips tickle mine as he grins.

"Just a few more words."

I rotate my hips and clench around him, making his body tighten around me.

"Eli."

"Yes."

"Fuck me already."

"Damn." He begins to move, in long steady strokes, panting and groaning, but holding my gaze in his. "I fucking love it when you talk dirty."

"I kind of like it too," I admit, and moan when he slips his hand between us and presses on my already screaming clit. "God, Eli, I'm gonna come."

"That's right." He kisses my neck and hooks one of my legs over his shoulder, opening me wider, pushing deeper as he grabs my ass and pulls me harder onto him. "I'm right here with you."

His strength never ceases to amaze me, and the way his body is working me over is just too much. I can't help but cry out as I'm consumed by the orgasm, pulsing around him and rocking against him, as I continue to ride the aftershocks.

Eli rests his forehead on mine and swears under his breath, as every muscle in his body tightens and he follows me over into his own release.

We're both gasping for breath and sweaty when Eli slips out of me and collapses on the bed beside me, his arm draped over my stomach.

"Well, good morning."

He chuckles and kisses my shoulder. I gaze over at him, and can't resist pushing his hair back off of his forehead.

"You're so handsome."

"Thank you." He kisses me again, then rolls away. "We have to get up."

"Why? I thought we decided we aren't going in to work today."

"We're not." He shoots me a naughty grin. "I have a surprise for you."

"What kind of surprise?"

"A surprise surprise." He rolls his eyes as he saunters into the bathroom. "But you'll need to stop over at your place and pack a bag for the weekend!" He yells out at me.

"Okay, I'll just go over there now, take a shower, and get ready."

"No."

My head whips up at the tone of his voice as he comes back into the room.

"No?"

He shakes his head and takes my hand in his. "We'll be showering together."

"Eli, I'm as adventurous as the next girl, but I don't think I can go another round right now."

He chuckles as he kisses my knuckles. "I can't either, *cher*. But I'm not letting you out of my sight that long. Besides, it's my mess. I should clean it up."

"Well, when you put it like that…"

***

An hour later, we're settled in Eli's car and headed out into the Bayou.

"It's amazing how, just a few minutes outside the city, we're in the middle of nowhere." I stare at the forests, the swamps, and wonder if there are alligators in the water.

"Not so different from most cities," he reminds me. He links his fingers with mine and kisses my hand before resting them on his thigh.

"Where are we going?"

"I thought we'd spend the weekend at the Inn."

"Oh, fun!" I grin and shimmy in my seat. "I've been dying to see it."

"We'll have my nosy sister and brother hanging around, but I think you'll enjoy it."

"You have such a great family." I gaze over at him as he drives effortlessly down the interstate. "They may be nosy, but they love you."

"Nosy," he insists with a grin.

"If you hated it, you would have left long ago."

His jaw clenches and his hand tightens on the wheel, but he takes a deep breath and finally nods. "True."

I tilt my head and watch him closely. There's something here he's not telling me, but rather than pry, I leave it be for now and decide instead to start telling him a bit about my past.

"I got it after I left my ex-husband," I say, and turn to look out the passenger window. "Because after being told every day that you're not good enough, it's easy to buy into it. But I'm not that person. I am enough."

"You're more than enough, *cher*." He kisses my hand again. "Look at me."

I turn to face him and am surprised to see him smiling.

"You're a strong woman, Kate. Which is a good thing, because it takes a strong woman to put up with my family."

He didn't make it awkward. Or turn it into a long soul-searching conversation.

He simply accepts me.

"I love your family."

He nods and changes lanes. "Tell me about your family."

"I love them too." I grin as I think of my ma and da. "My parents live in County Claire, Ireland."

"Did you grow up in Ireland?"

"No. I grew up outside of Denver. My da got a job there before I was born, so he and Ma moved there. Had me. Then about three years later, my da's brother and sister-in-law were killed in a car accident, leaving their son, Rhys, behind. So he came to live with us. He's really more like my big brother than a cousin."

"Rhys O'Shaughnessy? The baseball player?"

"Yes, that's him. You watch baseball?"

"When I can. Sam loves baseball, thanks to Beau."

"Where is Sam's dad?" I ask, as Eli takes an exit off the freeway and we merge onto a two-lane highway, headed deeper into the bayou.

"He's never met Sam." Eli shrugs, then shakes his head. "Gabby got pregnant right out of high school. When the boyfriend found out, he cut out right quick."

"That's horrible."

"It's probably for the best. Sam is loved by a great family."

"I agree with that, but it has to be hard for Gabby."

"We help her," he insists.

"Of course you do, but Eli, it's not just about being a single mom. She's *single*. I'm not saying that men make everything better, but I imagine she gets lonely. She has a young boy to care for, a business, and a large, successful family. She has a lot of responsibility."

He rubs his hand over his lips, thinking. "True. I don't think she's dated since Sam was born."

"Maybe she's not interested, and it's certainly none of my business, but I doubt it's as easy as she wants all of you to believe it is."

His eyes slide to mine. "You're an intelligent woman, Kate."

"Well, that we knew." I laugh and lean over to press my lips to his shoulder. "I'm excited to see her inn."

CHAPTER ELEVEN
ELI

"Oh, my God, Eli," Kate gasps and grips my thigh with her strong hand. It's the same tone she uses when she's about to come, and it makes my cock twitch reflexively, but I just grin over at her in the passenger seat.

"Pretty, isn't it?"

She turns her wide green eyes to me, her mouth dropped open, and then back to the plantation as we drive up to it. "Those oak trees are incredible! And the house! No wonder Gabby loves running this place. I'd never leave."

I smirk and look at the green, lush land, trying to see it for the first time. The white, three story home with it's pillars, black shutters and wrap around porch, and second floor balcony sits back from the road about one hundred yards. Leading to it is a row of oak trees, creating a tunnel to the majestic home and the land it sits on. Sunlight filters through the leaves and limbs, sprinkling the green grass in light.

"How old are those trees?" Kate asks.

"About six hundred years," I reply, and pull around the side of the house. "They've been here far longer than the house."

"They're amazing." She bites her lip and continues to stare at the trees, and I can't resist reaching over and tugging the delicate skin from her teeth, then smoothing the pad of my thumb over it. "I want to see everything," she says, as she nuzzles my palm with her cheek.

"And I'll show you." I kiss her lips quickly before we climb out of the car and walk around to the front of the house.

"Uncle Eli!" Sam exclaims and tosses his ball in the air, catches it, and runs over to hug me. "Are you really stayin' here tonight?"

"We are," I confirm. "You remember Miss Kate?"

"Hello, ma'am," Sam says, and holds his hand out for Kate's, making my lips twitch.

"You can call me Kate," she offers with a smile, but Sam shakes his head no.

"I'm not supposed to call adults their real names," he says seriously.

"Can you call me Miss Kate?" she asks, and squats down so she can look him in the eye. Sam looks up to me for confirmation.

"You may."

"Okay, Miss Kate." He offers her his toothless grin just as her phone rings.

"Oh, this is Rhys FaceTiming me. Sam, do you know who Rhys O'Shaughnessy is?"

"Only the best baseball player on the whole Chicago Cubs team," he replies in awe. I step back, shove my hands in my pockets, and watch Kate with my young nephew. She grins and accepts the call.

"Hey, handsome."

"Hey. Whatcha doin'?"

"Actually, I have a young man here who is your biggest fan. Would you mind saying hi?"

"I get to say hi?" Sam asks with a big smile.

"Sure, here." Kate turns the phone for Sam, and instead of getting embarrassed or shy, he launches into a million questions.

"Oh, my gosh! You're the best batter in the league! What kind of bat do you have? How do you hit the ball so hard? Do you have to practice every day?" He takes the phone and sits on the porch, chattering at Rhys, who is chuckling and trying to get a word in edgewise.

"That'll keep them both busy for a few minutes," Kate says, and loops her arms around my waist, her face tilted up to mine. "Rhys loves kids."

"You might have just made my nephew's year."

"Well, I have ulterior motives." She grins as her hands travel up my back and down again, over my ass.

"Do tell," I reply and kiss her forehead.

"I was thinking about doing this." She stands on her tiptoes, but she's still too short to kiss me, so I happily oblige her, leaning down to take her lips with mine. It starts as a soft, simple nibble, and quickly escalates to tongues and panting and me gripping onto her lower lip with my teeth.

"There's a child ten yards away," she whispers against my mouth.

"I know." I cup her face in my hands, kiss her forehead one more time, and breathe in her fresh, Kate scent, then lead her down the brick walkway between the enormous, ancient oak trees. "They were planted hundreds of years before the house," I begin.

"It's so cool out here," she says.

"Yes, thanks to the river just on the other side of that levy, and with the way the trees were planted, it creates a wind tunnel effect. No one ever imagined that air conditioning would be a thing. This was the first form of AC."

"Amazing. Look at how some of the branches rest on the ground!"

Jesus, I can't take my eyes off of her. She's pulled her thick, auburn hair into a knot at the back of her head. She's wearing a strapless sundress and flip flops.

I wonder if she's wearing panties under there.

I intend to find out very soon.

"This is seriously the most beautiful thing I've ever seen."

"You'll get no argument from me," I reply, my eyes trained on her gorgeous face, just as she turns to me and smiles shyly.

"Way to lay on the Southern charm," she says.

"I am Southern, and it may have sounded charming, but it doesn't make it less true."

"Miss Kate! Miss Kate!" Sam comes running down the walk at full speed, the way only a young boy can, with Kate's phone waving in the air. "He wants to talk to you!"

"I'm dizzy," Rhys says dryly, as Kate takes her phone and smiles at her cousin.

"He looks happy," she says.

"He talks more than anyone I've ever met in my life, and that includes you. Cute kid."

"I have to go tell Mom!" Sam takes off back to the house, and I begin to follow him.

"I'll be up at the house, *cher*. Take your time." She shakes her head, as if to keep me here, but I simply kiss her hand and smile. "I have to say hi to Gabby."

Her soft laugh follows me as I saunter behind the excited boy to the house. I glance around at the freshly mowed grounds of the plantation and the flowers around the house. Birds are singing in the trees, and the breeze Kate mentioned brushes through my hair.

Why haven't I ever noticed before how lovely it is out here?

Because I haven't noticed much for years. I haven't given two fucks about anything for years.

Except for my family and the business, and not necessarily in that order.

I climb the steps of the porch, then turn and look out at the trees and the amazing woman chattering away at her phone, smiling and laughing.

She's the reason I've come alive.

***

"Gabby makes incredible cookies," Kate says, as she pops the last bite of an oatmeal raisin in her mouth and tilts her head back to the let the sun warm her cheeks. "I could get used to this."

"What, cookies?"

"Cookies and sunshine and just…" she shrugs.

"Just what?"

We're wandering through the gardens behind the house, toward the slave quarters and caretaker's home, which is where Beau currently lives. I take her hand in mine and bring us to a stop, turn her to me, and cup her neck in my hand. "Just what?"

"Just being happy." The last word is said in a whisper, tugging at something unfamiliar in my gut. Before I can pull her into my arms, she smiles and continues walking. "What's over there?"

"Slave quarters," I reply. "Gabby had them refurbished, just enough to make them safe, so guests can learn and check them out."

"You owned slaves?" she asks with a gasp.

"Not me personally, no." I chuckle and tuck her hair behind her ear. I can't fucking stop touching her. "Many generations ago, slaves lived here, yes."

She frowns and bites her lip.

"It was two hundred years ago, Kate. That wasn't uncommon in the South."

"I know."

"This way." I lead her away from the slave quarters, through a rose garden in a riot of color.

"I want to check them out," she says, pointing to the small slave buildings.

"Later. Let's walk through the gardens."

"What's over there?" She squints her eyes, looking in the nearby field. "With the fence?"

"That's the cemetery."

"Is it old?" she asks with glee.

"Yes." I raise a brow. "Do you have a thing for cemeteries?"

"I know it sounds weird, but yes. Especially old ones. They're so interesting. Can we go look?"

"Let's go."

She walks quickly through the gardens, barely paying attention to the flowers. The gate to the graveyard is rusty, and a bit stuck, and I make a note to have it repaired, as I wrench it open and Kate hurries inside.

"I bet this is creepy at night," she says reverently, looking about like she doesn't know where to start, then makes a beeline for the very back and studies each headstone as she walks by. "There are dates here that go back to the 1700's."

"And there are graves on the property older than that, but the Boudreaux family started this graveyard around that time."

"Why aren't these graves above ground like the ones in the city?"

"Because the water table is different here. We're close to the river, but we sit higher. Even during Katrina, we didn't flood. We simply had wind damage."

"Amazing." She folds her arms and continues to walk through. The headstones have moss grown over them. Some are so faded that you have to really get close to read them. Several oak trees are planted throughout the space, giving shade and shelter from the elements, but their roots have made some of the stones go a bit cockeyed.

It is exactly what it looks like: an old cemetery.

"Oh, there are babies," she murmurs sadly, trailing her fingertips over a lamb carved in the stone.

I simply nod, my hands shoved in my pockets, my fingers rubbing the half dollar I keep there. The closer we get to a certain grave, the more nervous I become.

And that's ridiculous. He's been dead for two fucking years.

"The dates are getting more recent. Here's 1977." She sighs. "And these are sisters. Look," she points at the dates on the stone. "They were only two years apart. Died in the same week."

"They were spinster aunts," I inform her, remembering the stories I'd been told of the old maids. "They lived together, here, their whole lives. They were odd."

"Odd?"

I grin. "This is the Bayou, dawlin'. Let's just say they enjoyed the eccentricities that living here brought them. And if you ever made one of them mad, well…Bad things usually happened."

"They were witches?"

"Of course not." I chuckle and kiss her cheek. "They were simply Bayou women."

"Oh, this one looks new."

It is new.

She reads the stone and her eyes grow wide. "Your daddy."

I nod and read the stone for myself.

Beauregard Francois Boudreaux
1947 - 2012
Beloved Husband & Father
I've adjusted my sails.

"I've adjusted my sails," Kate reads aloud, and looks at me with a raised brow.

"Daddy always said, you can't control the wind, but you can adjust your sails. It was his way of reminding us that you can't control most of what happens in life. You can only control your reaction to it. I imagine he did the same in death." I smirk. "I'm quite sure he's running Heaven by now."

"I met him once," she says. "You get your height from him."

"Yes, and if you ask Maman, I got my stubbornness from him too."

"Naturally." She tilts her head as she watches me. The coin in my pocket is hot in my fingers, from me rubbing it hard, but I can't stop. "You're tense."

"As I always am when I'm around my father."

"You didn't get along?"

I shrug a shoulder, every instinct in me screaming at me to shut it down, walk away from the conversation and take Kate back to our room where I can sink inside her for about two days.

"I loved him fiercely," I say instead, surprising me. "And there were days that I hated him just as much."

"Those are extreme emotions."

"I spent my entire life trying to live up to what he wanted me to be," I say quietly, and remember the man now six feet under the ground. His loud laugh. His cold hazel eyes. His disapproving shake of the head.

"I'm sure he was very proud of you."

"No," I reply, and let Kate fold herself into my arms for a long hug. "He wasn't."

"How do you know?"

"He told me."

"What?" She pulls back with a frown. "He *told* you that he wasn't proud of you?"

"Let's sit." I guide her to the bench beneath a nearby magnolia tree. She sits facing me, waiting to hear more.

Am I seriously going to tell her something that I've never spoken aloud before?

"He told me to pull my head out of my ass and do what I was born to do, which was take care of my family's business."

She blinks for several seconds. "That seems harsh."

"He was right." I sigh and rub my hand down my face. "He'd already groomed Beau to take over as CEO of Bayou Enterprises, which makes sense because he's the oldest. I have a master's degree in business, but I spent ten years partying, taking advantage of the perks that money brings. Fucking random women."

I sigh and shake my head. "I was irresponsible and old enough to know better. I would have been disappointed in me too."

"You're not those things now," she says.

"No," I agree. "Sitting beside my father as he took his last breath, his last words being, 'You can be so much better than this'," will turn a man around." She takes my hand in hers and places a sweet kiss to my knuckles. "So, I focused all of my energy on the business, on the family. I work stupid hours."

"That's a good description."

"It's accurate. Working twenty-hour days is stupid, but I can't stop. I work, I look in on my family, and I go back to work.

Occasionally, I call up one of the several women I know to hook up with and scratch that particular itch, and then I go back to work."

Kate flinches. "You seem to respect women more than that."

"Of course I respect women," I reply. "My mother would kill me herself if I treated any woman with anything other than respect. But sex is sex, Kate."

She nods. "I'm following."

"Women don't usually understand that."

"I do." She shrugs. "I haven't been divorced long, and the relationship I just came out of was...*combative*. I'm not looking to replace it."

"Combative," I repeat, and just like every time she begins to talk about the hell—a hell I don't even fully understand yet— that her ex-husband put her though, my hands want to clench and I want to simply kill him.

With my own bare hands.

"Mmm," she confirms with a nod.

"He hit you."

"I told you he did."

I nod. "What else?"

"What do you mean?"

"Don't play stupid, Kate. You're a smart woman. Did he ever put you in the hospital?"

"Pshaw," she tips her head back, staring up into the branches above, but doesn't directly answer. I grip her chin in my fingers and thumb and pull her gaze back to mine.

"You don't have to tell me everything, just don't ever lie to me, Kate. Did he put you in the hospital?"

"Once," she whispers. I close my eyes and take a deep breath. "So, you see," she clears her throat, "I'm in no hurry to jump into anything serious."

"I wasn't trying to warn you off, *cher*."

"I know. But even if I did want something serious, this," she points back and forth between us, "has an expiration date."

"Really."

"I'll be gone in a few weeks. But I need to make something very clear, Eli."

"Keep going."

"While you're doing…*stuff* with me, you're not doing that same stuff with anyone else."

Is it any wonder that I can't get enough of her? She's fucking adorable.

"What kind of stuff?" I grin as she blushes.

"You know perfectly well what kind."

I lean in and tuck her hair behind her ear, then drag my nose over the apple of her cheek to her ear and plant a kiss there, making her shiver.

"Walks around the Quarter?"

"No." She sighs as I nibble down her neck, then back up again and kiss the tip of her nose.

"Pizza on the balcony?"

"Now who's playing dumb?"

"I want to hear the words."

"You always want to hear the words." Her hands grip onto my T-shirt. I love that I can turn her on so easily. She's so fucking responsive.

I grin wickedly and kiss her forehead, and then it occurs to me: My life has been in black and white for the past two years, and the minute she walked through my office door, everything was in blazing color.

I don't know what the fuck to do with that.

Except enjoy her, for every moment she's here.

"What is the stuff that we do?" I ask again.

"The sex stuff."

"You can do better than that."

"Do you have any idea how many Hail Marys I'm going to have to say because of you?" she demands.

"A lot," I reply with a laugh. "I haven't seen you go to church while you've been here."

"I only go when I'm visiting my parents." She shrugs one slender shoulder. "Okay, I'll make it clear. While you're fucking me, you don't fuck anyone else."

Fuck.

I have to swallow hard as I stare down at her determined green eyes. Fuck someone else? I can't think of anyone else.

"And you can't fall in love with me," she adds primly.

"I can't?"

"No. No love. Just friends, and laughs, and…stuff."

I narrow my eyes.

"And sex. I'm not saying the other word again today."

I watch her for a long moment, then tug her into my lap, cup her face in my hands, and kiss the fuck out of her. "You're all I see, Kate. I don't give a shit about other women. So you don't have to worry about me fucking anyone but you for as long as you're here."

"And no love."

Why does that statement make my heart hurt?

"I don't do love, *cher.*"

"Me neither."

Liar.

"But one other thing," I say, my lips against hers.

"What?"

"You're going to say fuck again today. You're going to say it a lot."

"Why does that turn you on?" She giggles and sinks her fingers into the hair on the back of my head.

"Because hearing those dirty words come out of your pretty mouth makes me hard." I kiss her, long and deep, then pull away when we're both gasping for breath. "Jesus, everything you do makes me hard."

"Maybe it's just been a while since you got laid."

That's what I thought too.

"No, it's you. It's just you."

CHAPTER TWELVE
KATE

"Are you sure you don't want to go to Mama's for dinner?" Gabby asks us as she gathers her handbag and car keys and settles Sam's baseball cap on his head.

"We'll be fine here," Eli replies with a grin, sips his sweet tea, and keeps his sexy, naughty eyes on me. "I'll show Kate around."

"I thought you showed her around yesterday," Gabby replies dryly. Eli simply shrugs one shoulder and takes another sip of his tea, watching me. God, he's potent. He showed me around yesterday, all right. Around his body, and mine, and I'm pretty sure he discovered erogenous zones that I didn't even know I had.

And muscles. I'm sore today. *Sore.* My inner thigh muscles are singing. How does that happen?

"How is it that you don't have any guests tonight?" I ask.

"I always have an empty inn on Sunday nights. That gives me time to catch up on laundry and cooking for the upcoming week, and I can get away to Mama's for dinner."

"Convenient for me," Eli says, and laughs when Gabby glares at him.

"You're my brother."

"That's the rumor," he says with a smile.

"No, you are," Sam adds solemnly. "Nannan says so. Plus, you look alike. I don't have any brothers."

"No, you don't," Gabby says with a laugh.

"I want some, though," Sam adds.

"Let's go." Gabby sighs and shakes her head. "Clean up your own messes, big brother."

"Yes, ma'am," he replies in that slow, sexy accent that never fails to make me weak in the knees, and the grin spreads over his face when Gabby's engine starts and drives down the driveway. "Alone at last."

"We're alone quite often," I remind him.

"Mm," he replies, leaning his hands on the kitchen island, just staring at me with that smirk on his face as I lean on the breakfast bar opposite him.

"Are you going to just…do me here on the counter?"

"*Do* you?" He tilts his head back and forth, as if he's considering it. "Probably. But first, I'm going to cook for you."

"Cook for me." It isn't a question. "You cook."

"I cook just fine, thank you very much." He cocks a brow.

I bet he does. He does everything very well.

"And what are you going to cook?"

"You'll see." He turns to the fridge and begins gathering supplies, moving about the kitchen as if he's perfectly comfortable here. Which kind of throws me, because let's face it, watching the uber successful billionaire businessman, who admits to being a workaholic, work in the kitchen like it's second nature is…*hot.*

"Where did you learn to cook?"

He chooses a knife from the butcher block and begins chopping up an onion.

"Mama taught us all to cook."

"What do you want me to do?"

"Just look gorgeous and keep me company."

"Charming," I reply with a sigh. He's in another black T-shirt and blue jeans, which I think is unusual for him, but look amazing on him. His forearms flex and bunch as he chops. Just like they bunch when he's over me, gripping onto the mattress as he thrusts in and out of me. His whole body gets tight. And this man isn't short on muscles.

I want to lick him.

"Kate?"

"Huh?" I blink rapidly and try to focus. "What did you say?"

He sets the knife on the cutting board and smiles. "What were you just thinking about?"

My first reaction is to say *nothing*, but instead I walk very slowly around the island toward him. "I was thinking about licking you."

He leans his hips against the island and crosses his arms, making his biceps flex, and just like that, I want to tear his clothes off.

"Is that right?"

I nod.

"Where would you like to lick me?"

I grin and drag a fingertip down his neck. "Right here."

He swallows hard, making me even wetter. I love turning him on.

"You're distracting me," he says evenly, and it would bruise my ego if his eyes hadn't just dilated and the pulse in his neck sped up.

"I think that's the point."

He shakes his head and returns to chopping. "I'm cooking dinner."

"I don't particularly give a crap about dinner."

He smiles, like he always does when I don't use the usual curse words, but doesn't look me in the eye.

"You'll give a shit later, *cher*. You'll need the energy for what I have planned."

"That sounds fun." I cup his very firm, stellar ass in my hand and kiss his bicep. "Let's skip to that part."

He laughs, turns and lifts me into his arms, my legs wrapped around his waist, and kisses me mindless, until I can't think; I can't even feel my fingertips.

But I can sure as heck feel the pulsing between my legs.

The next thing I know, he sets me on the counter top, plants a smacking kiss on my lips and backs away, returning to the cutting board just a few feet away.

"Stay."

I stick my lower lip out in a pout and bat my eyes at him, but he just reaches over and smooths the pad of his thumb over my lip, drags his knuckles down my cheek, and whispers, "Trust me. Let me feed you. Let me pamper you a bit. I like it."

Well, how in the heck am I supposed to say no to that?

"Can I snack while you cook?" I ask, as he chops through celery surprisingly quickly.

"Sure." He passes me a celery stalk. "Wine?"

"Always."

He pours us each a glass of white, we clink our glasses together, and take a sip before he resumes chopping and I munch my celery.

"You feed me a lot."

"You're a good eater."

I pause with the celery halfway to my mouth and frown at him.

"What are you implying?"

"That you eat well?" He asks with a shrug.

I glance down at my small-ish chest and flat-ish stomach and then back at him. "Am I fat?"

He busts out laughing, not breaking his stride in his chopping.

"No, Kate. You're not fat. You enjoy food. And in doing so, I enjoy watching you eat. I'd feed you every meal every day if I could."

Oh.

"Can I have more celery?"

He grins, passes me the celery, and kisses me soundly before pulling away to get back to work.

Sitting here, watching him cook, is not a hardship in the least.

***

Dinner was delicious. Eli is just one big surprise after another. It's amazing to me how *normal* he is. The whole family, really, and it shouldn't, because I've been so close to Van and Dec for so many years, but this family is rich beyond my wildest dreams, yet they're as grounded and down to earth as anyone else. There aren't servants bustling about. Their cars are new and expensive, but no Aston Martin.

And on a Sunday afternoon, I'm lying on the couch with this powerful man, who has the ear of governors and high-powered people, who runs a multi-billion dollar enterprise with ease and efficiency.

He's snuggling me, on his back, with me lying on his chest, watching some stupid movie on cable, while his fingertips glide up and down my bare arm, my shoulder, my neck and into my hair and back down again.

If I could purr, I so would right now.

"We have the whole house to ourselves, and you want to watch a movie?" I ask lazily. He plants his lips on my head, takes a deep breath, and hugs me tight before his fingers resume their trek over my skin.

"Is there something else you'd rather do?"

"Well…" I grin and kiss his heart, over his T-shirt, breathing him in. He smells good. Clean. A little citrusy. I shift my pelvis over his and feel him start to harden, and his fingers still on my shoulder. "Yes."

His fingers sink into my hair as I kiss down his torso, lifting his shirt as I go, and plant wet kisses over his flat, chiseled abdomen. His breathing speeds up, but he's quiet; the only sounds are the TV and my lips smacking on his smooth, warm skin.

I could kiss his stomach all day long.

His T-shirt slips back down, and I frown up at him. "Can we dispose of this, please?"

He sits up and pulls his shirt over his head, tosses it on the floor, and shuts the TV off before lying back down. "Better?"

"Hmm." I push up to kiss his lips, tug on the lower lip with my teeth, then work my way down his throat, chest, and back to his stomach, enjoying the ridges of the muscles there. "I thought the six-pack was a myth. Or the work of Photoshop."

"Not if you work your ass off for it," he replies. His breath hitches when my tongue finds the groove of that V in his hips and trace it down to where it disappears into his jeans. I make quick work of the button and zipper, and smile when I see he's not wearing underwear.

Convenient.

His erection springs free into my hand, and I immediately grip it and pump it twice. Eli tosses his head back and groans, then turns his hot eyes back on me as I slowly lick from his scrotum to the tip in one long, fluid motion and rub the underside of the head on the flat of my tongue before taking him in my mouth and sucking, not too hard, but enough to get his attention.

And by the way his hand tightens in my hair, right at the scalp, where it feels so darn good when he pulls, I've got his attention.

"Fuck, that feels good."

I take him deeper, until the head is at the back of my throat, and I swallow, massaging him, loving the way it seems to grow even bigger in my mouth, firm my lips and pull up, lick the head, and repeat the motion.

"Look at me."

My eyes find his. They're hot, narrowed just a bit. His mouth is open as he pants. The hand not gripping my hair is behind his head, and his whole body is heaving.

It's sexy as hell that I can turn him on like this after just a few moments.

I lick down his shaft and over his tight balls, lightly suck them, then work my way back up to take him into my mouth once again. He begins to gently guide me into a pace that he likes, barely thrusting up to meet me. Not forcing me, but rather guiding me, and I love it.

"Grip your lips just a little tighter."

I comply and he hisses out a breath.

"Fuck, baby." His hips are moving faster, and suddenly, he's pulling my hair, but I stay where I am. "Kate, I don't want to come in your mouth."

I hum and stubbornly stay put, but after only two more pushes and pulls with my mouth, he grips onto my shoulders and pulls me up his body, claims my mouth with his, and effortlessly reverses our position, pinning me beneath him on the cushions of the couch.

"I was having fun," I pout.

"That's not how this works, *cher*." He nibbles my lips, brushes his nose over mine, and then plants soft kisses on my cheek.

"How what works?" I ask breathlessly. Good God, this man can kiss. Is this legal in the state of Louisiana?

Probably not.

"This." He repeats softly as he continues to pepper my skin with kisses. "You're not going to just suck me off and make me come and call it a day."

"Well, that wasn't really my plan. I was just having fun."

"Hmm." He kisses my collarbone. "I'll be back. I don't have a condom on me."

"Wait." I grip his arms, keeping him still. "I have the birth control covered."

He raises a brow. "Are you sure? I don't mind using them." He kisses my collarbone again. "I've never *not* used them."

"I don't mind," I whisper. "Unless there's something you need to tell me."

He offers me a wicked smile and kisses me deeply.

I glide my hands down his naked back to his ass, under his loose jeans, and hold on tight as he presses his pelvis to mine, grinding against me and making me even wetter, if that's even possible. Is there anything sexier than a man's ass when it's barely covered by undone jeans?

No. No, there's not.

"Eli," I whisper.

"Yes, baby."

"My clothes are still on."

He grins against my lips and settles over me, his elbows planted on either side of my head. "Yes, they are."

"Take them off," I demand softly and wiggle beneath him, still gripping his ass, and the arch of my foot rubbing over his denim-covered calf.

"No."

He grips onto my hair and tilts my head to the side as he drags his lips down my jawline to my neck and proceeds to drive me out of my ever-loving mind with his talented mouth and tongue. My nipples have puckered, my hands grip him tighter, one still on his ass, the other now buried in his soft hair.

My hips tilt up, pressing against his hard on, and I want him inside me.

Now.

"Eli, please. Need you inside me."

"I'll get there," he replies lazily, and works his way around to the other side of my neck.

"Can we go a bit faster here?" I ask breathlessly, and then groan when his tongue skims over my sweet spot. "God, I love it when you hit that spot."

"I know," he whispers and does it again, making my toes curl.

"Eli." I'm whining, and I hate myself for it, but for the love of all that's holy, why isn't he naked and inside me?

"Kate," he says and bites the tender skin at the top of my shoulder. "It's Sunday."

I frown, but then sigh when he finally pulls my shirt up my body and guides it over my head. "What does the day of the week have to do with anything?"

He pulls the cups of my bra down and slowly circles one puckered nipple with his tongue, then blows on it and repeats the motion on the other side.

Moving as slowly as humanly possible.

He's trying to kill me.

"You're in the South. Don't you know that we don't do *anything* quickly on Sunday?" He's kissing down my stomach now, and I'm a bit self-conscious because hello, I don't have a six pack. Or any kind of pack.

But he doesn't seem to mind as he moves down my body, and I'm expecting him to pull my denim shorts off, but instead, he bypasses the center of my universe and begins kissing my legs.

My legs.

"Really?" I demand with a laugh, earning a sharp bite on the inside of my right thigh.

"Patience, Kate."

"Not patient."

He chuckles and drags his fingernails down my outer thighs, calves, to my bare feet and back up again while his mouth does something completely crazy to the back of my knee.

Apparently, he didn't find all of my erogenous zones yesterday.

"Oh, my God," I murmur, and can't keep my hips from shifting and moving. He's going to make me come without even *touching* me.

How is that possible?

"Open your eyes, sugar." My gaze meets his, and I'm surprised to find his eyes on fire, watching me as he unzips my shorts, guides them down my legs, and tosses them over his shoulder. "No underwear for you either?"

I shrug and smile at him, but he doesn't return it. He's still watching me intently, braced on the back of the couch, as his fingers glide up my inner thigh and brush, ever so gently, over my lips, my clit, and then…my stomach.

Really? He's not going to hang out in the one place that's screaming for him?

I must frown because a wicked smile breaks out over that impossibly handsome face of his and he cocks a brow. "You don't like that?"

"You're teasing me."

"Yes." He watches my face as his fingers find my core again, but it's just his fingertips tickling over my lips, the crease where my leg meets my center. I reach for his wrist to guide him inside, but he quickly grips my hand in his, kisses it, and places it above my head. "You're not controlling this." His lips are barely touching my own. "You're going to be patient, and enjoy. It's Sunday."

"You've never been lazy on a Sunday in your life," I whisper against his lips. Jesus, I can't catch my breath.

I'm going to die of asphyxiation before I get to come. That's not fair.

"There's a first for everything," he replies softly, bites my lower lip, then resumes the torture happening between my legs. He glances down. "Fuck me, you're wet."

"That happens when you do stuff to me," I reply and circle my hips.

"*Stuff?*" he repeats. "What kind of stuff?"

I'm not strong enough to fight him on my language. I don't care if I swear. All I can focus on is having him over me, in me. Now.

"When you kiss me and touch me and tease me with fucking me," I reply, and feel very satisfied when his eyes widen.

"I do love hearing those filthy words come out of your pretty mouth," he murmurs in that slow Cajun accent that makes me crazy. His fingers are rubbing my lips harder now, gliding effortlessly through my wet folds. Finally, he scoots down, kisses my navel piercing, slides one finger inside me, and plants his mouth on my clit, not sucking, just *being* and I cry out, gripping the cushions at my hips, pushing my hips up to grind on his lips.

He pulls the finger back out, and gently licks over my lips, clit and folds, plants the flat of his tongue over my clit, and pushes two fingers inside me; I push up onto my elbows, watching as he turns me inside out.

"Oh, my God, Eli, you're gonna make me..."

He pulls away, kisses me between my navel and pubis, and grins when I growl at him.

"Your pussy is so soft," he says, as though he's just making casual conversation. His fingers are moving in and out, slowly, methodically. If he'd just press his thumb on my sweet spot, I'd come spectacularly.

But I have a feeling that's not going to happen yet.

"You have this spot..." he shoves his fingers all the way in, and makes a *come here* motion that makes me see stars. "Right behind your pubic bone. Don't close your eyes," he orders. I look up at him as his fingers pick up speed. He's watching me as he pushes on that spot again.

"How didn't I know about this spot before?" I ask breathlessly, and then cry out when he settles the tips of his fingers there and rubs gently.

His eyes flare in male satisfaction. "You're good for my ego, *cher*."

"You're good for my," I swallow, "pussy."

"Fuck yes, I am." He rubs a little harder and I arch up off the couch. "Come, baby."

And that's all it takes, his voice, his breath on my skin, his fingers doing crazy amazing things inside me, and I come apart. I go blind, my core tightens, and I ride the wave of the orgasm as it shoots through me.

When I open my eyes, Eli is smiling down at me. He pulls his fingers out and covers me, guides himself inside me until he's balls-deep, and stays there, not moving.

I grip onto his cock with my muscles and grin when he swears under his breath. His jeans are still on, which for some reason, I find very sexy.

Everything about him is fucking sexy.

I grip his ass and pulse against him. "Move, Eli."

He shakes his head and tips his forehead against mine. "Not yet."

His whiskey eyes are trained on mine. He watches me as he pulls his hips back, then pushes back in slowly. "Your face is so expressive," he whispers. "And this feels so fucking amazing."

"The ridge of your cock rubs against that spot you've discovered," I whisper.

"Like that?" His smile is more than a little naughty.

"So good."

I bite my lip and tighten on him as he drags in and out of me. His eyes are on me, hands buried in my hair, gripping onto my scalp as he moves, and it occurs to me: this is what the fuss is all about. This is how a woman is supposed to be touched, looked at.

Respected.

Protected.

It's so unfamiliar to me, and sad at the same time, because I was *married* damn it, and I had no idea. How is it that sex with the man I was supposed to love was just…*empty*? And sex with Eli is…*everything*?

But Eli and I agreed. No love. Just fun.

This has an expiration date.

"Stop," he demands and begins to move faster, a bit harder.

"Stop what?"

"Thinking." He does something with his hips that has me gasping for breath, and in this moment, I can't remember my own name. "Grip my cock, Kate."

He pulls one of my legs up onto his shoulder to open me wider, and he sinks deeper inside, bumping my pubis with his, and holy shit, I see stars.

"Eli."

"That's right, baby." He smiles down at me. "You're amazing. I can see it building. Come for me."

I bite my lip and close my eyes, bear down on him, and fall apart all over again, shocked that it's so soon.

"Fuck," he whispers as he cups my ass and clutches me close to him, grinding inside me as he finds his own release. "Fuck, Kate."

"Yes," I sigh. "You just fucked Kate."

"As soon as I can move, you're getting spanked for that."

"You like it when I say fuck."

"I like spanking you too."

I feel him grin against my chest where he's resting and smile in return. I rather like the spanking myself.

I like Eli. And that could be dangerous.

CHAPTER THIRTEEN

I'm gonna spank your ass for that.

And, boy, did he.

I grin and bite the end of my pen as I sit at my desk. I had a productive morning, but now all I can do is daydream about being at the inn…Making love until the wee hours of the morning…Breakfast with Gabby and a very chatty Sam… Walking in the gardens.

Eli finding my G-spot.

I also thought that was a myth. Apparently, I was wrong.

So very wrong.

I giggle and touch my suddenly very warm cheeks. Is it hot in here?

"Hilary!" Mr. Rudolph calls from his office, and I roll my eyes. That's the third time today that he's called me Hilary.

Seriously, I've been here for three weeks. Shouldn't he have figured out by now that I'm not Hilary? Kate isn't a hard name to learn.

I walk briskly into his office. "My name is Kate, Mr. Rudolph."

He glances up and flicks his hand, as if it doesn't matter. "Whatever. I need you to run the month end tax reports for payroll." He goes on about the other tasks he wants me to handle—tasks that are normally *his*—and keeps checking his watch. He seems twitchy. Nervous. Even his brow is sweaty.

He's kind of creepy.

But then, he looks up at me, and his brown eyes are kind. "Thanks for doing all of this. Kate, right?"

I nod and turn to leave his office, my to-do list out of control.

"I'm leaving for the rest of the afternoon," he informs me, as he follows me out of his office and closes and locks the door. "I'll see you in the morning."

He wipes his fingers over his mouth and hurries out, and I'm just...*pissed*. It must be nice to not have to work much. The man is out of the office more than he's in it. He leaves every day at 1:30, like clockwork. Which really annoys me. Why would Eli have someone with such a poor work ethic working for him?

I set the list Mr. Rudolph just handed me aside, and decide to get some of my own work done. I examine the spreadsheet of all of the transfers of large sums of money that are unaccounted for so far, and try to find a common link. The amounts are all different. They range in size of a few hundred dollars to several thousand. It seems that lately, they've gotten bigger. One was almost ten thousand dollars. But they're not sent on the same day, or even on a regular schedule.

The only consistent thing is that they're transfers to Western Union. No name on these reports.

Don't you have to have an I.D. to pick up money from Western Union? I call a local branch, and sure enough.

Okay, who were they sent to?

Just as I'm about to start digging to find a name, something else occurs to me. The time of day the transfers were made were all around 1:00 in the afternoon, give or take a minute or two. I flip through them all, and sure enough, every single one is around the same time.

Interesting.

I glance at the time on the computer and frown. Mr. Rudolph leaves at 1:30 almost every day. I find each transaction in the computer, and I search for the name of the recipient at Western Union.

H. Peters.

Who in the hell is H. Peters?

I frown and pull up the roster of employees, not finding an H. Peters in the bunch.

Well, shit.

I dial Savannah's office number, but get her voice mail, so I dial her cell.

"Hello?" I can hear road noise and raise a brow.

"You've left early."

"Lance asked me to meet him at home," she replies with a sigh.

"Why?"

"No idea. What's up?"

"I have a small lead, and I'm going to need some help. Is there a person that you prefer I use internally to do some snooping, or can I call in my own private investigator?"

"We usually use someone internally, but let's bring in someone from the outside for this."

I nod in agreement. "Will do, thanks."

I place a call to Adam, a local investigator that a colleague recommended, and leave him a voice mail, outlining what I need, then hang up and study the transactions again. I've looked through them a hundred times, but didn't see the time stamp similarities until today.

What else am I missing?

"You look serious."

I gasp and throw the papers on the desk, startled, then cover my heart with my hand and sigh. "You scared me, Hilary."

"Sorry." She grins. "I have to go run some errands, but do you want to meet up for happy hour this afternoon? Say, around four?"

I frown and shake my head. "No, thanks. I had a long weekend. I really just want to go home and relax."

"A long weekend, huh?" She leans on the doorjamb and crosses her arms. "Who is he?"

I laugh and shake my head at my new friend. "You're incorrigible. It's not always about sex, you know."

"Of course it's always about sex." She laughs and tucks her hair behind her ear. "And you're having some. I can tell. I want to hear all about it. And you look like you could use a drink."

I sigh and start to shake my head again, but she rolls her eyes. "You're not saying no. Meet me at Huck's at four."

"Fine. Have a lemon drop waiting for me."

"Can do."

***

"So, talk. Who is it?" Hilary asks, as I sit and take a sip of a delicious lemon drop.

"Not telling." *No way, nohow.*

"You're not fun. I need details."

"I'm not telling you who it is, but I'll spill some details about the sex itself."

"Right on." She shifts in her seat and signals to the waitress for another drink.

"How long have you been here?" I ask.

"A little while. I'm a drink ahead of you. You have to catch up."

I take another drink and lick the sugar on the rim of the glass. I love this damn sugar.

It's probably why my hips are so wide. Damn hips.

"So, was the sex good?" Hilary asks.

"The best sex that was ever invented," I confirm, and click my glass to hers.

"Impressive." She sighs and rests her chin in her hand. "Does he do fun oral stuff?"

"Indeed."

"Good. If a man won't go down on you, it's a red flag. Life's too short for that."

I giggle and nod. "For sure. My ex-husband refused to do that. It should have been a clue to his ass-hattery."

"My ex-husband only wanted to have missionary sex," she says with a wrinkle of her nose. "What's the fun in that?"

"Missionary is good," I reply.

"Yes, but every time? Let's switch it up a bit."

"True."

"Was he a pushover, or did he wear the pants? Pun intended." She sips her Bloody Mary through a straw and leans in.

"Oh, he's bossy for sure."

"I love the bossy ones."

I nod in agreement, then watch in wonder as she drains her Bloody Mary and signals to the waitress for another.

"Slow down there, Speedy Gonzales."

She giggles and shakes her head. "I'm celebrating."

"Oh! What are we celebrating?"

"My new car." She smiles proudly. "I just bought a new Mercedes."

I blink at her, stunned. "Seriously? How can you afford that on our salary?"

"Oh, honey, where there's a will, there's a way." She winks and sips her new drink, and all the hairs on the back of my neck stand up. But before I can say anything, my phone rings.

"Hello?"

"We need you. Now."

"Dec?" I frown and immediately reach for my purse; I mouth *got to go* to Hilary, who just nods and waves me off, already paying attention to her own phone. I reach the sidewalk and pause. "Where am I going? What's happening?"

"Come to Savannah's, now."

"Is she okay?"

"No."

My stomach drops and a cold sweat breaks out on my skin that has nothing at all to do with the heat of summer.

"Is she alive?" I whisper.

"Yes. Get here."

"Wait! Where does she live?"

Declan swears under his breath. "Fuck, you don't have a car. Get to Charly's shop and she'll drive you both here."

"On it." I end the call and run to Charly's just two blocks over. She's locking up the front door, her phone pressed to her ear, tears running down her pretty face. "Charly!"

"She's here. We're coming now."

"What is going on?"

"I'm not sure; Declan didn't want to waste time giving info, he just said Van's been hurt, and we need to get there. Get in."

We climb into Charly's car and she speeds off.

"How far away is her house?"

"Three minutes."

"How far is it normally?" I ask, and brace my hand on the dashboard as Charly weaves in and out of traffic.

"Ten."

I hold my breath and pray as Charly gives the cab driver from my first day a run for his money in the crazy driving department, and finally she comes to a screaming stop in a driveway, cuts the engine, and we both go running for the front door.

"Van?!" Charly screams as she pushes inside. "Where is everybody?"

"Upstairs!" Beau calls, and we run through the beautiful home, up the stairs, and come to a halt when we find all three Boudreaux brothers and a man I don't know just outside of Van's bedroom. Beau is talking into the door.

"Who are you?" I ask the handsome, tall man with sandy-blonde hair and deep blue eyes. Eyes that look tortured and worried.

"This is Ben," Eli replies. "He's been a good friend for many years."

"Vanny, you have to open the door, baby. Let us in."

"What is going on?" Charly demands.

"Van called me," Declan says. "She was sobbing; I couldn't understand much, but she said she was home and needed help. I called everyone. But she won't come out of her bedroom."

I'm staring into Eli's scared, angry whiskey eyes. He pulls me hard against him and hugs me close, takes a deep breath, as if he needs this to anchor him, then lets me go and moves to the door.

"Savannah, Charly and Kate are here. Will you open the door for them?"

"Only they can come in," comes a small voice from the other side.

"Jesus, what the fuck?" Beau asks, pushing his hand through his hair. Ben is silent, but clearly agitated, as he paces back and forth.

The door opens a crack and I lead Charly inside and immediately feel the blood leave my face.

"Christ," Charly says, as we both rush to her side. Savannah is sitting on the edge of the mattress of her bed. It's been stripped bare, the sheets and blankets thrown about the room, along with lamps, the alarm clock, anything that could be thrown has been. There is glass shattered. Savannah is wearing her white dress shirt, but no pants. I immediately cover her with a white bed sheet. "What happened, baby?"

Van's hollow eyes are on mine, and I know. I know exactly what happened. I want to fall apart, but I pull myself together and know that I have to get through this for Van.

"Where did he hit you?"

Tears fill her eyes. "He kicked my ribs."

I lift her shirt and bite my lips to keep from crying out at the blazing bruises across her ribcage.

"Where else?"

She shakes her head, but she's cradling her right arm against her.

"Is your arm hurt, honey?"

She nods. She's begun to shake. "Yeah, he pulled it behind my back really hard."

I look up at Charly, who has tears streaming down her face. "Tell the boys to call an ambulance."

"No." Van shakes her head and starts to stand, but I keep her next to me.

"Yes. Savannah, you're hurt."

"Can we come in?" Dec asks from the doorway.

"I don't want them to see this," Van whispers.

"They need to," Charly says, and nods at Dec. The four big men fill the room, and all four look like they're about to kill someone.

"What happened, baby?" Beau asks softly, his voice in direct contrast to his tense body.

"Let's finish figuring out where she's hurt," I interrupt. "He wrenched your arm behind your back?"

Savannah nods, and won't look any of the men in the eyes.

"Are you afraid of us, *bebe*?" Eli asks quietly as he squats in front of her.

"No, of course not. I'm embarrassed," she replies quietly, and watches Eli's face as her tears spill over. "How could I let this happen?"

"What *did* happen, Vanny?" Declan asks.

She swallows and looks at me. "My shoulder is dislocated. I'm pretty sure. I think a rib is broken."

The men all still and watch very carefully as I smooth her tears from her cheeks. "Okay. What else?"

She shows me her wrist, which has bruises in the shape of fingers around it. "Check my other shoulder," she says.

I pull her shirt away and we all gasp at the sight of more finger-shaped bruises on her opposite shoulder.

"He pulled my arm around my back and held onto my shoulder with the other hand."

"And kicked you in the ribs," I confirm, and Van nods.

"Why are you wet, honey?" Charly asks, and I frown as I realize that Van's hair and clothes are all sopping wet.

She starts to shake her head, but Eli takes her face gently in his hands and says, "Why are you wet, my sweet girl?"

Ben stomps into the bathroom and swears ripely. Beau follows, then both men come back into the room.

"He tried to drown her in the tub," Beau says, as Declan calls for an ambulance. "He's a dead man."

"Why?" Savannah asks, still staring into Eli's face. "I don't understand. He called me and said he wanted to tell me something, at home, in private. So, I came home. And he was in here, pacing back and forth. He looked…*frustrated*. Said that he'd been fucking some young thing that decided that she couldn't fuck him anymore because he's married and it's wrong. So, it's my fault.

"I told him that was easily fixed. He can fuck whomever he wants, for the rest of his life, and I'll happily sign papers. But that only made it worse, because Daddy made him sign a prenup, and he won't leave me just to lose out on all the money after all these years."

"A fucking dead man," Beau repeats, and Ben simply leaves, the door downstairs slamming behind him.

"Did he say he was going to kill you?" I ask her.

She nods stiffly, shaking in earnest now, shock setting in. "He kept holding my face in the water, until I thought for sure I was going to die, and then he'd pull me back out. Oh, my God," she breaks down crying. "And then he dragged me back in here by the hair and…"

"And what?" Declan asks.

"I don't want you to hear it," she says to her brothers.

"Vanny, we love you," Beau says softly. "It's okay."

She looks around the room, then settles her gaze on mine and whispers, "He raped me."

I swallow hard. I want to throw up. I want to run away. I don't want to hear this, hear how brutalized my best friend was by the man who was supposed to love her more than anything. But, instead, I lean in and kiss Van's cheek.

"You're safe. The ambulance is coming. We need to take pictures, Van."

"What?" she gasps.

"To press charges, we need photos," I repeat.

"Am I pressing charges?"

"If he lives long enough, yes," Eli confirms. He and his brothers are scary. Lance should be very afraid.

"Of course you are, honey," Charly says, and caresses Van's hair soothingly.

"You're leaving him," I say firmly. "This is it. No more."

"What do you mean, *no more*?" Declan asks.

Charly sighs and winces in pain. "Not the first time."

"What?" Beau demands, and Eli stands to pace, unable to keep still any more.

"But, it's the last," I repeat, before her brothers can ask more questions. "Eli, can you please have the locks on the house changed today?"

"Done."

Sirens call in the distance as the ambulance gets closer. My fingers shake as I push Van's hair behind her ear. I want to fall apart. For me. For Van. For this whole family that has been shaken to the core by an evil that none of us quite understand.

But I can't. Not yet.

"Come with me," Van whispers.

"Every step of the way, friend."

"Love you so much," she says, and begins to cry again.

"Love you more."

CHAPTER FOURTEEN
ELI

"Where the fuck is he?" Beau asks the room at large for the fourth time in twenty minutes, and continues to pace my office.

"We've been all over the city," Declan answers, clearly as frustrated as the rest of us. And, out of all of us, Dec is the calmest one. Seeing him agitated is always unnerving. "Maybe he skipped town."

"We'll find him," I reply and sip my brandy. "He can't go far. We've frozen his bank accounts."

"Maybe we shouldn't have done that," Beau replies. "If he uses the bank accounts, we know where he's been."

"He's not getting one more dime from this family," I reply coldly, my gut churning as I remember the look in sweet Van's eyes as they held mine and asked *why?*

Why?

Because he's a piece of shit. Because he wouldn't know what it is to be a man if it fucked him up the ass without lube.

Because he didn't know a good thing when he had it.

But none of that would have made her feel better. *Nothing* can make her feel better, except time and love.

"We should have known," Declan says as he rubs his face, his elbows planted on his knees. "*I* should have known."

"We all should have known," Beau replies in resignation.

"We did," I say, and sip the brandy. "We knew he wasn't a good man. Even if Savannah never would confirm it; we knew *something* wasn't right."

"It was her choice to be with him," Beau says, and holds a hand up when Declan starts to argue. "Think about it. She was young and convinced and proud, Dec. There was no talking her out of it."

"But it's our mother fucking job to protect her," I reply softly. "And we didn't."

We all blink at each other for a long minute. Our fists clenched. Our jaws tight.

"Dad would have killed that fucker himself."

"He would," I agree with a nod. "No one ever fucked with his family and lived to tell the tale."

"Dad never killed anyone," Beau replies with a half smile, as though the thought is entertaining.

"No one dared fuck with us before to test him," Declan says.

"He's going to pay," Beau says, and swallows his glass of brandy.

"He already has," Ben says, as he stalks into my office. We all still when we see him. He's sweaty, dirty, and has blood on his shirt.

"What the fuck?" Declan demands.

"What happened?" I ask, much more calmly than I feel.

"You don't need specifics," he replies, and takes my drink from my hand, gulping the brandy, and holds the glass out for more. "I found him."

"Is he alive?" Beau asks.

"He's wishing he wasn't, but yes."

"Do you need an attorney?" I ask my friend since childhood. He shakes his head and swigs more brandy.

"Not necessary. He's already turned himself in."

"He's turned himself in to the police?" Beau asks incredulously.

Ben nods and leans his hips on my desk.

"How did you pull that off?" Dec asks.

Ben simply smiles, a cold, hard smile that would make most grown men piss in their pants. "I made it very clear that it was either turn himself in, or I'd kill him."

"You would have," I say, with a bit of surprise, although it shouldn't surprise me. Ben has been in love with Savannah since puberty.

"Without hesitation," he replies coldly, and takes another sip of brandy. When his glass is drained, he slaps it on the desk and walks toward my door.

"Ben," Declan says, stopping our friend when he grips the doorknob. "What exactly is Savannah to you?"

Ben glances over his shoulder at Dec, shakes his head, his eyes suddenly sad, and leaves without a word.

"Fuck," Beau whispers. "This could turn into a shitstorm."

"It won't," I reply. "Our people will take care of it. He'll pay. Dearly."

"What an idiot," Declan says with disgust. "He did this over a piece of ass?"

"He did this because he's an evil son of a bitch," Beau replies. "It really has nothing at all to do with Savannah. It was never about her."

"I'm going to go grab a shower and then head up to the hospital," Declan says.

"I'll go with you," Beau replies, just as my phone rings.

Kate.

"Hello, *cher.*"

"Hi." Her voice sounds tired. "Gabby is here at the hospital with Van. She's going to stay with her tonight."

"They're keeping Van overnight?" I ask and check my watch. Damn, it's almost midnight.

"Yeah, it's late, and she's pretty hurt. They want to watch her. Can you please come get me? I wouldn't ask, but Charly already went home and—"

"Of course I'll come get you." I grab my keys and head for the door. "I'll be there in fifteen minutes."

***

I hate hospitals. The smell, the sounds. I fucking hate that Savannah is lying in a bed here.

I walk into her room and curl my hands into fists. Her face isn't marked at all. The fucker was sure to not bruise up her pretty face. But her arm is in a sling, and she's cradling it against her like it aches.

My own chest aches.

Gabby sees me first and runs to me, launching herself into my arms. Our girls are always so strong. So fierce. But they aren't afraid to lean on their brothers when they need us.

And, as far as I'm concerned, that just makes them all the stronger.

"It's okay, *bebe*," I murmur and kiss the top her of head. Gabby is not just the baby, she's also the smallest. The rest of us are tall, but she's petite. And if you didn't know her, you'd mistakenly think she's fragile.

"I just need a hug," she murmurs before pulling away and smiling reassuringly at Van.

"You're a sweet girl, *bebe*," I whisper in her ear. "Who has Sam?"

"He's with Mama. She took him home with her. I called Cindy and asked her to watch the inn for tonight."

I inwardly cringe, but nod. Cindy has been Gabby's friend since grade school.

And she spent an out-of-control, mistake of a night in my bed.

"How are you feeling?" I ask, as I lean in and plant my lips on Van's forehead. She's cool to the touch.

No fever from shock or infection.

"Sore," she says, and smiles as I pull away. *Strong women.* "I'll be okay."

I kiss Kate and drag my knuckles down her smooth cheek before sitting on the bed at Van's hip.

The looks that Van and Gabby exchange aren't lost on me. They'll grill me later.

"I have news." I take Van's hand in mine and look her dead in the eye.

"Tell me."

I exhale, wondering how much information I should give her. "He's in custody."

She closes her eyes in relief and her body seems to sag. "Thank God."

"He won't hurt you ever again." She frowns and looks back into my eyes.

"Is he in custody, or in the morgue?"

I grin ruefully. "He's not dead. Unfortunately."

"But he's hurt."

Strong and smart.

I nod, but don't elaborate.

"You've never lied to me, E. Not once."

"No, ma'am."

"So, why are you now?"

"I'm not lying."

Gabby snorts and I send her a hard stare, shutting her up.

"You're not telling me everything. How did you find him? Was he arrested?"

"I didn't find him."

She tilts her head to the side, and there she is. My Van. She narrows her eyes, and I know I'm in for it.

Thank Christ.

"What. The. Fuck."

"Ben found him." Her eyes widen, but I continue. "I haven't seen him yet. But I saw Ben. Swollen knuckles, sweaty. A little blood."

"Blood!"

"Don't you dare defend that fucker," Gabby says angrily.

"No, I want to know if it was *Ben's* blood!"

I smirk. "Honey, nobody makes Ben bleed."

She sighs in relief, but then frowns again. "So, Ben called the cops?"

"I honestly don't know how it went down. I'm assuming we'll find out tomorrow. Ben found him, and made him see that turning himself in was best for Lance's well-being."

Van's lower lip quivers, making my gut tighten. "He did that for me."

"We would do *anything* for you, *bebe*." She grips onto my hand with her uninjured one and squeezes, holding my gaze in hers, and an entire silent conversation passes between us.

I love you. Thank you. I don't know what I would do without you.

I love you. Always. You're welcome. You don't ever have to know what it is to live without us.

"Go home," she whispers instead. "Take Kate home. She's tired, but she won't admit it."

"I'm not tired," Kate lies easily.

"She's lying," Van says.

"I know," I reply with a grin and glance over at Gabby, who still has tears in her eyes. "You got this?"

"Of course." She grins, the dimples in her cheeks showing. "Vanny's stuck with me all night. It'll be like when we were kids and I'd sneak into her room and sleep with her because my room was haunted."

"Your room wasn't haunted," Van replies with a roll of the eyes. "You just liked my bigger bed."

"My room was haunted," she insists, talking to Kate now. "My things would be mysteriously moved. I heard voices."

"Those voices are in that hard head of yours," I reply and grin when she sticks her tongue out at me, just like she did when she was small. "But I am going to take Kate home now."

"Kate appreciates it," Kate says sarcastically. "She also loves it when you talk about her like she's not here."

"She's testy," Van says. "She's been bossing the nurses around all day."

"I'm right here," Kate says.

"I know how to reel that bossy side in," I assure Van, and laugh when Kate mutters *right here, people.* "We will check in on you in the morning."

"Good night."

I take Kate's hand in mine and kiss it as I lead her out of Van's room and into the hallway. As soon as we're out of view, she pulls her hand from mine and walks ahead of me to the elevator, keeping her distance as we wait.

"Are you okay?" I ask.

She simply nods, her eyes trained on the door of the elevator. *Another lie.*

I move to brush her hair behind her ear, but she flinches away from my reach. My first reaction is frustration. Does she think that I would hurt her? But then she turns her sad green eyes to me and just shakes her head, and I relax.

It's not me. She's hanging on by a fucking thread.

I nod once and keep my distance to the car. Halfway home, I try to take her hand in mine, but she pulls away and clasps her hands tightly in her lap. Her whole body is tense. Her eyes trained on her lap.

For the first time in my life, I want to make it better for a woman. I want to hold her and protect her, and *she's not mine.*

She's never going to be mine. And the thought of her leaving makes me feel…

I don't know what, it just makes me *feel.*

I park and she jumps out of the car, walking quickly to her loft.

"Kate. You're coming up to my place."

"No. I'm not." She doesn't stop walking.

"Yes, *cher*, you are."

She stops and turns to glare at me. "No, I'm not. I don't want you tonight, Eli."

"You're getting me."

"You know what?" she rails, her eyes fierce, her gorgeous hair a riot of curls around her face. She advances toward me, anger vibrating in every muscle of her body. "I don't need this. I don't need another *man* telling me what I will and will not do."

"You shouldn't be alone."

"Shouldn't. Won't. Can't." She gets up in my face, and I've never seen anything like her. She's on fire, standing out here on the sidewalk in the French Quarter, yelling at me. "You're an asshole!"

Shot to the gut.

"I've never claimed otherwise, *cher.*" My voice is perfectly calm. My hands are in my pockets, so I don't reach for her and pull her in.

Not yet.

"You just play with people and their emotions! You're just selfish and heartless!"

My eyes narrow on her face. Her eyes are tearing up, her cheeks rosy, and her bottom lip quivers as she shoves her fists into my chest, knocking me back a step.

She's surprisingly strong for such a little thing.

"You just hurt people!" she yells.

"Who are you talking to right now, Kate?" I ask softly. Her eyes focus on me, and her face crumples as she begins to cry. "Ah, *bebe.*" I hug her tight to me, and she fights me, trying to wrench her way out of my arms, but I hold firm. "Shhh. You're safe, Kate. Let go. Cry. Scream. Do whatever you need to, sweetheart. I have you. I'm not letting go."

"I don't want you to see this."

"God save me from proud women," I mumble into her hair, as I press kisses to the top of her head, breathing her in. She begins to cry in earnest now, gripping onto my shirt rather than trying to get away. I scoop her up into my arms and carry her inside as she buries her face in my neck and cries; loud, body-shaking sobs making their way through her as though the storm has finally washed over her and all she can do is ride it out and survey the damage later.

And it's killing me. I don't take her upstairs to the bedroom. Instead, I carry her into the living room, sit on the couch, and simply hold her in my lap, my arms tight around her, and let her cry.

I brush her hair off her face, wishing I had a cool washcloth. Her back is slender under my hands as I caress her slowly, trying to comfort her.

Finally, after long minutes, the sobbing slows, and she is reduced to hiccoughs, then sniffles. Her small body still shaking. Her hands still clinging to me, as if I could let her go.

Not happening.

"Made a mess of you," she whispers roughly.

"Doesn't matter," I reply in the same whisper. The house is quiet around us as we sit here, holding onto each other.

"I know what she felt," she whispers, but then doesn't elaborate, and I don't ask her to. Finally, she says, "I know how it felt every time he kicked her. Pulled her hair. Wrenched her arm. Held her down while he—" The last word comes on a sob, and I tighten my arms around her as I wish for the chance to have Kate's ex-husband alone in a room for just five minutes. "At least I was never almost drowned."

I have to swallow the bile that rises up in my throat.

"Do all men hurt women?" she asks softly.

"No."

She simply nods.

"I hate that this happened to her. She'll question herself for a long time. *What did I do to make him hurt me? Why wasn't I good enough, smart enough, for him? If I had just done this or that, he wouldn't have gotten mad.*" My hands reflexively fist in her shirt. "Long after the bruises fade, and her shoulder heals, she'll still be broken."

"Do you think you're still broken, Kate?" I ask softly. She stills, then loops her arms around my neck and hugs me close, burying her fingers in my hair, and I return the hug, enjoying the way she feels in my lap, pressed against me.

"Sometimes I think I'll always be broken," she whispers into my ear, tears in her voice.

I cup her cheek in my hand and tip her face up so I can look her in the eye. Her tears make me feel so fucking helpless. I don't do helpless.

Shit, I don't do *feelings.* Or I didn't, until I met her.

"Do you want to know what I think?"

"Maybe," she replies with a sniffle.

I grin and tuck her hair behind her ear, then let my fingertips trail down her wet cheek. "I think that you are smart, funny, and sexy as fuck."

She grins and her green eyes darken, making my cock stir.

"I also think you're stubborn." She sniffles and raises an eyebrow. "I know you're beautiful." She tries to look down, but I tip her chin back up with my finger. "You are beautiful. Every freckle on your gorgeous little body drives me crazy. But, more than that, Kate? You're strong. Determined. You have a backbone."

Tears fill her eyes again, and I can't stand it. I tip my forehead against hers. "You're not broken, *cher.* He hurt you. But no one broke you."

"Thank you for that," she whispers, and kisses my lips softly before tucking her face back into my neck and beginning to cry again. Softly now. A cleansing cry. The kind of cry that sweeps out the demons and makes room for the good.

Kate deserves so much good.

***

There's a buzzing in my pocket.

And a woman lying on top of me.

I open one eye and squint at the light in the room. We're still in the living room, stretched out on the couch, cuddled up much like we were at the inn when we watched the movie.

Well, pretended to watch the beginning of the movie.

Kate's face is snuggled against my heart, her arms wrapped around my sides, legs entangled with mine. The only way we'd be able to get much closer is if we were naked. And it feels fucking amazing.

Imagine that.

The buzzing begins again in my pocket.

"Are you going to answer that?" Kate asks without moving, making me grin. I fish my phone out of my pocket, with Kate's dead weight on me, and frown when I see Declan's name on the caller ID.

"Hey," I answer. "What's wrong?"

"Nothing, as far as I know," he replies. I can hear street noises. "You sound funny. Were you still asleep?"

"No," I lie, and Kate pokes me in the ribs and hisses, "No lying."

"It's after nine, Eli."

"Are you the morning police?"

"Don't you have to be at work?"

"That's the thing about being the boss. I can go into work when and if the desire strikes." I kiss Kate's head and grin again as she shimmies against me, getting more comfortable, and succeeding in making sure my morning semi-hard-on is now just a hard-on.

But then she looks up at me, and everything in me just goes...*tender.* Her eyes are swollen and red. Her hair tangled around her face. Lips swollen from licking and biting them as she cried.

If I have anything to say about it, she'll never have another reason to be devastated like this in her life.

And that's ridiculous because *she isn't mine.*

Except, she's mine for right now, and that's all that matters.

"Eli?"

"Sorry, what?"

"If you tell me that you're having sex while on the phone with me, I will deck the fuck out of you when I see you."

"You don't scare me."

"He's not having sex," Kate says into the phone, and giggles as she snuggles into me again.

I've never loved to snuggle. I mean, it's a necessity to snuggle right after sex. Otherwise, you're just a prick who wanted to fuck her. And I am, but even I know the importance of the obligatory snuggle.

That isn't what this is.

"I might have sex after we hang up," I clarify, earning another giggle from Kate.

"No, he won't. At least not with me."

I slap Kate's ass and laugh when she pinches my side. "What's up, Dec?"

"Just wanted to give you an update on Van. She's doing better this morning. Stiff and sore, but her ribs aren't broken, and there's no bleeding. They'll let her go to Mama's this afternoon."

"She'll love that," I say dryly.

"Gabby wanted her to go to the inn, but I put the nix on that. Van will try to help. If we have her go to Mama's, she'll be pampered and taken care of."

"She'll die of boredom in a week."

"Maybe in a week she can go to Gabby's," he reasons, and I agree. "Anyway, I wanted to let you know so you can look in on her at Mama's tonight. I'll be by too."

"Thanks."

"And just so you know, Eli, she doesn't look good."

"I know. I saw her last night. But she's going to be fine, Dec."

"Yeah. Yeah, she will."

We ring off and I toss my phone on the floor and hug Kate close. "Now, what's this about me not having sex this morning?"

"I don't have time."

"Do you have somewhere you need to be?"

"Yes," she laughs. "I need to go in to work. As it is, I'm very late."

"You're with the boss, Kate."

"No one else knows that." She moves to climb off of me, but I tug her back into my arms and turn us on our sides, her between me and the back of the couch, and kiss her softly.

"Are you okay?"

"Yes."

I lean back so I can look at her clearly, and aside from the puffiness and redness, I can see that she's telling the truth.

"Strong girl," I whisper and kiss her forehead.

"I'm also late."

"Are we back to this?"

"I'm serious, Eli. I have a mountain of work, and I have some leads that I'm following."

"What leads?" I ask.

"Let me see if they go anywhere. All I have are hunches right now. I'll fill you in as soon as I have anything solid." She smiles and kisses my chin. "So, I really do have to go to work. And so do you."

"I do." I sigh and don't move. "I'm going to go check on Savannah this afternoon."

"I'll go this evening."

"Just ride with me this afternoon."

"I can't." She rolls her eyes and I grin because she's adorable. "You and I aren't doing...*stuff*."

"If by *stuff* you mean kissing," I kiss her lips, "and touching," drag my hand down her side to her hip, "and fucking," pull her against me so she can feel my hard cock against her abdomen, "yes, we are."

"No one else knows that. I can't arrive late and leave early, Eli. But I will let you do stuff to me later."

"We're going to keep working on your vocabulary, *cher*."

She grins up at me as she slides her leg up mine and presses her center against me, making my eyes cross.

"I'm looking forward to it."

CHAPTER FIFTEEN

"How are you adjusting?" I ask Van as I lean back in my chair and prop the phone between my ear and shoulder, returning an email.

"You know I love the inn," she replies. It's good to hear the smile in her voice. "And I love Mama too, but after the eighth day, I was ready to make an escape."

"Mama enjoyed babying you for a while," I reply.

"I really could go home, you know. I'm feeling pretty much normal again. I need to work."

"You need to relax."

"I have work, Eli."

"We may fall apart around here without you," the sarcasm in my voice is thick, "but we'll muddle our way through. Just enjoy the inn. Get well."

"I forgot how much I love being out here," she concedes. "And Sam is so adorable. He brought me breakfast in bed this morning. Gogurt and Goldfish crackers."

"Breakfast of champions."

"Oh, I have to go take a call for Gabby. I'll call you later."

"Bye."

I hang up and sigh. I'm restless. It's been more than a week since Van was hurt. She's doing well. The past week has been a blur of police statements, long days at work, and short nights with Kate.

Kate.

She's been working her own ass off. She works late into the evening, and is up early again the next morning. I see her long enough to sink inside her sweet body, then curl up around her and sleep.

I rub my hand over my mouth as it occurs to me that *I miss her.*

What the fuck is wrong with me?

I turn my attention back to work, but it's no use. I can't focus. I can't think of anything but Kate, and quickly decide to rectify the situation.

"Put me through to Kate O'Shaughnessy's office," I instruct my assistant and grin when I hear Kate answer with an irritated, "This is Kate."

"This is Eli," I reply. "I need you to gather all of your notes and files on your project and come to my office, please."

"Is there a problem?" she asks.

"Ten minutes," I reply, rather than answer, and hang up the phone. I answer several emails and calls before Kate is announced and shown into my office. I gesture for her to have a seat, then stand, cross to the door, lock it, and return to my own seat behind the desk.

"Good morning." My voice is formal, professional, and makes Kate frown.

"Hello," she replies. "Eli, is something wrong?"

"No." I shake my head and steeple my fingers. "I just want an update."

She narrows her eyes on me for a moment. I cock an eyebrow and simply wait, and finally, she opens a file and begins to talk.

And I don't even know what the fuck she's talking about. Her words mean nothing to me. All I can think about his how that skirt fits tight on her hips and ass and her white blouse fits tight across her tits. She loves expensive underwear, which makes my cock hard and my heart pound, and I want to know what she's wearing under that outfit.

She crosses her legs, drawing attention to the sexy emerald green fuck-me heels on her slender feet, and I swallow hard as I picture her naked, sprawled on my desk, her legs over my shoulders with just those heels on.

Jesus Christ, I want her.

"Eli?"

"Yes."

"Did you hear a word I just said?"

"No."

She shakes her head and watches me like I'm crazy. And I am. I'm completely fucking crazy about her.

"Do you want me to go through it again?"

"No, I don't really give a shit right now."

"You don't care that someone is stealing from your company? That's the whole reason you hired me, Eli."

"Right now, in this moment, no. I don't give a fuck."

"What do you want, then?"

"You."

Her green eyes flare, and her pouty mouth opens in surprise. The pulse in her neck speeds up.

I'm going to bite her there.

"You called me up here to—"

"To fuck you." I finish her sentence for her, because I didn't call her up here to do *stuff*, as she calls it.

"We are not going to do that here," she hisses, looking scandalized, but I simply grin and lean over the desk toward her, keeping her gaze steadily in mine.

"Let me make it clear; we can have sweat dripping, sheet ripping, furniture breaking, screaming, trembling, hair pulling, ass smacking fucking for hours, or soft, sweet, quiet, intense lovemaking for days. You can have either or both, but we're not leaving here without me being inside you, sugar."

Her legs shift as she clenches her thighs together and she swallows hard, processing my words.

"Right, because we can just stay here for days."

"Don't tempt me. I can make that happen."

She tilts her head and watches me for a moment. "You're intense today."

"I'm intense every day." I stand and slowly walk around my desk to her, pull her to her feet, and smirk at how short she still is, even with those amazing shoes on her feet. I turn her in my arms, glide my hands around her sides to her belly and up to her tits, bury my nose in her hair and whisper in her ear. "You're going to have to be quiet while I fuck you. My assistant is just on the other side of that door."

"I can't believe you want to do this."

I don't want to. I need to.

"Do you think you can do that, Kate? Be quiet?"

"I'm not good at quiet," she replies breathlessly, and pushes her ass back against my already hard cock. I grip her tight skirt in my hands, gathering the fabric, pulling it above her sweet, round ass.

"Did you wear this skirt just to make me crazy?"

"No, but if it does, that's a great bonus."

I bite her earlobe, thankful that she wore her hair up today, giving me access to her neck. "It does. And so does this fucking amazing underwear."

She's wearing black lace today.

"Lean on the desk." She bends over, pushes her ass out, and gasps when I squat behind her, rip her underwear, and toss them onto the desk.

"Those were expensive."

"And I don't give even one fuck," I murmur, as I drag my fingertip from the top of the crack of her ass, over her anus, and through her already sopping wet folds. "You're already turned on."

"Mm," she moans softly.

"No noise," I remind her, right before I pull her pussy lips into my mouth and suck, push my tongue into her, then over her folds, making sure she's good and wet. Her hips are moving desperately, searching for release, but before she can come, I stand and sink two fingers inside her while I unfasten my pants, desperate to be inside her. Jesus, it feels like I'm about to come out of my skin. I'm hot, swollen, and breathless.

I push into her from behind as I tilt her face back and kiss her hard, masking her moans. She can't stay quiet.

And that's another fuck that I just don't give.

I get only two pumps in, then pull out, spin her around, lift her onto the desk, pushing anything in our way aside so she can lie back, and coffee spills all over my iPad, right before my monitor tips over and cracks the screen.

"Oh, no!" Kate gasps, but I laugh as I prop her legs on my shoulders, kiss her ankle, and push back inside her.

"Thank God for the cloud," I murmur, and begin fucking her hard and fast. Her eyes are on mine, she's panting, and her cheeks are flushed. She licks her finger and reaches down to rub her clit. "Yes, baby, rub yourself. Fuck, that's hot."

She clenches around me, and I can't hold back. I come hard, and feel her come with me, milking my cock with her muscles. She covers her mouth with her free hand, trying to keep quiet, and failing miserably.

I pull out and help her off the desk.

"Just needed to take the edge off?" she asks, and begins to shimmy her skirt down her legs, but I stop her and lead her to the couch.

"I didn't say we were done." I strip us both out of the rest of our clothes and cover her body with mine on the couch.

"We already had furniture breaking sex," she says with a grin. "Or, electronic breaking anyway."

"And now we'll have the slow and sweet," I whisper against her lips. "You're beautiful, *cher*."

"You're charming," she whispers back. I love how shy she gets when I give her compliments, and turns it around on me, calling me charming.

I'm just being honest.

"Your eyes are so green," I murmur and slide my already recovering cock through her folds, up to her clit, and down again. She gasps and closes her eyes. "Open."

"You're so bossy," she moans and bites her lip.

"You like it."

"I like it *so much*," she groans and circles her hips, inviting me back inside. I pin her hands over her head with one of my hands, cup her face with the other, and kiss us both mindless as I sink inside and stop, balls deep, and enjoy how tight, wet, and hot she is.

"No one has ever turned me inside out the way you do," I say against her mouth, then tug her lower lip with my teeth. "You make me forget myself. You make me fucking crazy."

"You do the same for me," she says, and whimpers as she circles her hips again. "Please move."

"You need me to move, baby?"

"Yes." She pushes against my hands, using my strength as leverage to lift her hips, creating just a tiny bit of eye-crossing friction.

"Ask me," I reply.

"Please."

I pull out slowly and push back in and stop again, making her frown.

"Ask me better than that."

She narrows her eyes on me, earning a cocked brow from me. "Eli?"

"Yes, Kate?"

"Will you please—" she clenches her muscles on my cock, making me swear under my breath. "Please fuck me?"

"Now you're just using the dirty words to get what you want," I say, but comply, moving slow and steady, in and out, and she smiles up at me. A gorgeous, full-on, happy smile, and my heart catches.

"I love the way you feel inside me."

Heart fucking catches.

I can't respond. I'll say something ridiculous. Instead, I pick up the pace and grind my pubis on hers, hitting her sweet spot, and watch her come apart beneath me, pulling me with her.

I release her hands and lie on her chest, in her arms. I can hear her heart, thundering in her chest. I can't see it, but I brush my hand down her side, over the sexier than fuck tattoo there. *I am enough the way I am.*

She's so much more than enough.

She sinks her fingers into my hair and holds me tight.

"You're a sweet man, Eli Boudreaux."

She kisses my head, and suddenly, everything in me simply calms. This feels…*right.*

It feels like home.

And that's ridiculous.

Isn't it?

"I hate to have to be the party pooper, but I really do have to go back to work," she says softly, but continues to hug me to her, gliding her fingers through my hair. I could sleep like a baby, right here.

"I have work too. But this feels good."

"Hmm," she agrees. "I like your hair."

"My hair?" I ask with a laugh.

"It's soft. And it feels good in my fingers." She rubs my forehead with her fingertips and I sigh. This woman can touch me as much as she wants, whenever she wants. "I like it."

"I'm glad."

"And I like your ass."

"Are you making a list?" I ask with a grin.

"Shh." She continues to make me sleepy and calm with her fingers. "I like your ass. It's firm, and you have the sexiest dimples right above it."

"I'm happy you like them."

"You have lots of likeable parts."

"What about the most important part?" I ask and glance up at her to wiggle my eyebrows.

"God, you're such a man."

***

"Hey, Van, it's Eli."

"Two calls in one day? I'm fine, Eli. Seriously."

"I'm happy to hear that, but that's not why I'm calling this time."

"What's wrong? Do I need to come to the office?"

I laugh and shake my head. "No. You're not coming in to work. I need your advice. You're Kate's best friend. I want to do something nice for her. Surprise her. She's been working hard, but I don't know what to do. Give me ideas."

There's a long, pregnant pause.

"Is this Eli *Boudreaux*? My brother?"

"Funny."

"So, what exactly is happening between you and Kate, Eli? And don't tell me it's none of my business."

"It's none of your business," I reply, just to rile her up.

"Really?"

"Kidding. Honestly, I like her. A lot. We spend time together."

"You're fucking her."

That pisses me off for reasons I can't explain. Yes, I am fucking her, but it's more than that, and to hear it put like that makes it sound…*cheap*.

"We are engaging in a physical relationship, yes."

"Is that it?"

"Are you going to help me or not?"

"I will if you answer my question."

I sigh and drag my hand down my face. I washed up after she left my office, but I swear I can still smell her on me, and it makes me want her all over again.

This is getting ridiculous.

"She's not like the others, Vanny," I say quietly…voice aloud for the first time what's been brewing in my head for weeks. "I like her. I respect her. And I want to do something special for her."

"Are you going to ask her to stay when the job is done?"

"No," I reply without hesitation. Van sighs.

"Okay, stubborn ass, I know exactly what you should do."

***

Her head is bent over her desk as she reads through what look like financial reports. She doesn't even see me as I lean against the doorjamb, watching her work. It's early evening, at least two hours past the time that the last person left for the day.

I do believe I've met my match in the workaholic department.

"I see you," she murmurs without looking up. Is it any wonder that I'm crazy about her?

"It's time to go, *cher*."

"I have a few more things before the weekend."

"Kate, it's almost eight on a Friday evening. It's the weekend."

"I'm almost done."

I cross to her desk and tip her head back with my finger under her chin. "Shut it down. I have a surprise for you."

Her eyes flare in happiness. "You do?"

"Yes."

She begins plunging her hands in my pockets, patting me down. "Where is it?"

"This is a new side to you."

"I love surprises."

So noted.

"What is this?" She pulls the half-dollar out of my pocket and gazes at it. "Does this say 1860?"

"It does. Dad gave it to me when I was just out of college. He used to carry two of them. He gave the other to Beau."

"What does it mean?"

Smart girl. "They were handed down from my great-grandfather as the first measurable profit from the company. And Dad said that it was to remind us that every penny we make is important, whether it be fifty cents, or fifty million dollars."

"I like that." She replaces the coin in my pocket and keeps searching. "I can't find my surprise."

"Well, we have to go to it. I don't have it on me."

"Oh." She pouts, but then stands and launches herself into my arms. "Thank you."

"You don't even know what it is."

"It doesn't matter. Thank you."

"You're welcome. Let's go."

She locks her desk and gathers her things, and then frowns as I escort her down the hall.

"You know, you shouldn't come down to my office."

"Everyone is gone, Kate. We're the only ones here."

"Still." She sniffs as she steps into the elevator, then does a little happy dance. "What's the surprise?"

"I'm not telling," I reply with a laugh and tug on a piece of her hair.

"Can I guess? Is it…?" She bites her lip as she thinks. "Is it a show?"

"No."

"Is it…Dinner?"

"No." I pull her in for a hug and kiss her head. "Stop trying. You'll never guess."

"Give me a hint."

"You must be impossible to live with at Christmas."

She simply grins and climbs into the car, a bundle of nerves the entire drive through town.

"We're leaving town?"

"We're not going far."

"You're a good surprise giver."

I laugh and glance over at her where she's watching me with happy eyes. "Is that such a thing?"

"Yes."

I pull into the parking garage at the airport, and Kate watches me with shocked curiosity. "Where are we going?"

"You'll see."

"But, I didn't pack a bag! I don't even have a toothbrush, since I took my spare out of my purse—"

I yank her to me and kiss the fuck out of her, just to shut her up, then lead her into the baggage claim area. I watch as her eyes skim over the people waiting for their bags, and when they land on a familiar face, she smiles and runs to her friend.

"Oh, my God! What are you doing here?"

The tall, dark man who was speaking with Kate's friend steps away, gathers his own bag, and waves at Lila as he walks away.

"Eli! This is Lila," Kate announces, as she and the dark-haired, beautiful woman turn to me.

"I know," I reply with a grin and shake Lila's hand. "Pleasure to meet you in person."

"Likewise."

"Wait. Why didn't I know that you were coming?" Kate asks Lila, as they lead me back into the parking garage. I'm happy to bring up the rear with Lila's small suitcase in tow.

"Well, I was going to come down in a few weeks for a job interview anyway, and then Eli called and asked if I'd like to come see you, and *hello*! Of course I did! So, I called and had my interview moved to Monday, and here I am."

Suddenly, Kate launches herself into my arms and hugs me tight. "Thank you," she whispers into my ear.

"My pleasure, *cher*."

"First things first," Kate says, after we all get settled in the car. She and Lila are sharing the back, so they can talk without one of them craning their neck to see the other. "Who was that tall drink of water you were chatting with at the baggage claim?"

"Noticed that, did you?" Lila asks with a laugh.

"Um, hello, he was *hot*."

I growl as I catch Kate's eye in the rear-view.

"Did he just growl?" Lila asks with a laugh.

"He does that," Kate says. "Spill it."

"All I know is, his name is Asher, and he's in town for some work thing." She shrugs. "That's it."

"You didn't get his number?"

"No."

"Did he get yours?"

"No."

"What is wrong with you?"

Lila laughs and kisses Kate's cheek. "Let's talk about you. How are you?"

"I'm good."

There's a moment of quiet. "I believe you," Lila finally replies.

"You really didn't get his number?" The girls bust up laughing, and it makes me smile to hear Kate so happy. So carefree.

I plan to keep her that way.

"I think this calls for girls' night out tomorrow night," Kate says suddenly. "I'll call Van, Gabby, and Charly, and we'll hit the town."

"Excellent idea! I haven't seen them in forever."

"Do you know my sisters?" I ask.

"Yep, I met them a few times when we were all visiting Kate at college. This is gonna be epic."

"So fun," Kate agrees. "We'll start at Café Amalie and flirt with Joe."

"Who's Joe?" Lila asks as I growl again.

"My favorite waiter."

"Is he hot?" Lila asks.

"So hot," Kate answers, and I grip the steering wheel tighter.

"I'm so in," Lila replies.

Chapter Sixteen
Kate

"Can I borrow these earrings?" Lila asks, holding my silver chandelier earrings up to her lobes and looking in the mirror to my right. "They go with my shoes."

"Your shoes?" I chuckle and look down, and sure enough, she's right. "You're going to have a hard time walking in the Quarter in those heels. Trust me."

"It's GNO," she says with a shrug. "I'll be fine. I'll kick them off and dance barefoot at the bar."

"Ew. You won't want to do that on Bourbon."

"Are you saying the French Quarter is unsanitary?"

"At night it is," I confirm, and smooth lip gloss on my lips. I step back and take stock. My hair is down, and thanks to the products Charly recommended, it hangs in pretty waves past my shoulders. Makeup is done, bolder than usual, because hello, girls' night. "Is this dress okay?"

Lila examines me thoughtfully, then nods. "The color matches your eyes, which I kind of hate you for, because I can't wear green, and it shows off your boobs. Excellent choice."

"Right on." Lila is gorgeous, as usual, in a one-shoulder little black dress and strappy silver heels. Her black hair is also down, straight and sleek. Makeup put together.

She's always put together.

"You look awesome," I say, and offer her a fist to bump.

"We're hot bitches," she agrees, just as the front door opens and Charly yells, "We're here!"

"It was a good idea to meet here," Gabby says, and holds a bottle of liquor up. "We'll have shots before we leave."

"Why do I feel like I'm back in college?" Van asks and hugs Lila tight, still careful of her shoulder. "Hi, sugar."

"Hello, friend."

"You all look amazing," I announce and find shot glasses. Charly pours us each a shot of Patron.

"Should Van be drinking with pain meds?" Gabby asks.

"I haven't taken a pain med in a week," she says with a roll of the eyes. "But maybe I should try it. It could be fun."

"Hey, Karen used to swirl her meds in her martini for a reason on *Will & Grace*," Lila reminds us.

"Bingo," Van agrees with a laugh, and we all take a shot, then another.

"Are we ready to go?" I ask. "We have a reservation at Café Amalie in fifteen minutes."

"Let's go wreak havoc on the streets of New Orleans, ladies," Charly says, and leads us out the door and to the sidewalk. "Lila, honey, those shoes are gonna be a bitch when you're drunk and walking through the Quarter."

"Told you," I say and smirk.

"They're pretty," Lila says.

"Oh, they are that," Charly agrees. "Trust me, I know good shoes. But you'll need to be careful."

"I'll hold onto you," I tell Lila, and loop my arm through hers.

"Oh, good, we'll both be on our asses," she laughs.

"Are you saying I'm clumsy?"

"Yes," they all say at once, making me laugh. The walk to Café Amalie is short, and we're seated quickly.

"Ladies," hot waiter Joe says, as he approaches the table. "Welcome."

"Hi, Joe," I say with a smile. "Ladies, this is Joe."

"Well, hello, Joe," Charly says, blatantly looking Joe up and down. "You're delicious."

"As is the food," Joe says without missing a beat, and I mentally high-five him.

"You're going to get along with us just fine," Gabby says with a laugh.

"What can I bring you to drink?" he asks, and lays his hand on my shoulder.

His very big, very firm hand.

"Lemon drop?" he asks with a wink.

"I really love you, Joe." He laughs and takes all of our drink orders, and when he's gone, Charly lets out a low whistle.

"Dear, sweet God, the things I could teach that man."

"I don't know, I think Joe looks like he already knows his way around a woman," Lila says, and watches Joe unabashedly at the bar.

"He's good with his hands," I agree.

"He touched your *shoulder*," Van reminds me with a grin.

"Exactly. And that woke my girl parts up, so there you have it."

Joe delivers our drinks, and Gabby keeps craning her neck to see the iron entrance.

"Who are you looking for?" I ask.

"Cindy is going to join us, but she didn't know if she'd be able to make it here, or if she'd meet up with us later for dancing."

"So, who is this Cindy?" I ask and glance toward the bar, just in time to see a woman walking away toward the rest room. I'd swear it was Hilary from work, but she's gone before I can tell for sure. "I remember you mentioned her before."

"She's been a friend of mine for a long time," Gabby says, and smiles at Joe as he sets her mojito in front of her. "You'll like her. She's fun."

"Are you having dinner tonight, ladies?" Joe asks.

"Maybe just appetizers?" Charly asks.

"I don't know, we're going to be drinking. A lot," I remind her. I glance back toward the bar, hoping to see the woman again, but she's not there. I must have been mistaken.

"May I suggest then that you put something on your stomachs?" Joe asks seriously.

"I'm starving, so yes," Lila says, and orders her entrée. The rest of us follow suit, then clink glasses when Joe leaves. "These drinks are strong!"

"I know. I'm only allowed to have one," I reply. Dinner is full of laughs, awesome food, and lots of flirting with Joe, who takes it all in stride. When it's time to leave, night has fallen over New Orleans. The air has cooled comfortably, and the walk over to Bourbon Street is lovely. We find a fun club with a DJ, claim a large table, and settle in for a night of dancing and laughter.

And lots of drinks.

"To good friends and shenanigans!" Charly announces, as we all hold our drinks in the air and take a sip. "Let's dance!"

Gabby and Lila join her, just as a beautiful young woman approaches the table. Gabby hugs her, tosses her purse on the chair next to mine, and pulls her with them to the floor.

"That must be Cindy," I say to Van, as we watch the girls dance on the mostly empty dance floor.

"Yep," Van says with a nod. "She's a nice girl. Kind of slutty, but nice."

That makes me smirk, just as I've taken a drink of my lemon drop, and I clamp my hand over my mouth so I don't spew it everywhere. "Van!"

"It's true," she says with a laugh. "I'm so glad you're here."

"Me too. How are you feeling? Really?"

"Much better." She smiles, and when I would question her further, she shakes her head. "Let's not talk about it tonight, okay? Let's just have fun."

"Okay," I agree. She deserves this fun night. "Although, now that I have you alone, can we talk business for a minute?"

"Sure."

"I have the PI looking into some things, but he still hasn't gotten back to me. I'm a bit concerned about Mr. Rudolph."

"Why? Has something happened?"

"It's all circumstantial," I reply with frustration and sip my drink. "I discovered that all of the transfers were made at about the same time of day. Less than an hour before he typically leaves for the day. And Van? He leaves super early, like around 1:30, almost every day. I do the majority of the work he should be doing. What's up with that?"

"I should have told you, and it didn't occur to me," Savannah says. "His daughter is very sick. She's been in the Children's Hospital for a while, and that's where he goes every afternoon."

"Oh, that's horrible."

"He's a nice man. He's been with our company for longer than a decade."

"But, if his daughter is so sick, he has medical bills to pay. This doesn't make him look any more innocent."

But Savannah shakes her head adamantly. "No, we have excellent insurance, and anything they don't cover, Eli is picking up. We take care of our own, Kate. Mr. Rudolph's daughter is getting excellent care, and he has no out of pocket expenses for it. It wouldn't make sense for him to skim money. He's still making the same salary, despite needing to be gone so much."

"Geez, remind me to work for you guys from now on," I say with some surprise. "That's very generous."

"If you're loyal to your employees, they'll be loyal to you. That's what Daddy always used to say."

"Makes sense," I reply, and chew my lip as I think over this new information. It still doesn't add up.

"Oh, hello, Kate."

I glance up in surprise to find Hilary standing by our table, a wide grin on her face. She's looking between me and Van, and I cringe inwardly.

Crap. How am I going to play this off?

"Hi, Hilary. Do you know Savannah?"

"Of course. Hello, Ms. Boudreaux."

"When we're not in the office, I'm Savannah," she replies, and smiles at Hilary.

"Van and I went to college together," I say, hoping that Hilary won't ask any questions, and wondering just how long she was standing nearby, listening to our conversation.

"I see. It's not what you know, it's who you know, right?"

I tilt my head, but before I can say anything further, the others return from the dance floor.

"Hi, I'm Lila." Lila holds her hand out to Hilary, who shakes it and continues to smile.

"Hilary."

Introductions are made, and Hilary is invited to join us, and rather than decline, like I was hoping she'd do, she takes a seat and settles in across from me.

Darn it.

Another round of drinks is delivered, and suddenly a tall, handsome man is standing next to Charly, inviting her to dance.

"Darling, I'm a nightmare dressed like a daydream. Trust me, you don't want a piece of this." She pats him on the cheek and the man walks away, a look of pure confusion on his face.

"I wonder if he's confused because he got shot down, or if he's never listened to Taylor Swift before?" I ask.

"To Taylor Swift," Gabby says, holding her glass high. "For giving us fantastic one-liners for years."

"The girl writes some great ones," Lila agrees. "Oh! Fun drinking game. Every time someone uses a Taylor line in conversation, we take a drink."

"You're on!" Gabby says.

"This is so fun!" Cindy agrees, and we all drink in honor of the daydream line.

"Let's dance some more," Gabby says.

"Everything will be alright if we just keep dancing like we're twenty-two," Cindy says, we all drink, and then hit the dance floor while Pitbull and Ke$ha sing about Timber.

Charly and Van stay behind and are approached several times by cute men, and when the men leave after being shot down, they drink.

I wonder what lyrics they just used.

When we're all back at the table, our minds a little fuzzier, Hilary sits back in her seat and nudges her head to the side, indicating that I should look. "Three o'clock," she says.

"Which one? The bald one?" I ask.

"Fuck no, the one with the tattoo sleeve," she replies.

"Ah, I see him. Is that Mr. Starbucks?" I ask. "Louis?"

"Yes." She grins when Louis cocks his brow at her and shrugs a shoulder like, *you wanna*? "Looks like I'm getting lucky tonight, ladies."

"Lucky bitch," Gabby says with a frown, just as a waitress sets a basket of peanuts right in front of me, which Van quickly picks up and places at the other end of the table.

"You don't like peanuts?" Gabby asks.

"I'm allergic," I reply and shrug.

"Remember that time in college when you accidentally ate some and your face got all swollen? It was horrific," Van says with a dramatic shiver.

"Okay, back to me," Gabby says impatiently. "Do you know how long it's been since I got laid? *Years.*"

"Good Lord," Lila says in sympathy. "Honey, we can fix that. Like, right now."

"Oops! I'm out! Thanks for the drinks, guys." Hilary jumps up and scrambles over to Louis, who has just stood and paid his own tab, then they leave together with his tongue down her throat.

"She seems kind of fun," Charly says thoughtfully and sips her drink.

"I don't like her," Lila says with a shake of the head.

"Why?" I ask.

"I don't know. Just something about her."

"Anyway, back to me," Gabby says primly. "I haven't gotten laid in forever."

Just as the words leave her mouth, a shorter man, in his mid-thirties approaches her, leans in and says, "Why don't you let me help you out with that, sugar?"

Gabby blinks at him for a moment, then says, "I knew you were trouble when you walked in."

"Huh?" he asks in confusion as we all laugh, raise our glasses in salute, and drink.

"That means no," Van says helpfully, and the guy saunters away, shaking his head.

"Come on, Gabby," Lila says, "Why you gotta be so mean?" More drinks.

"That was creepy," Gabby says.

"It's okay, I'm not getting laid either," Charly says. "It's been longer than a minute."

"You could always call Ryan," Van says with a smug smile. "He'd do you in a hot second."

"We are never, ever getting back together. Like, ever," Charly says, and we all laugh and drink.

Damn, these drinks are good. And strong. Am I still drinking lemon drops? I don't even know.

Maybe.

"But he was good in the sack," Charly clarifies. "And he did this thing with his tongue—"

"Stop," Eli says as he walks up to the table. "I don't need to know what any man does to you with his tongue."

"Why are you here?" Van demands. "It's *girls'* night out. Only girls."

"Ah, shake it off, Vanny," Gabby says, prompting us all to drink. "Declan's right behind him."

"Hi, Eli," Cindy says from next to me. She's been very quiet all evening, listening, laughing, and now that Eli's here, she's chatty?

I look between her and Eli, and frown.

"Have you fucked her?" I ask, probably way too loudly, but once I'm this drunk, I can't stop the words.

Damn words.

Cindy blinks rapidly, but Eli doesn't react at all. No frown. No denial.

Nada.

"Did you just say fuck?" Savannah asks in surprise.

"Yeah. I know, it's new. Eli's been teaching me."

"He's teaching you to say fuck?" Lila asks. "That's cool. Way to go, Eli."

He's watching me with hot eyes, but he's not giving anything away. He won't answer me.

Which, of course, means yes.

I turn my blurry gaze back to young, perky, skinny, perfect-skinned Cindy. "Was loving him like red?" I ask, and we all drink.

"It was fire-engine red," she confirms, and I kind of want to smack the hell out of her.

"Uh," Lila says, but Declan interrupts.

"Why are you all using Taylor Swift lyrics?"

"New drinking game," I say. "If we use the lyrics in conversation, we drink."

"We've been using a lot of them," Gabby says sloppily. "It's fun."

"Do you guys want a drink?" I ask them and signal for the waitress. "You should play."

"No, we're your drivers," Eli says. His jaw ticks, just a bit, and I think maybe he's mad at me, but I don't care.

I didn't fuck Cindy.

"No drinks for them," Van says to the waitress. "But another round for us."

"So, does that mean you're not ready to go home?" Declan asks with a laugh.

"Are you guys going all the way back to the inn tonight?" I ask Van and Gabby.

"No, we're staying at Mama's. She's at the inn with Sam and the guests."

"Cool."

"Eli, will you please give me a ride home?" Cindy asks, and bats her eyes at the man who's been spending every night in *my* bed, but before I can curl my hand into a claw and tear her fake-eyelashed eyes out, Declan speaks up.

"I get that honor, *cher.*"

Eli is watching me.

Eli is watching me.

I grin and stand, make sure I'm steady on my feet, and say, "Excuse me."

"Where are you going?" Eli asks.

"Over there. Alone."

I nod decisively, walk to the bar, and get there just in time. My feet are slow. I'm glad I didn't wear heels.

"Hi there," the tall man next to me says. He's hot. Both of him.

"Hi."

"Having a good time?" he asks.

"Yes." I blink, and then exclaim, "I know you!"

"You do?"

"Yes! You were on the plane with Lila yesterday. Asher?"

"That's right." He shakes my hand and grins. "Is Lila with you this evening?"

"Yep. She's my BFF. We drink together. One time, in college, we made out, but it was no biggie."

"Okay," he laughs.

"You didn't ask her for her number," I accuse him, and poke my finger in his chest. He looks down at it.

"You just assaulted an officer."

"I did?" *Oh, crap.*

"Yes. I might have to arrest you."

"With handcuffs?"

"Would you like me to arrest you with handcuffs?"

"Hell to the yes!"

"Kate?" Eli's voice is cold and hard, and I'm sure he looks all scary and stuff.

"I'm talking to the hot Asher," I inform him. "I assaulted him, and he's a cop, and he's going to put me in handcuffs."

"No, I don't believe he will."

Asher laughs. "There's nothing going on here, man."

"Come see Lila!" I take his hand and lead him past Eli, who I glare at, because…*Cindy*, and am surprised to find that Gabby, Van, Charly, and slutty Cindy are all gone. "Where did everyone go?"

"Declan took them home," Lila says, and then her eyes go wide when she sees Asher. "Hi."

"We meet again," Asher says with a smile. He's super handsome, with dark hair and blue eyes and a great smile that's just a little crooked. Total hottie. I give her a thumbs up behind his back and sit down.

Eli joins me, lays his arm across the back of my chair and leans in to say in my ear, "We will talk later."

"About you fucking that young harlot?"

His eyes narrow. Yep, totally pissed.

"Among other things."

"Whatever," I say, and wave him off as if it doesn't matter. "You're not mine, Eli. Fuck whomever you please. There, there's a girl giving you the googly eyes right over there."

"Enough." His voice is cold and firm, and now he is glaring at me. I turn away and smile when I see that Asher and Lila have their heads together, chatting.

"So, I'm Kate," I say and hold my hand out to Asher, who shakes it with a smile. "But, I'm not telling you my last name, in case you really do want to arrest me."

"Her name is Mary Katherine O'Shaughnessy," Lila says. "Do you want her social security number?"

"How do you know my social security number?"

"I'm your person. If something happens to you, I have to know all your shit. Just like you know mine."

"Oh, right. She's my person," I inform Eli, before I remember that I'm mad at him.

Even though being mad at him is stupid.

"Kate tells me that you and she had a thing going in college," Asher says with a wink to me.

"We totally did," Lila agrees. "You know how crazy college kids are."

"The threesome only happened one time," I add, and the *look* passes between Lila and me. You know, the one that BFF's understand that says, *play along.*

"And we decided that we much preferred lesbian sex when it didn't involve a man," Lila says.

"Makes sense," Asher says thoughtfully, and I hear a noise beside me. It's Eli.

Laughing his ass off.

"Do you find threesomes funny?" I ask him.

"They can be," he says, and wipes his eyes. "But I'm still laughing at your name. Mary Katherine? Really?"

"What's wrong with my name?"

"It is kind of funny," Lila says.

"Is that why Dec calls you Superstar?" Eli asks. "Because of Mary Katherine Gallagher on SNL?"

"Yes." He's totally killing my buzz.

"Fuck, that's funny," Eli says.

"That part is super funny," Lila agrees.

"Okay, it's kind of funny," I say. My buzz is dying, it's getting late, and now all I can think about is going to bed. "Will you please take me home?"

"Of course, *cher.*" Eli kisses my cheek and stands.

"Coming?" I ask Lila, who laughs at something Asher said that I couldn't hear.

"I'm gonna have Asher take me home," she says and smiles.

"Atta girl," I say and high five her. I fish the key to my loft out of my small purse and hand it to her. "I brought the extra key for you. See you tomorrow."

Then I point at Asher and make my serious face. "And, listen up, buddy. If you hurt her, I don't care if you really are a cop, I'll make your life hell. Okay?"

"Okay." He nods sincerely, and I back away.

"Okay then."

Eli leads me outside into the fresh, not-so-fresh, Bourbon Street air.

"Did you bring your car?" I ask. "'Cause it's not far. We can walk."

"We will drive, *cher.*"

He leads me to the car, gets me settled the way he always does, which always makes me feel special, then climbs in the other side.

"I'm not special," I sigh, surprised when the words actually come out instead of stay in my head where they belong.

"What are you talking about?"

"Nothing." I shake my head, sober enough to know that I do *not* want to repeat that. "Are you really not interested in the threesome story?"

"Oh, I'm interested. I'm a man, Kate."

"Yes, you are."

"Okay, tell me."

"It was fun," I begin and smile at him. How long should I let this story go? "I mean, it's hard to say no to any of you Boudreaux brothers, and in college, Declan was *hot.* Look at him now, he's still hot, but back then, holy crap."

"Stop." He brakes in front of our building and turns to face me in the seat. "Are you telling me that you and Lila fucked my brother?"

"Well—"

"Because, if you are, you're also telling me that you lied to me when you told me that you'd never been with Declan."

I frown. "Eli, it was a joke. We never did a threesome. We never even had lesbian sex. We kissed once, when we were drunk. I think Declan saw that, I'm not sure."

He shakes his head and pushes out of the car, and I follow.

"Seriously, Eli. I won't curse because of the Catholic guilt. Do you honestly think I'd have a *threesome?*"

He laughs and meets me on the sidewalk.

"That's not the part that made you mad," I realize. "It was the *who.*"

He shrugs.

"Why does the thought of me being intimate with Declan make you so mad?" I ask softly and cup his face.

"It's not rational," he says and kisses my forehead. "But it's probably because he's my brother, and I've laid a claim on you, and the thought of him seeing your body, being inside you, loving you, is completely out of the question."

"Well, it was a joke."

He takes my hand and leads me inside. I'm still a bit wobbly on my feet, so he wraps his arm around my waist.

"Now." He helps me out of my shoes. "Let's talk about Cindy."

"Oh." I make the *I just ate something disgusting* face and sag my shoulders. "I don't want to."

"I do."

"Can't we just have sex?" I ask and tug his white T-shirt out of his jeans, then glide my hands over his hard abdomen. "I love your stomach."

"It was one night, Kate."

"I don't care."

"It was a mistake. She's much younger than me, and Gabby's friend, but we were drunk, and it just happened."

"I don't care, Eli." But I do. I so do. I walk away from him and take a deep breath. "Okay, I don't lie. Yes, I care. I *hate* it."

I turn back to him, and he's standing there, his hands in his pockets, watching me.

"Why?" he asks.

"I don't know. We've both been with other people, and we'll be with others again when this is done." His jaw ticks at that. "It's not rational to hate it, but I do. I don't want to think about you touching her, or anyone else. I don't want to think about some other bimbo seeing you naked, or touching you, or being intimate with you. Does that make me a crazy jealous fuck buddy? Probably. But that's the way it is."

"One," he says in a low voice as he advances toward me. "You are not now, nor have you ever been, my *fuck buddy.* That's disrespectful to both of us, and I won't have that."

I frown, but he holds his hand up, stopping any words that might have come out.

"Two, I agree. I know you were no virgin when I met you, but I don't want to think about your partners. Nor do I want to think about you with anyone after me. Because this is just between you and me, Kate.

"And three," he whispers as he stops just inches in front of me. I can feel the heat from his body; I can smell his shampoo.

I want him to touch me.

"Three, all I can see, all I can think about, is *you.* I want you. You don't just cross my mind once in a while, you live in it."

My eyes widen as I watch him carefully, completely sober now. He's still not touching me.

"We said this would only last for as long as you're here. Only us. No one else, and damn it, Kate, that hasn't changed for me."

"Me too," I whisper. "Eli?"

"Yes."

"I really need you to touch me now."

He takes a deep breath, his hands flexing in and out of fists at his sides, his eyes traveling from my eyes to my lips and back again.

"I want you," I whisper.

He backs me up to the wall, and finally presses his body to mine, takes my face in his hands, and plants his lips on mine, kissing, nibbling, devouring me in the most delicious way. This man can kiss like no one I've ever met.

He kisses like it's his damn *job.*

His hands skim down my sides as he slides my dress down until it's magically pooled at my feet, and I'm standing before him in a black strapless bra and black thong.

"Fuck, Kate."

"Yes, fuck Kate," I agree with a grin, but when his eyes find mine, they aren't laughing. "What is it?"

He shakes his head and kisses me again, and his hand dives under the scrap of lace to cup my pussy in his hand.

"This?" He pushes two fingers inside me, and I'm so wet they glide in effortlessly. "This is mine, Kate. Do you understand?"

I nod and bite his lip, and cry out when he presses the flat of his palm against my clit and makes me come, right here, this fast, against the wall. His whiskey eyes are watching as I cry out.

"That's right, *cher*. Mine." He pulls his hand out, lifts me, and carries me up the stairs to the bedroom. Before I know what's happening, he's discarded my underwear, stripped out of his own clothes, and joins me on the bed.

Just when I think he's going to spread my legs and slide inside, he flips me over, presses my legs together, straddles them and slides his cock inside me, with my thighs pressed together and my ass just barely in the air.

And, holy hell if it's not the best thing *ever*.

Like, *ever*.

"Oh, my God," I groan. I can't move much with him pressing me into the mattress, holding me down with his body, and in this position, his cock feels even bigger, and hits that amazing spot every single damn time he pushes inside me.

"What are you feeling?" he asks, out of breath.

"You," I reply.

"More."

"I can feel the head of your cock pushing on my spot. I can feel your hands on my hips, holding me down. Your legs on my thighs. Oh, yeah, right there."

"Good girl," he murmurs, and slides his hand up my spine and into my hair, then grips my hair at the scalp, so there's no slack, and pulls.

Hard.

"Shit, yes," I moan.

"You like to have your hair pulled, Kate?"

"I guess so."

"You guess?"

"This is new."

"No one's ever pulled your hair?"

"Not like this."

He chuckles and pulls just a touch harder and begins to seriously fuck me. Hard. His hips slap against my ass, and I feel the most amazing orgasm working its way through me.

"Eli!"

"Say it again."

"Eli. I'm gonna come."

"Come, baby." He releases my hair, leans over and bites my neck, near my shoulder, and that's it. It's over. I come hard and long, clenching him tightly and crying out.

"Fuck," he growls and follows me, grinding into me as he comes, then collapses next to me. "Mine."

CHAPTER SEVENTEEN

"Good morning," he whispers in my ear. I'm on my stomach, my arms under my pillow. I can feel him against my side, rubbing my bare back with the flat of his hand, kissing my cheek, and I want to just stay, right here, forever.

"Mm," I reply.

"Open your eyes," he says. I can hear the smile in his voice.

"Mm mm," I reply and frown, making him chuckle.

"For me?" He kisses my cheek again and cups my ass in his hand, then drags that amazing hand back up my spine and brushes my hair off my back, so he can kiss my neck and shoulder.

I'm awake.

"Your skin is so soft," he murmurs, dragging his lips across my shoulder. "I love your freckles."

"My mother calls them angel kisses. Every time an angel kissed me in heaven before I came to her, I got a freckle." I smile and suddenly miss my ma. I manage to get one eye open and smile at a rumpled Eli lying next to me, his head braced in his hand as his fingers travel over my skin. He's smiling softly at me.

"Good morning," he says.

"Good morning," I reply. "What time is it?"

"Don't worry about it." He kisses my cheek again, and I close my eye. I feel him move around, and then hear the shutter on his phone.

"Did you seriously just take a picture of me?" I ask, and open my eye again to glare at him.

"I did," he replies. "You look beautiful in the morning."

He's such a damn charmer.

I quickly pull his phone from his fingers and turn over, scoot up against him, and hold the phone out to take a selfie of the two of us.

"Morning selfie," I announce, and we both smile at the phone. I snap the picture, but before I lower it, he kisses my cheek, so I snap that too.

"Keep the phone up," he whispers, and turns my face to his, kissing my lips.

I snap that one as well.

"Kissing selfies," I whisper and he kisses my nose. "You're sweet in the morning." I set his phone aside and turn to snuggle in his arms, press my face against his solid, muscular chest, and take a long, deep breath when he closes his arms around me and holds me close.

"I'm not sweet, *cher.*"

"Mmm hmm," I reply and rub my nose against him. "Sure you're not. You smell good."

He chuckles and kisses my head.

"Your hair smells good."

"It's the new shampoo I bought downstairs," I reply.

"I like it."

I sigh and could definitely fall back to sleep right here, in Eli's arms, but I have a feeling we need to get up and out the door to work.

"Seriously, what time is it?"

"After seven," he replies.

"What?" I pull back and try to get out of bed, but he tugs me effortlessly back into his arms. "Eli, we have to get up."

"Five more minutes."

"I don't have five minutes to give you."

"Yes, you do." He hugs me again, rubs his hands down my back and kisses my forehead. "Let me just enjoy having you in my arms for five more minutes."

"Well, it does feel good," I concede, and snuggle against him.

"Nothing feels this good," he whispers, making me grin. I don't care what he says, in these quiet moments, he's very sweet.

If I'm not careful, I could tumble right over into love with him.

It's a good thing I'm the very definition of careful.

"Eli?"

"Hmm."

"I don't want to, but I have to get up."

"I know." He sighs and loosens his grip on me. "Thanks for the extra five minutes."

I grin and roll away, then gasp when I see the time. "It's almost eight!"

"Yes."

"You said it was after seven."

"It is."

I glare at him, but he just stares at me with humor-filled eyes.

"Oversleeping on a Monday means the rest of the week is going to be crappy," I announce, as I stomp into the bathroom, pull a brush through my hair, then tie it back and stare in despair at my makeup-free face in the mirror. "I don't have time for makeup."

"You're beautiful without it," Eli says calmly, as he hands me a steaming mug of coffee and kisses my cheek. "Stop freaking out."

"I don't want to be late," I reply, before gratefully sipping the coffee. "Where did this coffee come from?"

"Timer on the pot," he replies. "You're fine, *cher*." He wraps his arms around my waist and finds my gaze in the mirror as he kisses my cheek. "You didn't sleep that late."

I lean back against him and enjoy the feel of his chest pressed against my back for just a moment before slipping out of his arms and reaching for my makeup.

And then my phone rings.

Of course.

"Rhys is FaceTiming me at 8:00 on a Monday morning?" I ask with a frown. Eli just shrugs and saunters into his closet to dress. "Rhys, I can't talk now."

"Just give me ten," he replies, and I can tell just by looking at him that something is very wrong.

"What is it?"

"You didn't watch last night's game?"

"No," I reply guiltily. "Sorry."

"I'm hurt." The sarcasm is thick. "I thought you watched every game."

"Right. Of course I do. What's wrong?"

"I got hurt." He swallows and winces as he shifts in his seat. "Tore my rotator cuff."

"WHAT? Oh, my God, Rhys—"

"I'm fine."

I look into his green eyes, and I know he's lying. "No, you're not."

He sighs and pinches the bridge of his nose. "I'll need surgery. I'm out for the season."

"Rhys." I wish I could hug him. Baseball has been his life since he was five years old. It's been the one constant in his life, even after his parents died.

It's his life.

"I'm going home to Denver," he continues. "I'll see the doctors there, do some therapy. I'll be fine."

"Rhys."

He sighs again, and finally he says, "Careers end because of this, Kate. I can't lose baseball. I'm only twenty-eight, for Godsake."

"I'll be home in a couple weeks, tops, and I'll take care of you."

He smirks. "I don't need a mommy."

"Maybe I just need to be there to be helpful."

He clears his throat and talks to someone else in the room. "I have to go. I wanted to fill you in."

"Have you called Ma and Da?" I ask.

"They're next. Love you. See you soon."

"Love you too."

"He'll be okay," Eli says from the doorway, fastening the cuff-links on his shirt. I nod and set the phone aside, quickly brush on some mascara and lip gloss, resigned that this is as good as it gets today, and walk out of the bathroom.

"I know. Let me get some clothes on, and let's go."

***

"Hi Kate, this is Adam, the private investigator you spoke with last week?"

"Yes! Please tell me you've found something." I shift in my chair, gathering papers and a pen to make notes with.

"I have; I just hope it's something you can use. You mentioned that there is no employee named H. Peters at Bayou Industries, in any department."

"That's right."

"I had to do some digging into each of the employees and their families, and let me tell you, there are a lot of people who work there."

"Tell me about it."

"You have an employee there named Gerald Rudolph. Didn't get to him until I hit the 'R's. All of the hair on my body stands on end.

"We do."

"His wife's maiden name is Hannah Peters."

Bingo. I shimmy in my seat, doing the happy dance.

"Thanks, Adam. Can you email that information to me?"

"Sure thing. There is other info in the reports too, including a description of the woman who picks up the checks."

"Great job, Adam. Thanks again." I immediately call Eli's office and sigh in relief when he answers. "I need a meeting with you, Beau, and Van ASAP."

"What's wrong?"

"Nothing. We're about to wrap this case up."

There's a long pause, and then, "Be in my office in thirty minutes."

"But Van is at the inn."

"She's at the doctor for a check up. She'll be here."

He hangs up, and I sit for a second and frown at the phone. Why did he sound so...*cold*? Solving this case is what I was hired to do. He should be happy that it's almost over.

I use the next twenty minutes to print out all of the information I've gathered, along with the email from Adam when it comes through.

The elevator seems to take forever. This is the part of my job that I love so much. The part when I get to sit before those who hired me and tell them who and how. The satisfaction of knowing that the job was done well. My whole body is humming with excitement when I walk into Eli's office and see that Beau and Van are already there.

"Thanks for meeting with me."

The door closes behind me, and I sit in a seat between Beau and Van, facing Eli.

"Who is it?" Beau asks immediately.

"Gerald Rudolph."

"Impossible," Eli says calmly.

"No, it's not impossible." I explain the suspicions I brought to Van's attention over the weekend, and then show them the evidence that Adam sent over. "His wife's maiden name is Peters. Hannah Peters. Every transfer went to Western Union to an H. Peters."

Savannah is shaking her head. "This doesn't make sense. He has no reason to steal, Kate. He makes a very good salary. He's been with us for a very long time."

"That's how it usually is," I reply gently. "The person responsible is typically someone that is trusted. Loyal, even."

"I guess that people make poor decisions when they have a lot of stress in their lives," Savannah says slowly.

"Thank you, Kate," Eli says and stands, showing me the door. He's suddenly a stranger, and I don't like it. "We will go over this evidence, and discuss, and let you know if we need anything further."

"Are you okay?" I ask, frowning at him.

"Of course."

I stop in the middle of the office and stare at him. Finally, he simply leans in and whispers in my ear. "We will talk later. Have a good afternoon."

And with that, I'm shown through the door.

I return to my office and decide to make additional copies of all of the reports I just gave to Eli.

Why was he so cold just now? Not four hours ago he was holding me tight, being so sweet, so tender. Treating me like I'm special and sexy and someone he enjoys being with.

And, in his office, he was distant, as if he's never seen me naked or been inside me.

How can men do that? Go from hot to cold in a matter of hours?

Is he mad that I solved the case and the person responsible is someone he likes?

Or maybe…

I sit back and stare at the wall as it occurs to me that me solving this case means that I'm leaving. My time here is almost over.

And that just makes me sad.

I've loved spending time with Savannah and Declan again. I didn't realize how much I missed them until I had them available to me all the time.

But, most of all, I've enjoyed Eli. He's amazing sexually, and has given me a new confidence physically that I'll always be indebted to him for. He showed me how a woman is supposed to feel when she's with a man, in and out of bed. He makes me laugh. He turns my body inside out and makes it sing.

And I suspect that I wasn't as careful as I thought I was, and I've already done the irresponsible thing and fallen in love with him.

I don't do love.

He has been honest with me from the beginning. He's attracted to me, enjoys me, but he doesn't love me.

And I *am* leaving. I have a life in Denver. A job that sends me all over the country. I need to make sure that Rhys is going to be okay.

I have responsibilities.

"Are you okay?" Hilary asks, as she walks into my office, pulling me out of my daydream.

"Hi," I reply with a grin. "I'm okay. Just a lot on my mind."

"Wanna talk about it?"

I shake my head no with a sigh.

"I'm your friend, you know. You can always talk to me about stuff."

"I appreciate that. How was your weekend with Louis?"

"Even better than the last time," she says with a wink, and sits in the chair in front of my desk. She sets a to-go container on my desk. "I brought you lunch."

"You didn't have to do that. Is it lunch time already?"

"It is," she confirms. "I tried a new soup recipe and had a ton left over. This is why I rarely cook for myself. Cooking for one is just a waste of food."

"I hear you. Thanks." I take the lid off and sniff it. She even warmed it up for me. "Smells great. So, what else did you do this weekend?"

"I took Louis shopping. I needed some new shoes." She lifts her leg and shows me a gorgeous pair of sling-back Choos. "And I might have needed a new bag too," she says with a laugh, and shows off a gorgeous black Gucci handbag.

Wow.

"Those are gorgeous," I agree.

"Your friends are fun," she says with a smile, changing the subject.

"I know." I swallow, but keep my face impassive. This is the job. Lying. I'm excellent at it when I need to be.

"I didn't realize you were so close to the Boudreaux family."

"I wouldn't say we're super close," I reply easily. "I did go to college with Savannah, and when I decided to move down here, she offered me a job."

"Convenient."

So, Hilary has a bitchy side.

"I'm going to work through lunch," I say, ready for Hilary and her crappy attitude to leave. "Thanks again for the soup."

"Anytime." She stands and heads for the door. "I'm out for the day."

"Oh?" I check the clock. "At noon?"

"I have to go to the doctor. Yearly fun stuff." She wrinkles her nose, then waves and saunters off.

And I can't help but feel like I'm missing something.

I open the soup and take a bite and think back on the past few weeks with Hilary. She has more experience than me in this position, but I know she doesn't make enough money to buy close to five thousand dollars worth of shoes and handbags.

Unless she has a ton of credit card debt.

Which, she might. I mean, not everyone manages money well.

But...

One thing's for sure, she makes a heck of a soup. I continue slurping it up, eating it quickly. I was hungrier than I thought.

Where there's a will, there's a way. Hilary's statement the day we met for happy hour when I asked how she could afford her new car passes through my mind.

New shoes and bags.

Leaving early from work.

And she was at the club when I was talking to Savannah about my suspicions regarding Mr. Rudolph!

I wonder how much she really heard?

Having eaten all of the soup, I close the lid and come to a complete and utter stop. Written on the top in marker is **H. Peterson**, with the 'on' almost completely worn off.

H. Peters.

It can't be!

I scratch my neck, which has just begun to itch, and log into the employee time clock program to bring up Hilary's logs, print them out, and compare her comings and goings to the dates of the transfers.

Sure enough, every day there was a transfer, Hilary clocked out right around 2:00. Not long after Mr. Rudolph would have left for the hospital.

I page down Adam's email, looking for the description of the woman who picks up the checks.

A woman in her mid-thirties. Blonde hair, average height, average build.

Hilary.

I swallow, but realize my tongue suddenly feels thick. My throat itches. Cheeks are tingly.

"Shit!" I stare down at the empty bowl and my heartbeat triples. It's getting harder to breathe. My lips feel funny.

"Kate?" Mr. Rudolph is standing in the doorway, frowning. "Are you okay? Your face looks swollen."

I shake my head and pull my purse out of my drawer, looking for my EPI pen, but I don't have it. "Peanuts."

But my mouth is so swollen, it sounds like *veanuth.*

"What?"

"Ate peanuts," I repeat and point to the bowl. "Ambulance."

I'm struggling for breath now. My eyes are swelling shut.

I'm going to die. The bitch killed me!

"I need an ambulance," I hear Mr. Rudolph say. "She has an allergy and can't breathe."

And suddenly, everything goes black.

***

"Kate?"

Someone is yelling at me. I try to open my eyes, but can't. Everything is dark. My throat hurts.

"Kate, did you eat peanuts?" The same voice keeps shouting at me. I can only nod.

"It's a nut allergy," I hear another person say, as I'm being wheeled in a bed. "Gave her an EPI shot, and got her airway open."

"What's her name?"

"Kate O'Shaughnessy," someone says. I don't recognize any of the voices. Where is Eli? I want Eli. I can't see. I touch my face, and it feels totally foreign. "Here's her ID and insurance card."

Someone has been going through my purse.

"Okay, guys, wheel her back to room nine."

I'm shuffled about, lifted onto a new bed, changed from my clothes to a gown. All blind. My tongue is too big for my mouth. I itch *everywhere.*

"You can't talk to me, can you, Kate?"

I shake my head.

"I'm Dr. Coggin," the kind man says. "Just nod yes or no, okay?"

I nod yes.

"I hear you have an allergy to peanuts, and ate some?"

I nod.

"Do you know how much?"

I shake my head no.

"Are you itchy? Warm?"

I nod vigorously.

"Still having problems breathing?"

I hold my hand up and tilt it, as if to say *so-so.*

"Okay, we are going to give you some Benadryl and steroids in an IV, and it's going to make you sleepy, but it should calm all of this down. If you have visitors, can they come back to see you?"

I nod and lie back, frustrated that I can't talk or swallow. I'm quite sure I'm a drooling mess.

I want to cry, but my eyes are so swollen, my tear ducts don't work.

There's a prick in the back of my hand. "I'm putting in your IV, Kate. I'm your nurse, Mona."

I nod.

"Because this Benadryl is going directly into your bloodstream, you'll get sleepy pretty fast."

Good. Maybe I'll wake up half-way normal.

"Kate?"

My head turns at the sound of Savannah's voice. She takes my free hand in hers.

"Oh, my God, Katie, are you awake?"

I nod and squeeze her fingers, but the medicine is already making me tired. I need to tell her that it's all because of Hilary, but I still can't talk around my tongue, and now my body is feeling heavy from the drugs.

"Sleep, Kate," Van says. "You'll feel better when you wake up."

"Where's Eli?" I hear Beau ask Van as he also comes into my room.

"I don't know," Van responds. "We can't find him."

What does she mean they can't *find him*?

I moan, frustrated, but can't fight sleep as it slips over me.

CHAPTER EIGHTEEN
ELI

"Look, it's just government bureaucracy," Sal, the shipyard foreman, says in frustration. "It's their job to find these kinds of things."

"It's OSHA, Sal," I reply coldly. "I don't give a fuck if what you say is true, the bottom line is, you either fix that hydraulic system to their specifications, or they will shut down that whole line."

He shakes his head and paces his office in frustration.

"There's nothing wrong with it," he insists. "It's perfectly safe."

I raise an eyebrow. "Sal, you've been with us since I was a kid. I respect your opinion, and I'm not saying that it's *un*safe. I am saying that it didn't pass the OSHA inspection, and it has to be fixed. I don't want to be called back down here for another ass-chewing by that inspector. You know the regulations. We operate within them, one hundred percent of the time. If you don't want to work that way, I'll find someone else who does."

"Are you threatening me?" He scowls and props his hands on his hips.

"No. I'm explaining what I expect to happen. Get it done. You have twenty-four hours."

I walk out without another word, frustrated that I was brought in on this in the first place. I've just spent three hours away from the office, where I have to fire a man who I've known almost half of my life.

Fuck. And have charges brought against him.

But not before I sit down with him, man-to-man, to ask him just exactly what in the ever loving fuck he was thinking.

Not to mention, now that the case is closed, Kate will be leaving.

And why does the thought of that make me want to punch a wall? I've known since the day I met her this was temporary. We've had fun. I've enjoyed her.

I'll enjoy women after her.

I stop next to my car and shake my head before opening the door and lowering myself inside.

The thought of other women does nothing for me except turn my stomach.

I pull my phone out of my pocket and frown when I realize the sound had been off. Four missed calls from Beau, all over two hours ago.

He can be damn annoying.

I punch the button for voice mail and pull out of the shipyard.

"Eli, Savannah and I are on the way to the hospital. Something's happened to Kate." My heart stills, then trips over. "I'm not sure what's happening. Where are you?"

The next message fifteen minutes later: "I'm almost to the hospital. Answer your fucking phone."

I floor the accelerator and try to call Beau, but it goes straight to voice mail, as does Savannah's phone.

What the fuck has happened to Kate? Panic sweeps through me, picturing her broken and hurt in a hospital bed. Sweet, loving Kate is the last person on this Earth that deserves to be hurt. She's so damn *good*.

Living in a world without her is incomprehensible, even if she's not mine.

And she can't ever be mine.

But she'd sure as fuck better be okay.

I find parking, run into the hospital and ask for Kate's room number, rushing away as soon as the numbers are out of the receptionist's mouth.

It seems to take forever to find Kate's room, and just as I walk through the door, I see Kate reach up to Beau standing next to her, place her hand on the back of his neck, and pull his ear down to her lips.

"Hey, wrong brother—"

Beau puts a finger up, stopping me. Savannah and Lila are listening closely.

"Go ahead, Kate. What is it?" he says softly.

"Hilary," we all hear her rasp. "Not Mr. Rudolph. She stole the money, gave me peanuts. I have proof."

We all gather around her. I grip her leg, thankful that she's alive, but fucking pissed at how swollen her beautiful face is. She looks like she went ten rounds with the devil himself.

"Enough for me to go have her arrested now?" Beau asks anxiously. Kate nods, and Beau kisses her forehead and leaves immediately, pulling his phone out of his pocket as he hurries out.

"What's happened?" I ask Savannah and Lila, as I take Beau's place next to Kate. Her hand is small and warm in mine. "Are you okay, *cher*?"

"Wanted you," she says.

"Don't talk," Lila says soothingly. "Someone, *Hilary*, slipped her peanuts. She's very allergic."

"We told Hilary that at girls' night out," Savannah adds with mutiny in her eyes. "That little bitch knew exactly what she was doing."

"Lunch," Kate adds.

"She brought you lunch?" Lila asks and Kate nods. I brush her hair off her forehead and cheeks, kissing her lightly. I can't stop touching her, reassuring myself that she's okay.

"Thank God for Mr. Rudolph," Savannah adds. "He walked in just as the reaction happened. Her airway closed up. He called the EMT's and they brought her here. She's been sleeping since I arrived, and her tongue is just now small enough for her to talk."

"I knew I didn't like that woman," Lila adds.

"Sleepy," Kate says.

"Sleep, baby," I whisper in her ear. She tightens her grip on my hand. "I'm right here. I'm not leaving. I'll be here when you wake up."

She nods and slips into sleep.

"I'm going to make that woman's life a living hell," I announce calmly.

"Good," Lila says. "I'm going to go call Rhys and her parents. I'll be back."

Lila leaves and Savannah leans back in her chair and watches me quietly for a long minute.

"You're in love with her."

"I love her so much I can't breathe," I admit, surprised. "I think I just figured that out."

"But you're still going to let her leave." It's not a question. I glance up and hold my sister's gaze for a moment, then look back at the sweet woman lying in this bed.

"I am," I reply quietly.

"Eli—"

"It's the way it should be. She deserves so much more than me, Van. I am a toxic, broken asshole."

"Well, the asshole part is true enough, but the rest? No, you're not, Eli. You're one of the best people I know."

I shake my head and kiss Kate's hand. "No, I'm not. I'm your brother. You're supposed to think that."

"No, you're wrong there," she replies. "But I'm not going to fight you on this today. It'll keep."

We sit in silence, watching Kate sleep. She's so still. Lila returns, and not long after, Declan. He looks as distraught as I feel when he lays his lips on her forehead and kisses her softly, whispering how sorry he is, how we all love her, that she's going to be okay.

Words *I* should have said.

"Love you too," she whispers to Dec and opens her eyes.

"You're awake?" Dec asks.

"Hard to sleep with you hanging on me," she says, making Dec laugh.

"May I please come in?" Mr. Rudolph is at the door, looking shy and uncomfortable. I stand and shake his hand.

"Thank you. For everything."

He nods and approaches the bed, smiling kindly at Kate. "I see that you're feeling better."

Jesus, how bad did she look when they brought her in?

"Getting there," she says. "Tongue is smaller." Her eyes fill with tears. "Owe you 'pology."

"No," he says, and covers her hand with his. "Beau filled me in. It never occurred to me to tell you about Serena. She's been sick a long time, and everyone in the office knows. I would have suspected me too."

"Thanks," Kate says, and closes her eyes, tired again.

"Get well quickly, sweet girl," he says, and stands to leave. "I need to get over to see Serena. Take care of Kate."

"How long are they keeping her?" I ask after Mr. Rudolph leaves.

"Just until tomorrow. They'd let her go today, but she had so many breathing problems, they want to continue the IV steroids to make sure she's in the clear." Lila's gaze never leaves Kate as she relays the information to me. "She scared the shit out of me."

"All of us," Declan says. "Is it true that she wasn't breathing when the paramedics got there?" he asks Van.

She simply nods.

Hilary is going to wish she never stepped foot in Bayou Enterprises.

***

It's late. The hospital is surprisingly quiet, with just the occasional sound of footsteps walking past Kate's door. She's been in and out of sleep all day, and I haven't moved.

I know she's going to be okay, but I can't make myself leave her side. I sent Savannah, Declan, and Lila home hours ago, promising them that I'd stay, and call if there was any change.

Now I just want her to wake up, which is utterly selfish because she needs to sleep and get well.

The swelling in her face has gone down. Now, just her lips are a little puffy, and her eyes look a little bruised. Every once in a while during sleep, she'll scratch her arm or her neck.

She's still itchy.

She has one hell of an allergy.

I lean in and whisper, so as not to wake her, but I have to say this out loud, while I still can.

"You are so special, Kate. So beautiful. I'm going to miss you every day. You made the man who's incapable of love fall in love with you." My throat tightens, and I stop talking. I simply bury my face in her neck and breathe her in, already missing what she brings to my life. The light. The laughter.

Already missing who I am because of her.

***

"What are we doing today?" Kate asks two days later. And what a difference two days make. The swelling is completely gone, and it seems that she's back to her old, energetic self.

"Sleep," I reply, and close my eyes beside her, goading her.

"No. No sleep."

"You need to rest."

"Eli, I'm fine. All recovered. You can even have sex with me and I won't die."

"That's not funny," I reply calmly and turn to face her. "You could have died."

"I didn't," she says, and cups my cheek in her hand. "I'm fine. And you've kept me in bed—*not* for the fun stuff, I might add—for two days."

"Fun stuff?" I ask and kiss her forehead. "You want fun stuff?"

"Yes."

"Not yet."

"Eli, my face swelled, not my…*other places.*"

I laugh. I can't help it. She's so fucking funny when it comes to the swearing.

"These places?" I ask and brush the backs of my knuckles over her nipple, making it stand at attention.

"Yes," she whispers and closes her eyes. "That's a good place."

"What about this place?" I ask and drag the same knuckles down her stomach to her navel, circling it softly, loving that fucking piercing.

"That doesn't suck."

I grin and kiss her collarbone. God, she's soft. And expressive. She's addictive.

How am I going to live without her?

Because I will live without her.

But not today.

"And this?" I ask as my fingers drift down between her legs, lightly touching her warm skin. "What about this place, *cher?*"

"Best. Place. Ever." Her hips move, wanting me to press harder, deeper, but I hold back, barely tickling over her tiny pink pussy lips, watching in satisfaction as she squirms next to me. Her neck and cheeks pinken; her breath quickens. She grips the sheets at her hip opposite me and bites her lip. "That feels nice."

"Just nice, huh?"

Oh, we can do a whole lot better than fucking nice.

I kiss down her torso, lick the underside of her breasts, enjoying every gasp and moan that comes out of her delicious mouth. Her fingers find my hair and hold on tight as I nibble down her ribs, kiss a circle around her navel, then travel down between her legs. I spread her wide and growl when I see how wet she already is.

"You're so pink." I press a kiss to her pubis. "So wet." Her clit, making her gasp. "So sweet." I sweep my tongue through her folds, then pull back and look up into her shining green eyes. "I could do this all day."

"You'd kill me," she replies, and lets her head fall back as I grin and press a kiss to the delicate skin of her inner thigh, the crease where leg meets torso, then pay the same attention to the other side. "You *are* killing me."

"Just taking my time, *cher.*" It seems we always take it so damn fast, because I can't wait to be inside her, can't wait to feel her come apart at the seams. But this time, I want to enjoy every movement, every sigh, every moment. "You're quite fun, you know."

"I am?" She smiles down at me, decidedly happy with that compliment.

"You are." I lap at her now, from her pussy all the way to her clit and back down again. Her fingers tighten in my hair, pulling in the best way. She's sweet. Just a bit tangy.

Perfect.

"Eli, I want you inside me."

"I'll get there."

"No, really." I glance up at her tone. "This is *so good*, but I really want to feel you inside me. Please."

I kiss my way back up her delectable body, rest my hard cock against her folds, and prop myself on my elbows beside her head, careful to keep my weight off of her.

She takes my face in her hands and pulls me down to kiss her thoroughly, lapping at my lips, licking every drop of her own juices off of me, and if that isn't the sexiest fucking thing ever, I don't know what is.

I pull my hips back, and Kate reaches between us to wrap her little fingers around me, making my eyes fucking cross, then guides me inside her in one long, slow stroke.

"Oh, God," she whispers, her green eyes never leaving mine. "You always feel so good."

"It's all you, *cher*," I reply.

She shakes her head and bites my lip. "It's *us.*"

I close my eyes and lean my forehead against hers, unable to keep from moving any longer. She squeezes around me with each thrust in the most amazing way, making my balls lift and tighten, my spine tingle.

I'm not going to last like this.

"Look at me," she says softly.

"Bossy thing, aren't you?" I say as my eyes find hers. She doesn't reply. She simply lifts her legs higher on my hips and clamps down, hard, her pussy rippling as she comes in waves.

She doesn't cry out. She just grips onto my arms and lifts her head off the bed, resting her forehead on my chest as she comes harder than I've ever felt her. I'm helpless to stop the orgasm that tears through me, also so damn strong, but quiet.

She lies back and smiles up at me, trying to catch her breath.

"That's the best medicine ever."

I grin. "You'll never hear me complain."

I brush loose tendrils of hair off her sweaty cheeks and kiss her forehead, her nose, and her lips. When I move to pull out, she holds me close. "Not yet."

I'd move the earth for her right now if I could.

Her fingertips glide up and down my back, to my ass, then up again lazily. "I have to go to the office today," she murmurs.

I frown. "I thought you were done."

"I need to put together the last of my reports, then I need to pack."

Her eyes are sad as she looks up at me, almost as though she's silently begging me to ask her to stay. "When are you leaving?" I ask instead.

"Day after tomorrow."

"I want to spend every minute with you."

She smiles, then shakes her head.

"You don't have to. We know this is finished, Eli. We can just cut it off."

"No, I don't want that." I kiss her lips softly. "I want to spend every minute with you that you're here. I'll take you to the airport myself."

"Why?"

I swallow hard and call myself a selfish fucking bastard, and a coward, when I say, "Because I'm not quite ready to say goodbye."

"And if I am?" she asks. I pull up so I can clearly look her in the eye.

"Are you?"

She bites her lip, thinking about her response, and then finally shakes her head quickly. "No."

"Okay then. When are we going to the office?"

"After you fuck me again."

She grins naughtily and squeezes my ass, and just like that, I'm hard again.

"You know what those filthy words to do me."

"No, what do they do?" she asks with wide, innocent eyes.

"This," I whisper against her lips as I begin moving inside her again. "I'll just keep reminding you until you figure it out."

"Maybe I'll stop using the dirty words."

"Oh, I think we'll make sure that doesn't happen."

***

"Here." I walk into Kate's bedroom and hand her a glass of lemonade. She's been working most of the afternoon, packing her things. Why I'm here watching, I have no idea. The only explanation I have is I've suddenly become a masochist.

Because this fucking hurts.

"Thanks." She grins, kisses me quickly, then returns to neatly folding her sexier than fuck underwear and placing them in a suitcase.

"I haven't seen these before." I retrieve a pair of leopard print boy shorts from the bag and hold them up. "I like these. Put them on."

"No." She laughs and snatches them out of my hand, refolds, and returns them to the case, right after I pull a purple, lacy thong out.

"Wow. I haven't seen this either." It's dangling from my index finger when she grabs it and glares at me as she folds and replaces it.

"Stop undoing everything I'm doing."

"I just want to know why you've been withholding sexy underwear from me. You know how much I love it."

"I haven't been withholding it," she laughs with a shake of the head, making her hair move about her shoulders.

My fingers itch to dive into that thick, soft hair.

So they do.

I comb my fingers through her hair and watch it fall back to her shoulders, then repeat the motion.

"I have a system," she informs me primly. "And you're messing it up."

"I am?"

"Yes."

She sighs and closes her eyes as my fingertips rub her scalp.

"That feels good."

With her eyes closed, I retrieve a sexy red nightie from the suitcase.

"And who, exactly, were you planning to wear this for?"

She gasps and steals the scrap of lace from my hand.

"Seriously. Stop touching all of my underwear."

"You don't mind when I take it off of you, *cher*."

"That's different." She sniffs, her nose in the air. "And I wasn't *planning* on wearing it for anyone."

"Wear it for me, before you go." The request is quiet. Sincere. She watches my eyes solemnly as she sets it aside.

"I can do that."

"You're good at taking orders," I comment with a grin. She narrows her eyes at me.

"I'm no one's submissive."

"Indeed," I agree, and run a finger down her cheek. "But I like that if I make a request, you're eager to comply."

"Why do I do that?" she asks with a frown. "Is that what got me into trouble with my ex-husband? I was too *easy*?"

"You didn't get into trouble with your ex-husband," I say, and take her face in my hands, making her look at me. "He was an asshole who didn't know a good thing when he had it. He doesn't know how to treat a woman, Kate. And wanting to please people you love isn't a bad thing, when it's done sincerely."

"Thanks," she whispers.

"So, you'll wear the sexier than fuck nightie?" I ask with a grin, lightening the mood again.

"We'll see," she says with a wink. "I don't want you to think I'm a sure thing."

"Oh, sugar, that ship has sailed." I laugh and pull her in for a hug, delighted with her. "You make me laugh."

"Do I make you want to pack things?" she asks, making my heart still at the reminder of her leaving. "Because I need to finish this and you're distracting me."

"You make me want to undress you," I reply, but she backs out of my reach.

"Oh, no." She points a finger at me and glares.

"You don't scare me."

"No hanky-panky. This has to get done."

"*Hanky-panky*?" I ask with a laugh. "What, exactly, is *hanky-panky*?"

She giggles and backs further away. "You know what it is. I have to get this done, Eli. I don't have time for shenanigans."

"Oh, there will be shenanigans, *cher*." I slowly saunter toward her. She's run toward the balcony, caging herself in. "Admit it. You like the shenanigans."

"No. I don't." She giggles.

God, I love her giggle.

"You also like it when I get you naked."

"Stop it." Now she stands firm, her hands on her hips, as though she's a teacher and I'm an unruly student. "I'm serious, Eli. I have work to do."

I grin. "So do I."

CHAPTER NINETEEN
KATE

"I never did ask you what happened with Asher." I'm chatting on the phone with Lila. "I was too busy looking like a blow fish."

"A lot happened with Asher," she says.

"Was there sex?" I ask, and throw the last of my things in my carry-on bag.

"Oh, indeed, friend. There was lots of sex."

"Was it good sex?" I grin and flop on the couch, wishing Lila was still here, rather than back in Denver.

"Maybe the best sex that has ever been had on this planet. Every time."

"*Every* time?"

"Every. Time."

"So, was there the exchange of phone numbers?"

There's a pause, and I sit up straight, stare at my phone, then, "Seriously? Lila!"

"I don't have time for a relationship."

"Who said anything about a relationship? Just call him up now and again have the best sex on the planet."

"Impossible," Eli says as he walks through the door. "We have the best sex on the planet."

I laugh and hold up my hand, signaling that I just need one more minute.

"He lives in Seattle, Kate," Lila says with a sigh. "I never go to Seattle."

"Maybe he goes to Denver," I suggest.

"I'm not going to be in Denver much longer either."

"You're not? Why?"

"Because, while I was in New Orleans, I had that interview with Tulane University, and I have a new job beginning this fall."

"Shut the front door!" I exclaim, and jump to my feet, dancing around the living room. "I'm so excited for you!"

"Thank you. So, I have enough to keep me occupied for now."

"It's not like being occupied by the best sex on the planet is a hardship," I remind her dryly.

"Seattle, Kate."

"Fine." I sigh. "I guess it doesn't matter anyway, since you didn't get his number."

"When do you come home?"

"Tomorrow." I bite my lip and glance back at Eli, who's sipping a bottle of water and leaning against the countertop, watching me. "I get in around noon."

"Want me to pick you up?"

"Sure."

"Okay, send me your itinerary. I'll see you tomorrow. Go enjoy your sexy business man. Have the second best sex on the planet."

"You're sick," I reply with a laugh. "Bye."

"How is Lila?" Eli asks and joins me in the living room.

"Good. She got the job at Tulane." I grin and stand on my tip-toes, so I can kiss him. He still has to bend down to meet my lips.

"Good for her." He cups my neck in his hands and takes the kiss deeper, in that way he does that makes my toes curl and my fingertips tingle.

The man can seriously kiss.

"What would you like to do this afternoon?" he asks.

"I want to take one more walk through the Quarter. It's so pretty this afternoon."

"Grab your hat," he instructs me, making me grin.

"Yes, sir."

"Don't sass me."

"No, sir."

He swats my butt. "Smart ass."

"Yes, sir." I tug my hat onto my head, grab my purse, and Eli leads me down the steps to the sidewalk.

"Which way?"

"I get to choose?"

"Of course." I stop on the sidewalk and take him in, standing so tall, his dark hair moving in the summer breeze, his sunglasses hiding his whiskey eyes. He has a little dark scruff on his face, and his lips are tipped in a half-smile, as if he finds me amusing. His body is perfectly comfortable in a white button-down and jeans, and despite having had him mere hours ago, I want to climb him.

"*Cher*?"

"Oh, what?" I shake my head and look up into his face.

"Where would you like to go?"

"Oh. Let's start in here." I lead the way into the amazing botanical shop beneath my flat. "I love the way it smells in here."

"After you." He holds the door for me, then follows me in, hanging back as I wander through the racks and tables of lotions, soaps, oils, and extracts. I saunter through, smelling the potions.

"Hi there," a woman with long, thick dark hair and bright, happy blue eyes says from the checkout counter. "Can I help you find anything?"

"No," I reply with a grin. "I've been staying upstairs, and I've wanted to stop in to look around. The smells that drift upstairs are delicious. I stopped in briefly one day to buy shampoo, which I love, but I didn't have time to browse."

"Well, I'm Mallory, the owner, and just let me know if I can answer any questions."

I nod and smile, and before I'm done, I've gathered more shampoo and conditioner, cucumber lotion for my eyes, lip balm, and an eye-pillow full of lavender.

Mallory rings me up and Eli pays before I can pull my wallet out of my purse, earning a glare from me.

"You're not paying for anything when you're with me, Kate."

"Thank you. That was fun," I say with a smile, as we step out onto the sidewalk. "I should have gone in there before. I love girlie stuff."

"Well, you are a girl, so I guess that fits," Eli says with a laugh, and takes the bag of goodies out of my hand.

"You're quite chivalrous, you know."

"Mama raised me right," he replies. Damn that accent gets me every time. Especially when he was in my hospital room, whispering in my ear.

You made a man who's incapable of love fall in love with you.

He thought I was asleep, but I heard him.

Not that it changes anything. I'm still leaving tomorrow, and I refuse to be the one to tell him that I love him when I'm not full of medication.

Because, what if I was wrong? What if I was hallucinating?

How embarrassing would that be?

He takes my hand, kisses the back of it, and leads me down the sidewalk, toward Jackson Square, toward the sound of music and people and the smell of beignets.

I'm going to miss this.

I'm going to miss *him*.

I glance up, and for just a moment, the words are on the tip of my tongue.

"What is it, *cher*?"

"I just—" I take a deep breath and chicken out. "I'm going to miss this place."

He smiles softly and kisses my cheek, but doesn't say anything in return, and I swallow my disappointment and decide to simply enjoy our last day together.

***

"Another lemon drop?" Joe the waiter asks, as he delivers our Brussels sprouts.

"No," Eli answers for me, giving me a stern look. "I'd like to actually have a coherent conversation with you this evening."

"Come on," I reply with a laugh. "I'm fun when I'm drunk."

"You are fun," he agrees and spears a sprout with his fork, then holds it up to my lips. "But since this is my last night with you, let's keep it semi-sober."

"Deal." I chew the delicious vegetable and sit back in my seat, enjoying the courtyard of Café Amalie. "This place is so beautiful. I love the pretty lights in the trees. Isn't it pretty?"

"Yes," he replies, but when I look over at him, he's not looking at the trees. He's looking at me.

"Charmer," I whisper, and take the last sip of my drink.

"You look beautiful in this dress." He takes my hand in his and kisses my knuckles, sending electricity up my arm.

"Thank you."

"Your dinners," Joe announces, as he places our entrées before us. Dinner is delicious and filling, and when Eli suggests that we take a longer walking route back to his place, I readily agree.

I need to work off some of this food.

"Oh, look at this gallery," I breathe, and stop at a window with canvasses full of black trees and colorful leaves and backgrounds. They look almost…weepy. "I love this one with the yellows, golds, and oranges." I point to the one that has caught my eye. "It reminds me of Denver in the fall."

"Hmm," Eli murmurs and kisses my cheek before leading me further up the block. We stop several more times to admire window displays, walking slowly, hand-in-hand, laughing and talking.

Enjoying.

Did I ever honestly think this man was intimidating? Cold? Distant? It's amazing to me the difference in him from when I first walked into his office to that same man walking next to me tonight.

"What are you thinking so hard about?" he asks quietly, his accent thicker, perfect for this lazy, easy moment.

"Nothing."

"Now, that's a lie," he replies with a soft smile. "I can hear your wheels turning."

"I was thinking about you." I squeeze his hand a little tighter, and then bring it up to nuzzle it with my cheek. "And that I'll miss you when I leave."

He grows quiet for a moment, not responding at all, and then he surprises me.

"I've enjoyed every moment with you, Mary Katherine O'Shaughnessy," he says, making me smile at the way he says my last name with his accent. "You are a special woman."

We're standing in front of his townhouse now. Based on his last statements, I'm wondering if he's not saying goodbye.

"Thank you for a lovely evening."

"No, *cher*, I'm not cutting our night short." He leads me inside, up to the bedroom. "I just wanted to make sure I told you how much I've enjoyed you, in case I don't have enough blood supply to my brain later and I forget."

"Definitely charming," I laugh. Eli's phone rings, making him frown. He checks the display, dismisses the call, and sets his phone aside.

"I do believe I'd like to pamper you a bit this evening," he says, as he slowly saunters toward me.

"How so?" I ask, feeling a bit breathless at the look in his eyes, the way his body moves so effortlessly, his muscles bunching and moving beneath his smooth skin.

He's simply delicious.

"Well, I'll begin by slowly taking this dress off of you," he whispers. He's pressed against me now, his arms around me as he lowers the zipper on my back, pushes the black fabric off my shoulders, and watches it fall to my ankles. "You pulled the leopard print back out," he says with a cocked brow.

"You seemed to like it." I swallow at the hot look in his eyes as they lazily roam up and down my body.

"I didn't realize there was a matching bra."

"Of course there's a matching bra," I reply dryly. "There's always a matching bra."

"I do love your taste in underwear," he says, just before he hooks his fingers in the straps on my shoulders and tugs them aside, then lays his lips on my skin, kissing me gently all the way to the ball of my shoulder. He pays the same attention to the other side, just as his phone rings again.

"You should answer it," I whisper in his ear, then kiss him, just below his earlobe, on that soft skin that feels so good on my lips.

"No."

"It could be important."

He shakes his head and unhooks my bra in the back; his fingertips drag over my skin as he pulls it down my arms, then lets it fall. I tug his shirt out of his pants, then slide my hands up his stomach, over his smooth, warm skin.

God, I love touching him.

"This is supposed to be about you," he whispers against my collarbone.

"It is," I reply softly. "Touching you makes me happy."

He pauses, and then kisses me, right over my heart.

Tell him! My mind screams. *Tell him you love him and you don't want to leave!*

"Eli."

His phone rings again, and we both moan in frustration, but he ignores it.

"Eli, you really should answer it."

"Fuck no," he replies stubbornly. "Whoever it is can fuck off."

I slide my hands down the back of his pants and grip onto his very firm, very fine butt.

"I like your butt," I whisper, making him laugh.

"I'm glad you do," he says.

"I think you're wearing too many clothes," I say, just as my own phone rings. Our eyes meet and wait, and sure enough, as soon as mine stops, his starts. "Seriously. Answer. Something is wrong."

He swears and stalks over to his phone. "What." He frowns as he listens. "Are you sure?" He sighs and pinches the bridge of his nose, then scrubs his hand over his mouth in agitation. "Fine. I said fine, Beau. I'll be there in twenty."

He clicks off and turns to me with regret and anger written all over his face.

"You have to go."

"I'll be back in an hour."

I laugh and shake my head, then cross to him and simply wrap my arms around him and hug him tight. "It's okay, Eli."

"I swear, I'll be back in an hour. Two tops." He braces his hands on my shoulders and sets me away from him. "Take a hot bath, drink a glass of wine, relax. I'll come back and we'll pick this back up."

"Okay." I grin and kiss his chin, then his lips. "I'll go back over to my place and finish up a few things, so I don't have to do them in the morning. It'll buy me ten more minutes of sleep."

"I'll come get you when I get back," he promises, kisses me once more, hard and long, then tucks his shirt back in, grabs his keys and wallet, and rushes out. I take my time pulling my dress back on, not bothering with the bra, and walk over to my own flat.

Once I've finished gathering the last few things for tomorrow morning, sure that I'm ready for my flight, I take a hot shower, shave my legs, *again*, because really, you can never have legs that are too smooth, and decide to wear the pretty red nightie that Eli admired the other day.

He did ask nicely, after all.

I check the time on my phone, frowning when I realize he's been gone for over an hour. Should I go to bed and let him wake me up when he gets back?

It's getting late, and I have an early flight. I try his phone, to let him know that I'll be asleep, but I just get his voice mail.

"Hey, just wanted to let you know that I'm going to sleep for a while. Come on in and wake me up when you get home. See you soon."

I lie down, and the next thing I know, my phone is ringing. "'Lo?"

"It's Eli. I'm sorry, Kate."

"What time is it?"

"It's after two. I'm not going to make it back tonight. I got hung up here. I'll have to send someone to take you to the airport in the morning."

Um. Wait. What?

"Okay."

"I'm so sorry, Kate. I have to go. Please take care of yourself. Thanks for everything. Take care and safe travels."

And with that, he's gone.

"Thanks?" I ask the empty room. "Take care and safe travels?"

I sit and blink into the blackness. Did that really just happen, or did I dream it? I check my phone, and sure enough. It was real.

He's not coming back.

I stare at my phone as it goes black and feel my eyes well. He's just my *friend*. This shouldn't upset me at all. So I don't get to have sex with him one more time. So I don't get to feel the weight of him on top of me, or his lips on my skin. So I don't get to hear that sexy accent of his as he whispers in my ear because he's so darn turned on he can't help himself.

So I don't get to feel his hands on my back as he holds me, or see the special way he smiles at me when he thinks I'm being particularly adorable or ridiculous.

So what?

It's a clean break. Like ripping off the Band-Aid quickly. It's probably for the best.

And hurts worse than any slap in the face.

I thought I'd at least get to say goodbye in person.

I lie back and can't stop the tears that flood my eyes, and that only pisses me off more. I refuse to waste one more tear on a man. *Any man.* Especially a man who doesn't love me and says goodbye with *safe travels.*

No more tears.

Not one.

I roll onto my belly and bury my face in the pillow, crying angrily. Why did I let myself fall in love with him? Haven't I learned anything?

***

"Hey, superstar," Declan says, when I open the door for him and turn to gather my luggage.

"Good morning. Thanks for picking me up."

"No problem. Eli said he—"

"I don't care what Eli said," I interrupt, and then scowl. "That sounded really bitchy."

"Kind of." He helps me gather my bags.

"The moving people will come get the rest later today or tomorrow."

Declan nods and follows me down the steps. I glance to my left, and also coming down Eli's steps is Gabby's friend, Cindy.

She glances over at us, smiles and waves, and then walks to her car, climbs in, and leaves.

Are you fucking kidding me?

"She's a little slut," Declan mutters, as he loads my bags into the back of his car.

"So is your brother," I reply. "*That* is what he got hung up with last night?"

"Hey," Dec holds his hands up in surrender. "I honestly don't know. I was simply asked to come take you to the airport." He winces and offers me a sympathetic smile. "I'm sorry."

"Whatever," I reply and get in the passenger side. "It was over anyway."

"Was it?"

"It sure as heck is now."

CHAPTER TWENTY
ELI

I drop into the chair behind my desk, lean my elbows on the smooth wood and prop my head in my hands, gripping my hair in my fists. It's after eight in the morning, and I just got here.

I never went home.

All I want to do is sleep, so I'll take a cold shower, get dressed, and get back to work.

Back to my life.

But first, I dial Kate's number, needing to hear her soothing, sweet voice after the fucked up night I just had, and frown when I'm immediately sent to the automated voice of her mailbox.

Her plane has taken off.

And it's probably for the best.

"You okay?" Beau asks, as he walks into my office and flops into the chair across from me, looking every bit as exhausted as I feel.

"I feel the way you look," I reply. "I told Sal to replace that hydraulic. *I told him*. I made it very clear what would happen if he didn't."

"We just never planned on a guy being killed in the night shift because he didn't do it fast enough," Beau replies, and rubs his eyes with the pads of his fingers.

"It was pride," I spit out. "I bruised his fucking ego, so he drug his feet."

"Well, he can drag his feet all the way to the unemployment office."

I nod grimly. "That doesn't help that young man's widow and two small kids."

"We'll make sure they're very well taken care of."

"Something tells me she'd rather have her husband," I whisper sadly.

"Eli," Beau begins and scratches his scruffy cheek. "I wanted to tell you, I was really fucking proud of you last night."

I raise a brow and watch my older brother. He's my best friend, and we respect each other, but we're men.

We don't get mushy.

I shift in my chair, uncomfortable, but he keeps going.

"You handled the situation perfectly."

"I didn't do it alone," I remind him. "You were right there with me, taking on your fair share of the work."

"Yes, and I'll continue to, but you did great. Dad would have been impressed."

I smirk. "Right."

Beau cocks his head, narrows his eyes. "Dad loved you."

"I know."

And I do. But, he didn't respect me, and wasn't *impressed* by anything I did once in my life.

"You're a good man, Eli. A fair one. A good leader. *I'm* proud of you."

"Thank you."

"Is she gone?" he asks suddenly, changing the subject.

"Yes."

He sighs. "And you let her go."

"She doesn't live here, Beau. She has a life and a job."

He shakes his head at me. "I'm sorry you missed last night with her. She was good for you."

So am I. So fucking sorry.

"Did you at least call and say goodbye?"

"I'm not a dick, Beau. Of course. I called and wished her safe travels."

His jaw drops. "That's it?"

"What else was there to say? Discuss the weather? Exchange recipes? Pledge my undying love?"

"You're wrong," Beau says quietly, as he stands and shoves his hands in his pockets, the same way I do, looking very much like our father. "You are a dick."

"Never claimed otherwise," I mutter as he walks away. I check my phone, for what I'm not sure. She may have landed by now. I tried to call Declan earlier to ask him how she was this morning, but he's not answering my calls.

He's probably either asleep or bouncing on one of his groupies.

I'd give just about anything to hear her voice right now, to smooth the rough edges left from holding that young widow through the night while she cried long, heartbroken sobs against my chest for a man who's never coming home. From being awake for too fucking long.

From already missing her.

But she's gone, and I have a business to run. So I schedule a mid-morning mandatory meeting with the men at the shipyard and hurry to shower and dress to make it there on time.

This is my life. This is what's important. Kate was just a pleasant distraction. It's time to get back to business.

***

"I don't give a fuck. I want it done. *Today.* Understood?"

"Yes, sir."

"Good." I hang up and bring up an email, just as Savannah and Declan saunter into my office.

"I see you're just your usual puppies and rainbows self," Declan says dryly, as he lowers himself into a chair, a smirk on his face.

"What do you want?"

"We want to talk to you," Savannah says. She folds her hands in her lap, sitting straight in the chair, head high, the way she always does. But her eyes are sad, and that kills me.

"How are you, *bebe*?" I ask her softly.

"Worried about you," she replies.

"Alright." I sit back in my chair and rub my fingers over my mouth. "What's up?"

"We've come to point out that you're back to your old asshole ways," Declan says.

"How would you know?" I ask with a raised brow. "You haven't spoken to me in two weeks."

"And I'd rather not speak to you now either, but Van talked me into it."

"Since you're talking to me, would you like to explain *why* you'd rather not?"

"Because you're a fucking dick, and you made Kate cry."

"What?" I scowl at them both. "I haven't spoken to Kate since she left two weeks ago."

"Oh, we know," Savannah replies. "And you're back to your BK attitude."

"*BK*?"

"Before Kate."

"Is this an intervention?" I ask with a laugh, and immediately wish for a glass of bourbon.

"Yes, if you'd like to call it that," Van replies. "It's an asshole intervention."

"Noted. You can see yourselves out."

"You don't even want to know if she's okay?" Declan asks incredulously. "No, *so, how's Kate?*"

"So, how's Kate?"

His jaw and fists clench, but before he can say anything else, Savannah jumps in. "She's...*fine.*"

What the fuck does that mean?

"Why did you let her leave?" Savannah asks.

"I have a better question," Dec interrupts. "Why did you fuck Cindy while Kate was twenty feet away, worried about you, wondering when you were coming back?"

I blink at my siblings, not exactly computing what the fuck they're saying.

"Excuse me?"

"Cindy? Gabby's slutty friend? The woman that Kate and I saw leaving your townhouse as we took her luggage to the car. The leggy blonde with the big tits."

"So charming," Van murmurs, while she glares daggers at me.

"I didn't fuck Cindy." Just the thought has bile rising in the back of my throat.

"Bullshit. We *saw* her, Eli."

"I don't know what the fuck you think you saw, but I didn't fuck her. I wasn't home, Dec. I was at the shipyard. Jesus, I haven't been home since I left Kate that night."

"Wait." Van thinks it over and then nods. "That's right. He was at the shipyard. And what do you mean, you haven't been home?"

What's the point? Kate's not there. She won't be on her balcony with wine and pizza. Or next door listening to her music too loud. Or in my bed.

"I have work."

"So, you're living *here*? How?"

"I have clothes here. Showers. A couch. And I'm pushing thirty-one, so I can pretty much do whatever the fuck I want, little sister."

"Are you eating?" Savannah asks, and I simply sigh.

"Hello, pot, I'm kettle. Have you seen you lately? Your clothes are hanging off of you."

"We're not talking about me," she says defensively.

"You never answered why you let her leave," Declan says quietly. "You didn't ask her to stay."

"Her job was finished."

"You love her," Savannah reminds me softly. "You told me you love her so much you can't breathe."

And I haven't taken a deep breath in two weeks.

"You hurt her!" Declan exclaims.

"I don't deserve her!" I shout back. "What am I going to offer her? You've said it yourself, I'm an asshole. I'm consumed with my job. This," I gesture to my office, "is what I eat, sleep, breathe, fuck. I made a promise to Dad that I'd get my shit together and focus on this family and this company, and that's what I'm doing! No woman wants to take second place to a job!"

"Eli, Dad wouldn't want you to give up love for this company," Savannah says. "You don't have to put the company above anyone you love on your priority list."

"Daddy never made us feel like we were second place. He sure as fuck never made Mama feel that way. They were a team, E," Dec says quietly. "You have so much more to give than that."

I stare at Dec for a moment. "What did you say?"

"You have so much more to give."

"You need to take responsibility for your actions, son. Beau is going to need your help with the company. The family needs you. You have so much more to give this life than what you've been giving it. Riding along, screwing every pretty thing in a skirt, is not the way to live your life.

"The love of one good woman is worth more than all of those tarts combined. What your mama and I have had for the past thirty-five years? You can't buy it. You can't drink enough to fake it. It's soul-deep. I love her so much I can't breathe, Eli. Even when she makes me want to strangle her tiny little neck. She makes me feel so much. She gave me six amazing children. She makes me laugh.

"I want that for you. You are capable of so much in this life, Eli. I want you to love what you do. I know you're going to make our company better than I ever did. But more than that, I want you to fall in love. Have babies. Love her so much you can't *breathe."*

"But, you know what?" Declan continues as I blink hard, coming out of that moment with my dad that I'd forgotten. "It doesn't matter. Kate's not hard to please, Eli. All she's ever wanted was someone to be kind to her. To love her. To be someone she can trust to protect her. Someone to *fight for her*."

"And you just let her go," Savannah agrees.

I just let her go.

"Look, man, if you don't love her, fine. It's not a requirement to love Kate, although how anyone could *not* love her, I don't know. But calling her at 2:00 with *safe travels*, after everything you'd done and been through was a dick move."

Such a fucking dick move.

"I love you so much," Savannah says with tears in her eyes. "I saw how different you were with her. You smiled so easily. You were tender with her. It was the Eli that hasn't been around in a long time. And now that she's gone, so is he. And I miss him."

"I'll let her know that we misunderstood about Cindy," Declan says, as he and Van stand to leave.

"No." I shake my head as they both spin around to stare at me.

"What? Why?" Savannah says.

"I'll tell her." I swallow hard and stand, push my hands in my pockets, fingering the half-dollar.

"If you're planning to call her, she won't answer," Savannah warns me.

"I'm going to see her."

"She won't want to see you," Declan says with a smile. "I kind of wish I was gonna be there to witness this."

"You also have a dick side," I comment calmly. "Must run in the family."

"Rhys is there," Dec says. "He might try to beat the shit out of you."

"He lives with her?"

"Yeah, they share a place, since neither of them are there often. But, come to think of it, he has a bum shoulder. You can take him."

"Duly noted."

"Good luck." Van grins, and comes around the desk to kiss my cheek. "You *do* deserve her. No one else does."

I hug her tight and pray she's right. Because living without her is pure agony.

I need her.

***

Kate and Rhys's house is in a newer development in Denver. The homes are modest, but nice, with trim yards and enough space between houses to be comfortable.

I pay the cabbie and walk to the door, not sure what in the hell I'm going to say.

Sorry just sounds…lame.

I ring the bell and am not surprised when a tall, broad blond man answers the door.

"Yes?"

"Is Kate available, please?"

"Who wants her?"

"Eli Boudreaux."

His nostrils flair, eyes narrow, and just when I think he's going to slam the door in my face, he steps back, and gestures for me to come in.

"I'm Rhys," he says and holds his hand out for mine, which I shake firmly.

"I figured," I reply, as he leads me into a living area littered with chocolate wrappers, popcorn, and used wine glasses. "Did you have a party?"

"Something like that," he replies. "Kate has stepped out for a few minutes, which is convenient, because I'd like to have a word with you privately."

"Okay." I look him in the eye, ready for him to rip me a new asshole, but instead, he blows out a gusty breath and sits in the chair opposite me.

"If you're here to fuck with her head some more, you can just get the hell out of here now. I won't have her hurt anymore. Not by anyone. Ever again."

"I'm not here to fuck with her head."

He licks his lips and leans back in the chair, crossing his ankle over his knee.

"Look, Rhys, I understand that you're protecting her, which I respect. I have three sisters, and if anyone even looks at them sideways, I want to rip into them. I don't want to hurt Kate. I'm *nothing* like her ex-husband."

"There are few people out there like her ex-husband. He's a murdering sonofabitch motherfucker," Rhys says matter-of-factly.

I nod, in complete agreement, when one word brings me up short.

"Murdering?" I ask, much more calmly than I feel.

"I know a lot of people don't consider the loss of unborn life to be murder, but in this case, it was brutal murder, man."

I frown, lost, and then the conversation from the graveyard comes to mind.

"Did he ever put you in the hospital?"

"Once."

"Are you saying he—"

"She didn't tell you," he mutters and curses, pushing his hand through his hair. "Yes, he did."

"I know that he hurt her."

Rhys lets out a humorless laugh.

"Yes, he hurt her. He used her for a punching bag. For sport." He clears his throat and has to stand to pace the living room. "Look, this is her story to tell, but I'm going to tell it anyway, because you need to know what she had to overcome just to let you close enough to *touch* her, man.

"That fucker smacked her around regularly. Not usually in the face to leave bruises, or when I was in town, because he's a spineless asshole. But then she got pregnant."

I swallow hard, hating the words about to come out of his mouth, and feeling so fucking helpless it's almost crippling. I also stand and pace, unable to sit.

"She thought the baby would make him change." Rhys shakes his head. "Men like that don't change."

"No. They don't."

"So, she pissed him off one day. I don't know how. Sometimes all it had to do was rain for him to hit her. He knew she wanted that baby." Rhys stares at me, blinking hard. "All I know for sure is that he kicked her in the stomach, repeatedly, then threw her down the stairs. He made her miscarry, at fifteen weeks. It wasn't an easy miscarriage. She was in the hospital for a week."

Once.

"Please tell me that fucker is in jail," I say through the hot, burning rage boiling in my gut. "Because, if he isn't, I'm going to fucking kill him."

"He is. For now." Rhys's smile is cold. "And when he gets out, you'll have to get in line. So, I'm going to ask you, right now, what your intensions are with Kate, and you'd better be brutally honest with me."

"I love her. I'm not leaving here without her."

"Not good enough."

I raise a brow. "Love isn't good enough?"

"No." He shoves his hands in his pockets. "It isn't."

I mirror his stance, hands in pockets, in a stand-off with the man protecting my girl.

I like him.

"She scares the fuck out of me."

"Now we're getting somewhere." His lips quirk. "If she didn't scare you a little, she wouldn't be the one for you."

"I will take my own life before I ever even *think* about hurting her in any way. I'm not saying I won't be an idiot and say things that I'll regret, but I would never intentionally hurt her, Rhys. I'd never touch her in anger. She's...*everything.*"

He studies me for a long moment, and then finally nods. "Okay. I like you."

"They didn't have the milk and cookies ice cream flavor, so I got chocolate chip cookie dough," Kate announces, as she comes in the house through the entrance to the garage, lugging plastic grocery bags. "And you can stop judging me right now, Rhys O'Shaughnessy, because I deserve ice cream." She sets the bags down on the kitchen island, then looks up, and her eyes go wide when they land on me.

Fuck, she looks amazing.

"Someone came to see you," Rhys says.

"And you can show him out," she says to her cousin, and turns to march out of the room. "I don't have anything to say to him."

"Looks like this is going to be a challenge," he says, and claps his hand on my shoulder. "And something tells me few things are a challenge for you these days."

I smile and walk after her.

"I love a challenge."

CHAPTER
TWENTY-ONE
KATE

Earlier that day...

"Seriously? Weren't you in this exact spot, doing exactly this, when I went to bed last night?" Rhys is standing over me, hands on his lean hips, frowning down at me. I'm lounging on the couch, eating stale popcorn.

"What? I'm in the middle of a season of *Vampire Diaries*."

"How many seasons have you watched in the past three days?"

"Four." I scowl up at him. "I finished with *Orange Is the New Black*."

"Kate, you haven't eaten real food in days. And you smell... *ugh*."

"Then don't come in here." I stick my tongue out at him and return to my show. "By the way, Damon is hot in this show. Why are the hot guys always the jerks?"

"I'm a jerk?"

"You're not hot." I smirk and then squeal when he takes my popcorn away and sits at the opposite end of the couch with it. "Give it back!"

"No." He shoves a handful in his mouth, and then spits it back out again. "This is disgusting. When did you pop it?"

"I don't know." I shrug and reach for the Twizzlers. "Two days ago?"

"Now you're just being gross."

"I'm being lazy," I correct him, and cringe inwardly. I am gross. I do smell. I haven't washed my hair in a week. I don't remember what my own bedroom looks like because I haven't left the downstairs since I got home.

Not that I'm going to admit that to *him*.

"So, what's up with that chick, Elena?" he asks, pointing to the screen. "She's hot for a vampire."

"She's not a vampire. Well, her doppelganger is." I catch him up on the show, giving him the highlights, and sigh when the credits roll. "This is seriously good TV."

"Kate?"

"Yeah?"

"I'm worried about you."

"Why? Because I love the *Vampire Diaries*?"

He raises a brow and stares at me like I'm stupid. And I'm not stupid.

"There's no need to worry. I'm just taking some lazy time between jobs, that's all."

"You're sad," he says softly. "I can't stand it when you're sad. Have you talked to him at all?"

I shake my head no. "I don't want to hear from him."

"Maybe you should call him," he suggests.

"Maybe not," I reply.

"You're being stubborn."

He fucked another woman while I was right next door, pining for him! I'm so not telling Rhys that. Talk about humiliating.

But the most humiliating part? I *know* this. I know it, and I still miss him so much it hurts.

Because I'm a stupid girl.

And I'm sick of being stupid. And sad. And…smelly.

"You know what?" I say and stand, stretch, and ignore him when he winces at the smell of me. "You're right. I'm done sitting on the couch. I'm going to go take a shower and go to the grocery store."

"Good, you could use some sun. You're as pale as those vampires on that show."

"You know, you used to be nice to me. You used to love me."

"You used to smell good," he replies with a grin and crosses his arms as I saunter by. "Take a shower, and I'll love you again."

"Conditional love." I tsk tsk as I walk by. "There aren't supposed to be strings attached to love, Rhys. Maybe that's why you can't keep a girlfriend."

"I don't want to keep a girlfriend," he replies with a laugh. "Girlfriends expect stuff from you."

"Yes," I agree sarcastically, "like kindness and cuddle time and sex."

"Hey, I can handle those things. Especially the sex."

"Ew."

"But not the other strings like *commitment* and all of my time and nosing into my financial business."

"And monogamy."

He just smiles and I make puking noises as I walk upstairs to my room. I love Rhys. He always makes me feel better.

The shower feels amazing. I stay in long enough to wash my hair three times, shave my legs, and drain all of the hot water.

When I step out, I actually take the time to style my freshly washed hair and put on a bit of makeup; I pull on a cute pair of red capris pants and white button-down sleeveless shirt.

I feel almost human again.

My bedroom is a shambles. I never unpacked my suitcases when I came home from New Orleans. I quickly do that, throw some dirty clothes into the laundry, vow to burn the clothes I've been marinating in over the past two weeks, then bounce down the stairs to find Rhys in the kitchen, making me a list.

"Thanks, *dear*."

"You're welcome." He grins and checks his list. "I need some things. Don't get any junk food. We've had enough of that to last the rest of the year."

"Yes, sir." I give him a mock salute and take his list. "Since when do you eat parsnips?"

"I'm going to put them in smoothies. They're good for you."

"What *are* they?"

"A vegetable, smart ass."

"I'm getting extra Oreos, just to even it out. Yuck."

"No junk!"

"Whatever."

***

"They didn't have the milk and cookies flavor of ice cream, so I got chocolate chip cookie dough." These bags are so dang *heavy*. I seriously need to go to the gym once in a while. "And you can stop judging me right now, Rhys O'Shaughnessy, because I deserve ice cream." I pile the bags on the kitchen island, let out a sigh of relief, and look right up into the whiskey-colored eyes of Eli Boudreaux.

"Someone came to see you," Rhys says.

"And you can show him out," I reply, and turn to rush out of the room. I can't feel my feet, and I pray I don't fall on my ass. "I don't have anything to say to him."

I can hear their voices, but can't understand what they're saying over the rush in my ears. My skin is hot. I can't breathe.

Damn it! I was doing so much better today.

I walk straight through my bedroom to the balcony that overlooks my backyard. The sun is warm on my shoulders as I lean on the railing and take a deep breath, fighting tears.

Why is he here?

"You'll get burned out there in the sun, *cher*."

I will not turn around. But, oh, God, the sound of his voice is the most amazing sound I've ever heard.

"Look, Kate, I know I should have called you—"

"Why?" I ask without turning around. "Why would you call? The job was done. I came home. There's nothing to say."

"There's a lot to say."

"You're right." I turn now, and will myself to keep myself together until I throw him out on his arse. "There is one thing to say. Fuck you, Eli. All I wanted from you was respect and honesty. To be monogamous until I left. And you couldn't even do *that*. So, fuck you. Now, please leave."

"I didn't fuck anyone!" he exclaims with frustration. "Declan told me what you saw the morning you left, but she wasn't with me, Kate. I didn't go home that night at all. I haven't been home since I left you that night."

"Wait. What?" He advances, but I flinch, so he stops abruptly and shoves his hands in his pockets.

"I haven't been with Cindy, or anyone else, since the minute I met you. I have no idea what she was doing at my townhouse that morning."

"Why haven't you been home?" I whisper.

"Because you aren't there," he replies, almost reluctantly. "And I miss you."

"Look, thanks for clearing that up for me, Eli, but you didn't have to come all this way to tell me that. You could have just sent me an email."

"I'm in love with you," he says, his face intense, jaw ticking. He looks nervous. Unsure of himself.

And that kills me, because Eli is the most self-assured person I've ever met.

"Excuse me?"

"Fuck it," he whispers and takes me in his arms, clutching me to him almost desperately. His nose is in my hair, breathing deeply, his hands rubbing up and down my back.

And I'm not hugging him back. Not yet.

"I remembered something," he murmurs. "Remember when I told you about what my dad said to me when he was dying?"

I nod, and can't help but take a breath, inhaling Eli's strong, spicy scent. God, how I've missed him. My hands grip onto his arms as he continues.

"All I've focused on was the disappointment in his eyes, his voice. The *bad* things he said that day, and I've done everything in my power to make sure that he would be proud of me now."

He grips my shoulders and pushes me away, looking me in the eye.

"But something Declan said reminded me of what Dad said about what's important. That the love of one good woman is worth more than all the casual sex put together. That what matters is being in love, having a family.

"Kate, I thought I didn't deserve you because I work *so hard* to make Bayou Industries something my dad would be proud of, and I thought that in doing that, you'd always take the backseat to my career. But that's bullshit. I can have both. My parents did it effortlessly, because they *made* each other the priority."

"What are you saying?" I ask breathlessly.

"I'm saying," he says and swallows hard, "that you mean the world to me. I've been looking for you my whole damn life. I'm uninterested in a life without you. Not having you with me over the past few weeks has been a hell I don't wish on anyone."

"You hurt me," I whisper, as tears roll unnoticed down my cheeks. He sweeps them away with his thumbs.

"I hurt both of us," he replies softly. "I fell into such an easy love with you, I didn't even realize it was happening, until one day, it was everything."

"You don't do love," I reply.

"I didn't," he agrees with a half-smile. "But you made the man who was incapable of love fall in love with you."

I frown and tilt my head. "You said that to me in the hospital."

He nods solemnly.

"Eli, I don't know if I can do marriage and forever with *anyone* again. I don't know if I have that in me."

"Oh, baby." He kisses my forehead and hugs me to him again. "You do. But we can take this one day at a time. As long as you're with me, every day, nothing else matters, *cher*. We don't have to jump into anything."

My arms clutch him now, wrapping around him and holding him tight.

"I missed you too," I whisper into his chest.

"You're going to burn," he says and leads me into the bedroom. He lies next to me on my bed, turning us so we're facing each other, and I can't help the tears that spring to my eyes. "Don't cry."

"I thought you'd—"

"If I'd known you'd thought that, I would have called and told you differently right away. I had no idea. I'm so sorry."

I shake my head and close my eyes, then lean in and press my lips to his lightly. His hand drifts down my side to my hip, and he lets me take the lead, nibbling his lips, kissing his cheek. I pull my fingertips down his chin as his hand makes its way up my shirt.

"I missed your skin," he whispers.

"I might have missed your abs," I reply softly.

He raises a brow. "Might have?" He pushes me onto my back and unfastens the buttons on my shirt, nudges it aside and kisses my chest, over to my already puckered nipple, pulling it into his mouth through my bra.

"Probably." My hand drifts down his back to his butt. "And this too."

He chuckles and works his way down my stomach. "I think we should make a list. The first on mine is this sexy as hell piercing."

"A list of things I love about you?" I ask with a giggle. He raises his head, his eyes wide, and pushes back up to look me in the eye.

"Do you love me, Kate?"

"I love you very much," I reply sincerely. "All of you."

His eyes close and he tips his forehead against mine, then sends me that sexy, naughty grin of his. "Let's make those lists."

***

Two Weeks Later...

"I would have hired people to unpack your things," Eli says, as he wraps his arms around me from behind and kisses my cheek.

"That's silly," I reply, and hang the last blouse in the closet. "Besides, the thought of having strangers touch my clothes and underwear is not appealing."

"Well, when you put it like that," he agrees with a smile, and turns me to face him. He kisses me softly. "Welcome home, *cher.*"

"Thank you." I smile widely, happy to be here in *our* townhome in the French Quarter. "I love this place."

"I love you."

I smile up at him. "I know."

He swallows and cups my cheek in his hand. "Kate, Rhys told me about the baby you lost, and I've been meaning to find the right moment to tell you that I'm so very sorry for your loss."

I feel tears fill my eyes, but his words are a balm to my heart. "Thank you."

He kisses me softly, gently, his thumbs making circles on my cheeks, and I can't help but hope that there will be other babies.

Lots of babies.

"Is the family here?" I ask.

"We are." Eli's mama's voice comes from the bedroom, and when we step out of the closet, she's smiling widely. "Hello, sweet girl."

"I'm so glad you all came for dinner." I hug the petite woman before walking toward the door.

Just before I leave the room, I hear her say, "Your daddy would be so proud of you, Eli."

I grin and leave them alone, joining the others in the kitchen.

"Are you really living with Uncle Eli now, Miss Kate?" Sam asks excitedly.

"I am." I smile at the sweet little boy and smooth his unruly hair down, then snatch a fried potato out of a serving tray that the caterers brought.

Eli had this gathering catered. He didn't want me to have to deal with cooking dinner *and* unpacking my things.

God, I love that man.

"Are you okay?" Eli asks, as he wraps me in his arms and hugs me tightly, joining us in the kitchen.

"Why wouldn't she be okay?" Beau asks, as he uncovers the shrimp gumbo. "She doesn't start work until Monday, so you haven't had a chance to be a hard ass with her yet."

"How did your boss take it when you quit?" Van asks.

"He was fine when I explained that I didn't want to travel around so much, and that Bayou Enterprises offered me a position."

"I don't want to think about the positions Eli offers you," Charly grumbles, earning a glare from her mother.

Eli simply raises an eyebrow at me, a half-smile on his sexy lips.

"I'm great."

"You're amazing," he whispers in my ear. "And all mine."

I smile up at him, in the middle of the hustle and bustle of his family, laughing and talking, in our home, and know that I'm exactly where I'm supposed to be.

"All yours."

EPILOGUE
RHYS O'SHAUGHNESSY

Three Months Later…

"It's fine," I insist with a growl, glaring at the doctor. My coach, team physician, even the fucking *owner* of the team are all here in this meeting. "I can play."

"No, you can't," the doctor insists grimly. "You'll tear that rotator cuff again in a heartbeat."

"I've done the therapy," I insist. "I've done everything you've told me to."

"Yes, you have. Rhys, you and I both know that this happens to players every day."

"Not to me." I lean forward. "Not. To. Me."

"He's not saying you're out for good," Reggie, my coach reminds me. "You're just out for the season, and it's almost over anyway."

I'm staring at the doctor, who's looking back at me with tired, sad eyes. He and I both know the truth: the chances of me coming back are slim.

"What do I need to do?" I ask.

"Keep doing what you're doing. Keep up with the PT, get it worked over by a massage therapist regularly to keep the muscles supple. Exercise." He spreads his hands wide, as if to say, *what else can I say*?

"I'll be back next season," I promise the room, and I can't help but wonder who I'm trying so hard to convince, me or them?

"And we'll be excited to have you back," Mr. Lyon, the owner, replies. "Get yourself well, Rhys. That's the most important thing."

We all leave the boardroom, and I walk briskly to my car, anxious to get out of here. Summer is hanging onto Chicago like a pit bull with a bone. It's fucking hot.

I take off down the interstate, ready to be back in Denver, wishing Kate would be there to talk to. And, at just the thought of her, I know I need to hear her voice.

"Hello?" Her voice is full of smiles as she answers.

"Hey, kiddo."

"What's wrong?"

"I'm out for the season," I reply, and check my blind spot to switch lanes. "Doc just confirmed it. They made me come all the way to fucking Chicago to tell me that I can't play."

"I'm sorry. I thought you already knew that."

"I was trying to get back in before the postseason."

"What are you going to do?"

"Keep working on it. Exercise. Get it healthy."

"Do you have to be in Denver to do that?" she asks.

"No, I suppose not."

"Then get your butt to New Orleans. I have the perfect place for you to stay."

THE END